HIGH PRAISE FOR JACK KETCHUM AND *THE GIRL NEXT DOOR*!

"*The Girl Next Door* is alive. It does not just promise terror, but actually delivers it."

—Stephen King

"Ketchum [is] one of America's best and most consistent writers of contemporary horror fiction."

—Bentley Little

"Just when you think the worst has already happened...Jack Ketchum goes yet another shock further."

—*Fangoria*

"This is the real stuff, an uncomfortable dip into the pitch blackness."

—*Locus*

"The reader, even though repulsed by the story, cannot look away. Definitely NOT for the faint of heart."

—*Cemetery Dance*

"Realism is what makes this novel so terrifying. The monsters are human, and all the more horrifying for it."

—*Afraid Magazine*

"For two decades now, Jack Ketchum has been one of our best, brightest, and most reliable."

—*Hellnotes*

"A major voice in contemporary suspense."

—Ed Gorman

"Jack Ketchum is a master of suspense and horror of the human variety."

—*Midwest Book Review*

Other *Leisure* books by Jack Ketchum:

SHE WAKES
PEACEABLE KINGDOM
RED
THE LOST

THE GIRL NEXT DOOR

JACK KETCHUM

LEISURE BOOKS

NEW YORK CITY

A LEISURE BOOK®

June 2005

Published by

Dorchester Publishing Co., Inc.
200 Madison Avenue
New York, NY 10016

ISBN 0-8439-5543-0

Printed in the United States of America.

THE GIRL NEXT DOOR

"You got to tell me the brave captain
Why are the wicked so strong?
How do the angels get to sleep
When the devil leaves the porch light on?"
—Tom Waits

"I never want to hear the screams
Of the teenage girls in other people's dreams."
—The Specials

"The soul under the burden of sin cannot flee."
—Iris Murdoch, *The Unicorn*

I

Chapter One

You think you know about pain?

Talk to my second wife. She does. Or she thinks she does.

She says that once when she was nineteen or twenty she got between a couple of cats fighting—her own cat and a neighbor's—and one of them went at her, climbed her like a tree, tore gashes out of her thighs and breasts and belly that you still can see today, scared her so badly she fell back against her mother's turn-of-the-century Hoosier, breaking her best ceramic pie plate and scraping six inches of skin off her ribs while the cat made its way back down her again, all tooth and claw and spitting fury. Thirty-six stitches I think she said she got. And a fever that lasted days.

My second wife says that's pain.

She doesn't know shit, that woman.

* * *

Evelyn, my first wife, has maybe gotten closer.

There's an image that haunts her.

She is driving down a rain-slick highway on a hot summer morning in a rented Volvo, her lover by her side, driving slowly and carefully because she knows how treacherous new rain on hot streets can be, when a Volkswagen passes her and fishtails into her lane. Its rear bumper with the "Live Free or Die" plates slides over and kisses her grille. Almost gently. The rain does the rest. The Volvo reels, swerves, glides over an embankment and suddenly she and her lover are tumbling through space, they are weightless and turning, and up is down and then up and then down again. At some point the steering wheel breaks her shoulder. The rearview mirror cracks her wrist.

Then the rolling stops and she's staring up at the gas pedal overhead. She looks for her lover but he isn't there anymore; he's disappeared, it's magic. She finds the door on the driver's side and opens it, crawls out onto wet grass, stands and peers through the rain. And this is the image that haunts her—a man like a sack of blood, flayed, skinned alive, lying in front of the car in a spray of glass spackled red.

This sack is her lover.

And this is why she's closer. Even though she blocks what she knows—even though she sleeps nights.

She knows that pain is not just a matter of hurting, of her own startled body complaining at some invasion of the flesh.

Pain can work from the outside in.

I mean that sometimes what you *see* is pain. Pain in its cruelest, purest form. Without drugs or sleep or even shock or coma to dull it for you.

You see it and you take it in. And then it's you.

You're host to a long white worm that gnaws and eats, growing, filling your intestines until finally you cough one morning and up comes the blind pale head of the thing sliding from your mouth like a second tongue.

No, my wives don't know about that. Not exactly. Though Evelyn is close.

But I do.

You'll have to trust me on that for starters.

I have for a very long time.

I try to remember that we were all kids when these things happened, just kids, barely out of our Davy Crockett coonskin caps for God's sake, not fully formed. It's much too hard to believe that what I am today is what I was then except hidden now and disguised. Kids get second chances. I like to think I'm using mine.

Though after two divorces, bad ones, the worm is apt to gnaw a little.

Still I like to remember that it was the Fifties, a period of strange repressions, secrets, hysteria. I think about Joe McCarthy, though I barely remember thinking of him at all back then except to wonder what it was that would make my father race home from work every day to catch the committee hearings on TV. I think about the Cold War. About air-raid drills in the school basement and films we saw of atomic testing—department-store mannequins imploding, blown across mockup living rooms, disintegrating, burning. About copies of *Playboy* and *Man's Action* hidden in wax paper back by the brook, so moldy after a while that you hated to touch them. I think about Elvis being denounced by the Reverend Deitz at Grace Lutheran Church when I was ten and the rock 'n' roll riots at Alan Freed's shows at the Paramount.

I say to myself something weird was happening, some great American boil about to burst. That it was happening all over, not just at Ruth's house but everywhere.

And sometimes that makes it easier.

What we did.

I'm forty-one now. Born in 1946, seventeen months to the day after we dropped the Bomb on Hiroshima.

Matisse had just turned eighty.

I make a hundred fifty grand a year, working the floor on Wall Street. Two marriages, no kids. A home in Rye and a company apartment in the city. Most places I go I use limousines, though in Rye I drive a blue Mercedes.

It may be that I'm about to marry again. The woman I love knows nothing of what I'm writing here—nor did my other wives—and I don't really know if I ever mean to tell her. Why should I? I'm successful, even-tempered, generous, a careful and considerate lover.

And nothing in my life has been right since the summer of 1958, when Ruth and Donny and Willie and all the rest of us met Meg Loughlin and her sister Susan.

Chapter Two

I was alone back by the brook, lying on my stomach across the Big Rock with a tin can in my hand. I was scooping up crayfish. I had two of them already in a larger can beside me. Little ones. I was looking for their mama.

The brook ran fast along either side of me. I could feel the spray on my bare feet dangling near the water. The water was cold, the sun warm.

I heard a sound in the bushes and looked up. The prettiest girl I'd ever seen was smiling at me over the embankment.

She had long tanned legs and long red hair tied back in a ponytail, wore shorts and a pale-colored blouse open at the neck. I was twelve and a half. She was older.

I remember smiling back at her, though I was rarely agreeable to strangers.

"Crayfish," I said. I dumped out a tin of water.

"Really?"

I nodded.

"Big ones?"

"Not these. You can find them, though."

"Can I see?"

She dropped down off the bank just like a boy would, not sitting first, just putting her left hand to the ground and vaulting the three-foot drop to the first big stone in the line that led zigzag across the water. She studied the line a moment and then crossed to the Rock. I was impressed. She had no hesitation and her balance was perfect. I made room for her. There was suddenly this fine clean smell sitting next to me.

Her eyes were green. She looked around.

To all of us back then the Rock was something special. It sat smack in the middle of the deepest part of the brook, the water running clear and fast around it. You had room for four kids sitting or six standing up. It had been a pirate ship, Nemo's *Nautilus*, and a canoe for the Lenni Lennape among other things. Today the water was maybe three and a half feet deep. She seemed happy to be there, not scared at all.

"We call this the Big Rock," I said. "We used to, I mean. When we were kids."

"I like it," she said. "Can I see the crayfish? I'm Meg."

"I'm David. Sure."

She peered down into the can. Time went by and we said nothing. She studied them. Then she straightened up again.

"Neat."

"I just catch 'em and look at 'em awhile and then let them go."

"Do they bite?"

"The big ones do. They can't hurt you, though. And the little ones just try to run."

"They look like lobsters."

"You never saw a crayfish before?"

"Don't think they have them in New York City." She laughed. I didn't mind. "We get lobsters, though. *They* can hurt you."

"Can you keep one? I mean, you can't keep a lobster like a pet or anything, right?"

She laughed again. "No. You eat them."

"You can't keep a crayfish either. They die. One day or maybe two, tops. I hear people eat them too, though."

"Really?"

"Yeah. Some do. In Louisiana or Florida or someplace."

We looked down into the can.

"I don't know," she said, smiling. "There's not a whole lot to eat down there."

"Let's get some big ones."

We lay across the Rock side by side. I took the can and slipped both arms down into the brook. The trick was to turn the stones one at a time, slowly so as not to muddy the water, then have the can there ready for whatever scooted out from under. The water was so deep I had my shortsleeve shirt rolled all the way up to my shoulders. I was aware of how long and skinny my arms must look to her. I know they looked that way to me.

I felt pretty strange beside her, actually. Uncomfortable but excited. She was different from the other girls I knew, from Denise or Cheryl on the block or even the girls at school. For one thing she was maybe a hundred times prettier. As far as I was concerned she was prettier than Natalie Wood. Probably she was smarter than the girls I knew too, more sophisticated. She lived in New York City after all and had eaten *lobsters*. And she moved just like a boy. She had this strong hard body and easy grace about her.

All that made me nervous and I missed the first one. Not an enormous crayfish but bigger than what we had. It scudded backward beneath the Rock.

She asked if she could try. I gave her the can.

"New York City, huh?"

"Yup."

She rolled up her sleeves and dipped down into the water. And that was when I noticed the scar.

"Jeez. What's that?"

It started just inside her left elbow and ran down to the wrist like a long pink twisted worm. She saw where I was looking.

"Accident," she said. "We were in a car." Then she looked back into the water where you could see her reflection shimmering.

"Jeez."

But then she didn't seem to want to talk much after that.

"Got any more of 'em?"

I don't know why scars are always so fascinating to boys, but they are, it's a fact of life, and I just couldn't help it. I couldn't shut up about it yet. Even though I knew she wanted me to, even though we'd just met. I watched her turn over a rock. There was nothing under it. She did it correctly though; she didn't muddy the water. I thought she was terrific.

She shrugged.

"A few. That's the worst."

"Can I see 'em?"

"No. I don't think so."

She laughed and looked at me a certain way and I got the message. And then I did shut up for a while.

She turned another rock. Nothing.

"I guess it was a bad one, huh? The accident?"

She didn't answer that at all and I didn't blame her. I knew how stupid and awkward it sounded, how insensitive, the moment I said it. I blushed and was glad she wasn't looking.

Then she got one.

The rock slid over and the crayfish backed right out into the can and all she had to do was bring it up.

She poured off some water and tilted the can toward the sunlight. You could see that nice gold color they have. Its tail was up and its pincers waving and it was stalking the bottom of the can, looking for somebody to fight.

"You got her!"

"First try!"

"Great! She's really great."

"Let's put her in with the others."

She poured the water out slowly so as not to disturb her or lose her exactly the way you were supposed to, though nobody had told her, and then when there was only an inch or so left in the can, plunked her into the bigger can. The two that were already in there gave her plenty of room. That was good because crayfish would kill each other sometimes, they'd kill their own kind, and these two others were just little guys.

In a while the new one calmed down and we sat there watching her. She looked primitive, efficient, deadly, beautiful. Very pretty color and very sleek of design.

I stuck my finger in the can to stir her up again.

"Don't."

Her hand was on my arm. It was cool and soft.

I took my finger out again.

I offered her a stick of Wrigley's and took one myself. Then all you could hear for a while was the wind whooshing through the tall thin grass across the embankment and rustling the brush along the brook and the sound of the brook running fast from last night's rain, and us chewing.

"You'll put them back, right? You promise?"

"Sure. I always do."

"Good."

She sighed and then stood up.

"I've got to get back I guess. We've got shopping to do. But I wanted to look around first thing. I mean, we've never had a woods before. Thanks, David. It was fun."

She was halfway across the stones by the time I thought to ask her.

"Hey! Back where? Where are you going?"

She smiled. "We're staying with the Chandlers. Susan and I. Susan's my sister."

Then I stood too, like somebody had jerked me to my feet on invisible strings.

"The Chandlers? *Ruth?* Donny and Willie's mom?"

She finished crossing and turned and stared at me. And something in her face was different now all of a sudden. Cautious.

It stopped me.

"That's right. We're cousins. Second cousins. I'm Ruth's niece I guess."

Her voice had gone odd on me too. It sounded flat—like there was something I wasn't supposed to know. Like she was telling me something and hiding it at the same time.

It confused me for a moment. I had the feeling that maybe it confused her too.

It was the first I'd seen her flustered. Even including the stuff about the scar.

I didn't let it bother me though.

Because the Chandlers' house was right next door to my house.

And Ruth was . . . well, Ruth was great. Even if her kids were jerks sometimes. Ruth was great.

"Hey!" I said. "We're neighbors! Mine's the brown house next door!"

I watched her climb the embankment. When she got to the top she turned and her smile was back again, the clean open look she'd had when she first sat down beside me on the Rock.

She waved. "See you, David."

"See you, Meg."

Neat, I thought. Incredible. I'll be seeing her all the time.

It was the first such thought I'd ever had.

I realize that now.

That day, on that Rock, I met my adolescence head-on in the person of Megan Loughlin, a stranger two years older than I was, with a sister, a secret, and long red hair. That it seemed so natural to me, that I emerged unshaken and even happy about the experience I think said much for my future possibilities—and of course for hers.

When I think of that, I hate Ruth Chandler.

Ruth, you were beautiful then.

I've thought about you a lot—no, I've researched *you, I've gone that far, dug into your past, parked across the street one day from that Howard Avenue office building you were always telling us about, where you ran the whole damn show while the Boys were away fighting The Big One, the War to End All Wars Part Two—that place where you were utterly, absolutely indispensable until the "little GI pukes came strutting back home again," as you put it, and suddenly you were out of a job. I parked there and it looked ordinary, Ruth. It looked squalid and sad and boring.*

I drove to Morristown where you were born and that was nothing too. Of course I didn't know where your house was supposed to be but I certainly couldn't see your grand disappointed dreams being born there either, in that town, I couldn't see the riches your parents suppos-

edly thrust upon you, showered you with, I couldn't see your wild frustration.

I sat in your husband Willie Sr.'s bar—Yes!—*I* found *him, Ruth! In Fort Myers, Florida, where he'd been ever since he left you with your three squalling brats and a mortgage all these thirty years ago, I found him playing barkeep to the senior citizens, a mild man, amiable, long past his prime—I sat there and looked at his face and into his eyes and we talked and I couldn't see the man you always said he was, the stud, the "lovely Irish bastard," that mean sonovabitch. He looked like a man gone soft and old to me. A drinker's nose, a drinker's gut, a fat fallen ass in a pair of baggy britches. And he looked like he'd never been hard, Ruth. Never. That was the surprise, really.*

Like the hardness was elsewhere.

So what was it, Ruth? All lies? All your own inventions?

I wouldn't put it past you.

Or maybe it was that for you—funneled through you—lies and truth were the same.

I'm going to try to change that now if I can. I'm going to tell our little story. Straight as I can from here on in and no interruptions.

And I'm writing this for you, Ruth. Because I never got to pay you back, really.

So here's my check. Overdue and overdrawn.

Cash it in hell.

Chapter Three

Early the following morning I walked next door.

I remember feeling shy about it, a little awkward, and that was pretty unusual because nothing could have been more natural than to see what was going on over there.

It was morning. It was summer. And that was what you did. You got up, ate breakfast and then you went outside and looked around to see who was where.

The Chandler house was the usual place to start.

Laurel Avenue was a dead end street back then—it isn't anymore—a single shallow cut into the half-circle of woodland that bordered the south side of West Maple and ran back for maybe a mile behind it. When the road was first cut during the early 1800s, the woods were so thick with tall first-growth timber they called it Dark Lane. That timber was all gone by now but it was still a quiet, pretty street. Shade trees everywhere, each house different from the one beside it and not too close together like some you saw.

There were still only thirteen homes on the block. Ruth's, ours, five others going up the hill on our side of the street and six on the opposite.

Every family but the Zorns had kids. And every kid knew every other kid like he knew his own brother. So if you wanted company you could always find some back by the brook or the crabapple grove or up in somebody's yard—whoever had the biggest plastic pool that year or the target for bow and arrow.

If you wanted to get lost that was easy too. The woods were deep.

The Dead End Kids, we called ourselves.

It had always been a closed circle.

We had our own set of rules, our own mysteries, our own secrets. We had a pecking order and we applied it with a vengeance. We were used to it that way.

But now there was somebody new on the block. Somebody new over at Ruth's place.

It felt funny.

Especially because it was *that* somebody.

Especially because it was that place.

It felt pretty damn funny indeed.

Ralphie was squatting out by the rock garden. It was maybe eight o'clock and already he was dirty. There were streaks of sweat and grime all over his face and arms and legs like he'd been running all morning and falling down *thwack* in deep clouds of dust. Falling frequently. Which he probably had, knowing Ralphie. Ralphie was ten years old and I don't think I'd ever seen him clean for more than fifteen minutes in my life. His shorts and T-shirt were crusty too.

"Hey, Woofer."

Except for Ruth, nobody called him Ralphie—always Woofer. When he wanted to he could sound more like the Robertsons' basset hound Mitsy than Mitsy could.

"Hiya, Dave."

He was turning over rocks, watching potato bugs and thousand-leggers scurry away from the light. But I could see he wasn't interested in them. He kept moving one rock after the other. Turning them over, dropping them down again. He had a Libby's lima beans can beside him and he kept on shifting that too, keeping it close beside his scabby knees as he went from rock to rock.

"What's in the can?"

"Nightcrawlers," he said. He still hadn't looked at me. He was concentrating, frowning, moving with that jerky nervous energy that was patented Woofer. Like he was a scientist in a lab on the brink of some incredible fantastic discovery and he wished you'd just leave him the hell alone to get on with it.

He flipped another rock.

"Donny around?"

"Yep." He nodded.

Which meant that Donny was inside. And since I

felt kind of nervous about going inside I stayed with him awhile. He upended a big one. And apparently found what he was after.

Red ants. A swarm of them down there beneath the rock—hundreds, thousands of them. All going crazy with the sudden light.

I've never been fond of ants. We used to put up pots of water to boil and then pour it on them whenever they decided it would be nice to climb the front porch steps over at our place—which for some reason they did about once every summer. It was my dad's idea, but I endorsed it entirely. I thought boiling water was just about what ants deserved.

I could smell their iodine smell along with wet earth and wet cut grass.

Woofer pushed the rock away and then reached into the Libby's can. He dug out a nightcrawler and then a second one and dumped them in with the ants.

He did this from a distance of about three feet. Like he was bombing the ants with worm meat.

The ants responded. The worms began rolling and bucking as the ants discovered their soft pink flesh.

"Sick, Woofer," I said. "That's really sick."

"I found some black ones over there," he said. He pointed to a rock on the opposite side of the porch. "You know, the big ones. Gonna collect 'em and put 'em in with these guys here. Start an ant war. You want to bet who wins?"

"The red ants will win," I said. "The red ants always win."

It was true. The red ants were ferocious. And this game was not new to me.

"I got another idea," I said. "Why don't you stick your hand in there? Pretend you're Son of Kong or something."

He looked at me. I could tell he was considering it. Then he smiled.

"Naw," he said. "That's retarded."

I got up. The worms were still squirming.

"See you, Woof," I said.

I climbed the stairs to the porch. I knocked on the screen door and went inside.

Donny was sprawled on the couch wearing nothing but a pair of wrinkled white slept-in boxer shorts. He was only three months older than I was but much bigger in the chest and shoulders and now, recently, he was developing a pretty good belly, following in the footsteps of his brother, Willie Jr. It was not a beautiful thing to see and I wondered where Meg was now.

He looked up at me from a copy of *Plastic Man*. Personally I'd pretty much quit the comics since the Comic Code came in in '54 and you couldn't get *Web of Mystery* anymore.

"How you doin', Dave?"

Ruth had been ironing. The board was leaning up in a corner and you could smell that sharp musky tang of clean, superheated fabric.

I looked around.

"Pretty good. Where's everybody?"

He shrugged. "Went shopping."

"*Willie* went shopping? You're kidding."

He closed the comic and got up, smiling, scratching his armpit.

"Naw. Willie's got a nine-o'clock appointment with the dentist. Willie's got *cavities*. Ain't it a killer?"

Donny and Willie Jr. had been born an hour and a half apart but for some reason Willie Jr. had very soft teeth and Donny didn't. He was always at the dentist.

We laughed.

"I hear you met her."

"Who?"

Donny looked at me. I guess I wasn't fooling anybody.

"Oh, your cousin. Yeah. Down by the Rock yesterday. She caught a crayfish first try."

Donny nodded. "She's good at stuff," he said.

It wasn't exactly enthusiastic praise, but for Donny—and especially for Donny talking about a *girl*—it was pretty respectful.

"C'mon," he said. "Wait here while I get dressed and we'll go see what Eddie's doing."

I groaned.

Of all the kids on Laurel Avenue Eddie was the one I tried to stay away from. Eddie was crazy.

I remember Eddie walking down the street once in the middle of a stickball game we were playing stripped to the waist with a big live black snake stuck between his teeth. Nature Boy. He threw it at Woofer, who screamed, and then at Billy Borkman. In fact he kept picking it up and throwing it at all the little kids and chasing them waving the snake until the concussion of hitting the road so many times sort of got to the snake eventually and it wasn't much fun anymore.

Eddie got you in trouble.

Eddie's idea of a great time was to do something dangerous or illegal, preferably both—walk the crossbeams of a house under construction or pelt crabapples at cars from Canoe Brook Bridge—and maybe get away with it. If you got caught or hurt that was okay, that was funny. If *he* got caught or hurt it was still funny.

Linda and Betty Martin swore they saw him bite off the head of a frog once. Nobody doubted it.

His house was at the top of the street on the opposite side from us, and Tony and Lou Morino, who lived next door, said they heard his father beating up on him all the time. Practically every night. His mother and sister got it too. I remember his mother, a big gentle woman with rough thick peasant hands, crying over coffee in the kitchen with my mom, her right eye a great big puffy shiner.

My dad said Mr. Crocker was nice enough sober but a mean drunk. I didn't know about that but Eddie had inherited his father's temper and you never knew when it would go off on you. When it did, he was as likely to pick up a stick or a rock as use his hands. We all bore the scars somewhere. I'd been on the receiving end more than once. Now I tried to stay away.

Donny and Willie liked him though. Life with Eddie was exciting, you had to give him that much. Though even they knew Eddie was crazy.

Around Eddie they got crazy too.

"Tell you what," I said. "I'll walk you up. But I'm not gonna hang around up there."

"Ahh, come on."

"I've got other stuff to do."

"What stuff?"

"Just stuff."

"What're you gonna do, go home and listen to your mother's Perry Como records?"

I gave him a look. He knew he was out of line.

We were all Elvis fans.

He laughed.

"Suit yourself, sport. Just wait up a minute. I'll be right there."

He went down the hall to his bedroom and it occurred to me to wonder how they were working that now that Meg and Susan were there, just who was sleeping where. I walked over to the couch and picked up his *Plastic Man*. I flipped the pages and put it down again. Then I wandered from the living room to the dining area where Ruth's clean laundry lay folded on the table and finally into the kitchen. I opened the Frigidaire. As usual there was food for sixty.

I called to Donny. "Okay to have a Coke?"

"Sure. And open one for me, will ya?"

I took out the Cokes, pulled open the right-hand drawer and got the bottle opener. Inside the silverware was stacked all neat and tidy. It always struck me as weird how Ruth had all this food all the time yet had service only for five—five spoons, five forks, five knives, five steak knives, and no soup spoons at all. Of course except for us Ruth never had any company that I knew of. But now there were *six* people living there. I wondered if she'd finally have to break down and buy some more.

I opened the bottles. Donny came out and I handed him one. He was wearing jeans and Keds and a T-shirt. The T-shirt was tight over his belly. I gave it a little pat there.

"Better watch it, Donald," I said.

"Better watch it yourself, homo."

"Oh, that's right, I'm a homo, right?"

"You're a retard is what you are."

"I'm a retard? You're a skank."

"Skank? *Girls* are skanks. Girls and homos are skanks. You're the skank. I'm the Duke of Earl." He punctuated it with a punch to the arm which I returned, and we jostled a little.

Donny and I were as close to best friends as boys got in those days.

We went out through the back door into the yard, then around the driveway to the front, and started up to Eddie's. It was a matter of honor to ignore the sidewalk. We walked in the middle of the street. We sipped our Cokes. There was never any traffic anyway.

"Your brother's maiming worms in the rock garden," I told him.

He glanced back over his shoulder. "Cute little fella, ain't he,"

"So how do you like it?" I asked him.

"Like what?"

"Having Meg and her sister around?"

He shrugged. "Don't know. They just got here." He took a swig of Coke, belched, and smiled.

"That Meg's pretty cute, though, ain't she? Shit! My cousin!"

I didn't want to comment, though I agreed with him.

"*Second* cousin, though, you know? Makes a difference. Blood or something. I dunno. Before, we never saw 'em."

"Never?"

"My mom says once. I was too young to remember."

"What's her sister like?"

"Susan? Like nothing. Just a little kid. What is she, eleven or something?"

"Woofer's only ten."

"Yeah, right. And what's Woofer?"

You couldn't argue there.

"Got messed up bad in that accident, though."

"Susan?"

He nodded and pointed to my waist. "Yeah. Broke everything from there on down, my mom says. Every bone you got. Hips, legs, everything."

"Jeez."

"She still don't walk too good. She's all casted up. Got those—what do you call 'em?—metal things, sticks, that strap on to your arms and you grab 'em, haul yourself along. Kids with polio wear 'em. I forget what they're called. Like crutches."

"Jeez. Is she going to walk again?"

"She walks."

"I mean like regular."

"I dunno."

We finished our Cokes. We were almost at the top of the hill. It was almost time for me to leave him there. That or suffer Eddie.

"They both died, y'know," he said.

Just like that.

I knew who he meant, of course, but for a moment I just couldn't get my mind to wrap around it. Not right away. It was much too weird a concept.

Parents didn't just *die*. Not on my street. And certainly not in car accidents. That kind of thing happened elsewhere, in places more dangerous than Laurel Avenue. They happened in movies or in books. You heard about it on Walter Cronkite.

Laurel Avenue was a dead end street. You walked down the middle of it.

But I knew he wasn't lying. I remembered Meg not wanting to talk about the accident or the scars and me pushing.

I knew he wasn't lying but it was hard to handle.

We just kept walking together, me not saying anything, just looking at him and not really seeing him either.

Seeing Meg.

It was a very special moment.

I know Meg attained a certain glamour for me then.

Suddenly it was not just that she was pretty or smart or able to handle herself crossing the brook—she was almost unreal. Like no one I'd ever met or was likely to meet outside of books or the matinee. Like she was fiction, some sort of heroine.

I pictured her back by the Rock and now I saw this person who was really brave lying next to me. I saw horror. Suffering, survival, disaster.

Tragedy.

All this in an instant.

Probably I had my mouth open. I guess Donny thought I didn't know what he was talking about.

"Meg's *parents*, numbnuts. Both of 'em. My mom says they must have died instantly. That they didn't know what hit 'em." He snorted. "Fact is, what hit 'em was a Chrysler."

And it may have been his rich bad taste that pulled me back to normal.

"I saw the scar on her arm," I told him.

"Yeah, I saw it, too. Neat, huh? You should see Susan's though. Scars all *over* the place. Gross. My mom says she's lucky to be alive."

"She probably is."

"Anyhow that's how come we've got 'em. There isn't anybody else. It's us or some orphanage somewhere." He smiled. "Lucky them, huh?"

And then he said something that came back to me later. At the time I guessed it was true enough, but for some reason I remembered it. I remembered it well.

He said it just as we got to Eddie's house.

I see myself standing in the middle of the road about to turn and go back down the hill again, go off by myself somewhere, not wanting any part of Eddie—at least not that day.

I see Donny turning to throw the words over his

shoulder on his way across the lawn to the porch. Casually, but with an odd sort of sincerity about him, as though this were absolute gospel.

"My mom says Meg's the lucky one," he said. "*My mom says she got off easy.*"

Chapter Four

It was a week and a half before I got to see her again apart from a glimpse here and there—taking out the trash once, weeding in the garden. Now that I knew the whole story it was even harder to approach her. I'd never felt sorry. I'd rehearse what I might say to her. But nothing sounded right. What did you say to someone who'd just lost half her family? It stood there like a rock I couldn't scale. So I avoided her.

Then my family and I did our yearly duty trip to Sussex County to visit my father's sister, so for four whole days I didn't have to think about it. It was almost a relief. I say almost because my parents were less than two years from divorce by then and the trip was awful—three tense days of silence in the car going up and coming back with a lot of phony jolliness in between that was supposed to benefit my aunt and uncle but didn't. You could see my aunt and uncle looking at one another every now and then as if to say Jesus, get these people *out* of here.

They knew. Everybody knew. My parents couldn't have hidden pennies from a blind man by then.

But once we were home it was back to wondering about Meg again. I don't know why it never occurred to me just to forget it, that she might not want to be reminded of her parents' death any more than I wanted to talk about it. But it didn't. I figured you had to say *something* and I couldn't get it right. It was important to me that I not make an ass of myself over this. It was important to me that I not make an ass of myself in Meg's eyes period.

I wondered about Susan too. In nearly two weeks I'd never seen her. That ran contrary to everything I knew. How could you live next door to someone and never see her? I thought about her legs and Donny saying her scars were really bad to look at. Maybe she was afraid to go out. I could relate to that. I'd been spending a lot of time indoors myself these days, avoiding her sister.

It couldn't last though. It was the first week of June by then, time for the Kiwanis Karnival.

To miss the Karnival was like missing summer.

Directly across from us not half a block away was an old six-room schoolhouse called Central School where we all used to go as little kids, grades one through five. They held the Karnival there on the playground every year. Ever since we were old enough to be allowed to cross the street we'd go over and watch them set up.

For that one week, being that close, we were the luckiest kids in town.

Only the concessions were run by the Kiwanis—the food stands, the game booths, the wheels of fortune. The rides were all handled by a professional touring company and run by carnies. To us the carnies were exotic as hell. Rough-looking men and women who worked with Camels stuck between their teeth, squinting against the smoke curling into their eyes, sporting tattoos and calluses and scars and smelling of grease and old sweat. They cursed, they drank Schlitz as they worked. Like us, they were not opposed to spitting lungers in the dirt.

We loved the Karnival and we loved the carnies. You *had* to. In a single summer afternoon they would take our playground and transform it from a pair of baseball diamonds, a blacktop, and a soccer field into a brand-new city of canvas and whirling steel. They did it so fast you could hardly believe your eyes. It was magic, and the magicians all had gold-tooth smiles and "I love Velma" etched into their biceps. Irresistible.

It was still pretty early and when I walked over they were still unpacking the trucks.

This was when you couldn't talk to them. They were too busy. Later while they were setting up or testing the machinery you could hand them tools, maybe even get a sip of beer out of them. The local kids were their bread and butter after all. They wanted you to come back that night with friends and family and they were usually friendly. But now you just had to watch and keep out of the way.

Cheryl and Denise were already there, leaning on the backstop fence behind home plate and staring through the links.

I stood with them.

Things seemed tense to me. You could see why. It was only morning but the sky looked dark and threatening. Once, a few years ago, it had rained every night of the Karnival except Thursday. Everybody took a beating when that happened. The grips and carnies worked grimly now, in silence.

Cheryl and Denise lived up the street across from one another. They were friends but I think only because of what Zelda Gilroy on *The Dobie Gillis Show* used to call propinquity. They didn't have much in common. Cheryl was a tall skinny brunette who would probably be pretty a few years later but now she was all arms and legs, taller than I was and two years younger. She had two brothers—Kenny and Malcolm. Malcolm was just a little kid who sometimes played with Woofer. Kenny was almost my age but a year behind me in school.

All three kids were very quiet and well-behaved. Their parents, the Robertsons, took no shit but I doubt that by nature they were disposed to give any.

Denise was Eddie's sister. Another type entirely.

Denise was edgy, nervous, almost as reckless as her brother, with a marked propensity toward mockery. As though all the world were a bad joke and she was the only one around who knew the punchline.

"It's *David*," she said. And there was the mockery, just pronouncing my name. I didn't like it but I ignored it. That was the way to handle Denise. If she got no rise she got no payoff and it made her more normal eventually.

"Hi Cheryl. Denise. How're they doing?"

Denise said, "I think that's the Tilt-a-Whirl there. Last year that's where they put the Octopus."

"It could still be the Octopus," said Cheryl.

"Unh-unh. See those platforms?" She pointed to the wide sheets of metal. "The Tilt-a-Whirl's got platforms. Wait till they get the cars out. You'll see."

She was right. When the cars came out it was the Tilt-a-Whirl. Like her father and her brother Eddie, Denise was good at mechanical things, good with tools.

"They're worried about rain," she said.

"*They're* worried." said Cheryl. "*I'm worried!*" She sighed in exasperation. It was very exaggerated. I smiled. There was always something sweetly serious about Cheryl. You just knew her favorite book was *Alice in Wonderland*. The truth was, I liked her.

"It won't rain," Denise said.

"How do you know?"

"It just won't." Like she wouldn't let it.

"See that there?" She pointed to a huge gray and white truck rolling back to the center of the soccer field. "I bet that's the Ferris wheel. That's where they had it last year and the year before. Want to see?"

"Sure," I said.

We skirted the Tilt-a-Whirl and some kiddie boat rides they were unloading on the macadam, walked along the cyclone fence that separated the playground from the brook, cut through a row of tents going up for the ring-toss and bottle-throw and whatever, and came out onto the field. The grips had just opened the doors to the truck. The painted grinning clown head on the doors was split down the middle. They started pulling out the girders.

It looked like the Ferris wheel all right.

Denise said, "My dad says somebody fell off last year in Atlantic City. They stood up. You ever stand up?"

Cheryl frowned. "Of course not."

Denise turned to me.

"I bet you never did, did you?"

I ignored the tone. Denise always had to work so hard to be such a brat all the time.

"No," I said. "Why would I?"

"Cause it's *fun!*"

She was grinning and she should have been pretty when she grinned. She had good white teeth and a lovely, delicate mouth. But something always went wrong with Denise's smile. There was always something manic in it. Like she really wasn't having much fun at all despite what she wanted you to think.

It also disappeared too fast. It was unnerving.

It did that now and she said so only I could hear, "I was thinking about The Game before."

She looked straight at me very wide-eyed and serious like there was something more to come, something important. I waited. I thought maybe she expected me to answer. I didn't. Instead, I looked away toward the truck.

The Game, I thought. Great.

I didn't like to think about The Game. But as long as Denise and some of the others were around I supposed I'd have to.

It started early last summer. A bunch of us—me, Donny, Willie, Woofer, Eddie, Tony and Lou Morino, and finally, later, Denise—used to meet back by the apple orchard to play what we called Commando. We played it so often that soon it was just "The Game."

I have no idea who came up with it. Maybe Eddie or the Morinos. It just seemed to happen to us one day and from then on it was just there.

In The Game one guy was "it." He was the Commando. His "safe" territory was the orchard. The rest of us were a platoon of soldiers bivouacked a few yards away up on a hill near the brook where, as smaller kids, we'd once played King of the Mountain.

We were an odd bunch of soldiers in that we had no weapons. We'd lost them, I guess, during some battle. Instead, it was the Commando who had the weapons—apples from the orchard, as many as he could carry.

In theory, he also had the advantage of surprise. Once he was ready he'd sneak from the orchard through the brush and raid our camp. With luck he could bop at least one of us with an apple before being seen. The apples were bombs. If you got hit with an apple you were dead, you were out of the game. So the object was to hit as many guys as you could before getting caught.

You always got caught.

That was the point.

The Commando never won.

You got caught because, for one thing, everybody else was sitting on a fairly good-sized hill watching and waiting for you, and unless the grass was very high and you were very lucky, you had to get seen. So much for the element of surprise. Second, it was seven against one, and you had just the single "safe" base back at the orchard yards away. So here you were firing wildly over your shoulder running like crazy back to your base with a bunch of kids like a pack of dogs at your heels, and maybe you'd get one or two or three of them but eventually they'd get *you*.

And as I say, that was the point.

Because the captured Commando got tied to a tree in the grove, arms tied behind his back, legs hitched together.

He was gagged. He was blindfolded.

And the survivors could do anything they wanted to him while the others—even the "dead" guys—looked on.

Sometimes we all went easy and sometimes not.

The raid took maybe half an hour.

The capture could take all day.

At the very least, it was scary.

Eddie, of course, got away with murder. Half the time you were afraid to capture him. He could turn on you, break the rules, and The Game would become a bloody, violent free-for-all. Or if you did catch him there was always the problem of how to let him go. If you'd done anything to him he didn't like it was like setting free a swarm of bees.

Yet it was Eddie who introduced his sister.

And once Denise was part of it the complexion of The Game changed completely.

Not at first. At first it was the same as always. Everybody took turns and you got yours and I got mine except there was this *girl* there.

But then we started pretending we had to be nice to her. Instead of taking turns we'd let her be whatever she wanted to be. Troops or Commando. Because she was new to The Game, because she was a girl.

And she started pretending to have this obsession with getting all of us before we got her. Like it was a challenge to her. Every day was *finally* going to be the day she won at Commando.

We knew it was impossible. She was a lousy shot for one.

Denise never won at Commando.

She was twelve years old. She had curly brown-red hair and her skin was lightly freckled all over.

She had the small beginnings of breasts, and thick pale prominent nipples.

I thought of all that now and fixed my eyes on the truck, on the workers and the girders.

But Denise wouldn't leave it alone.

"It's summer," she said. "So how come we don't play?"

She knew damn well why we didn't play but she

was right too in a way—what had stopped The Game was nothing more than that the weather had gotten too cold. That and the guilt of course.

"We're a little old for that now," I lied.

She shrugged. "Uh-huh. Maybe. And maybe you guys are chicken."

"Could be. I've got an idea, though. Why don't you ask your brother if he's chicken."

She laughed. "Yeah. Sure. Right."

The sky was growing darker.

"It's going to rain," said Cheryl.

The men certainly thought so. Along with the girders they were hauling out canvas tarps, spreading them out in the grass just in case. They were working fast, trying to get the big wheel assembled before the downpour. I recognized one of them from last summer, a wiry blond southerner named Billy Bob or Jimmy Bob something who had handed Eddie a cigarette he asked for. That alone made him memorable. Now he was hammering pieces of the wheel together with a large ball-peen hammer, laughing at something the fat man said beside him. The laugh was high and sharp, almost feminine.

You could hear the *ping* of the hammer and the trucks' gears groaning behind us, you could hear generators running and the grinding of machinery—and then a sudden staccato pop, rain falling hard into the field's dry hard-packed dirt. "Here it comes!"

I took my shirt out of my jeans and pulled it up over my head. Cheryl and Denise were already running for the trees.

My house was closer than theirs. I didn't really mind the rain. But it was a good excuse to get out of there for a while. Away from Denise.

I just couldn't believe she wanted to talk about The Game.

You could see the rain wouldn't last. It was coming down too fast, too heavily. Maybe by the time it was over some of the other kids would be hanging around. I could lose her.

I ran past them huddled beneath the trees.

"Going home!" I said. Denise's hair was plastered down over her cheeks and forehead. She was smiling again. Her shirt was soaked clear through.

I saw Cheryl reach out to me. That long bony wet arm dangling.

"Can we come?" she yelled. I pretended I didn't hear. The rain was pretty loud over there in the leaves. I figured Cheryl would get over it. I kept running.

Denise and Eddie, I thought. Boy. What a pair.

If anybody is ever gonna get me into trouble it'll be them. One or the other or both of them. It's got to be.

Ruth was on the landing taking in the mail from her mailbox as I ran past her house. She turned in the doorway and smiled and waved to me, as water cascaded down the eaves.

Chapter Five

I never learned what bad feeling had come between Ruth and my mother but something had when I was eight or nine.

Before that, long before Meg and Susan came along, I used to sleep over nights with Donny and Willie and Woofer in the double set of bunk beds they had in their room. Willie had a habit of leaping into bed at night so he'd destroyed a few bunks over the years. Willie was always flinging himself on something. When he was two or three, Ruth said, he'd destroyed his crib completely. The kitchen chairs were all unhinged from his sprawling. But the bunks they had in the bedroom now were tough. They'd survived.

Since whatever happened between Ruth and my mother I was allowed to stay there only infrequently.

But I remember those earlier nights when we were kids. We'd cut up laughing in the dark for an hour or two whispering, giggling, spitting over the sides at whoever was on the bottom bunks and then Ruth would come in and yell and we'd go to sleep.

The nights I liked best were Karnival nights. From the open bedroom window facing the playground we could hear calliope music, screams, the whir and grind of machinery.

The sky was orange-red as though a forest fire were raging, punctuated by brighter reds and blues as the Octopus whirled just out of sight behind the trees.

We knew what was out there—we had just come back from there after all, our hands still sticky from cotton candy. But somehow it was mysterious to lie listening, long past our bedtime, silent for once, envying adults and teenagers, imagining the terrors and thrills of the big rides we were too young to go on that were getting all those screams. Until the sounds and lights slowly faded away, replaced by the laughter of strangers as they made their way back to cars all up and down our block.

I swore that when I got old enough I'd be the last one to leave.

And now I was standing alone at the refreshment booth eating my third hot dog of the evening and wondering what the hell to do with myself.

I'd ridden all the rides I cared to. I'd lost money at every game and wheel of fortune the place had to offer and all I had was one tiny ceramic poodle for my mother shoved in my pocket to show for it.

I'd had my candy apple, my Sno-Cone and my slice of pizza.

I'd hung out with Kenny and Malcolm until Malcolm got sick on the Dive Bomber and then with Tony and Lou Morino and Linda and Betty Martin until they went home. It was fun, but now there was just me. It was ten o'clock.

And two hours yet to go.

I'd seen Woofer earlier. But Donny and Willie Jr. hadn't shown and neither had Ruth or Meg or Susan. It was odd because Ruth was usually very big on Karnival. I thought of going across the street to see what was what but that would mean admitting I was bored and I wasn't ready to do that yet.

I decided I'd wait a while.

Ten minutes later Meg arrived.

I was trying my luck on number seven red and considering a second candy apple when I saw her walk slowly through the crowd, alone, wearing jeans and a bright green blouse—and suddenly I didn't feel so shy anymore. That I didn't feel shy amazed me. Maybe by then I was ready for anything. I waited until I lost on the red again and went over.

And then it was as though I was interrupting something.

She was staring up at the Ferris wheel, fascinated, brushing back a lock of long red hair with her fingers. I saw something glint on her hand as it dropped to her side.

It was a pretty fast wheel. Up top the girls were squealing.

"Hi, Meg." I said.

She looked at me and smiled and said, "Hi, David." Then she looked back at the wheel.

You could tell she'd never been on one before. Just the way she stared. What kind of life was that? I wondered.

"Neat, huh? It's faster than most are."

She looked at me again, all excited. "It is?"

"Yeah. Faster than the one at Playland, anyway. Faster than Bertram's Island."

"It's beautiful."

Privately I agreed with her. There was a smooth easy glide to the wheel I'd always liked, a simplicity of purpose and design that the scary rides lacked. I couldn't have stated it then but I'd always thought the wheel was graceful, romantic.

"Want to try?"

I heard the eagerness in my voice and wished for death. What was I doing? The girl was *older* than me. Maybe as much as three *years* older. I was crazy.

I tried to backtrack.

Maybe I'd confused her.

"I mean, I'd go on it with you if you want. If you're scared to. I don't mind."

She laughed. I felt the knife point lift away from my throat.

"Come on," she said.

She took my hand and led me over.

Somehow I bought us tickets and we stepped into a car and sat down. All I remember is the feel of her hand, warm and dry in the cool night air, the fingers slim and strong. That and my bright-red cheeks reminding me I was twelve years old on the wheel with something very much like a full-grown woman.

And then the old problem came up of what to say, while they loaded the rest of the cars and we rose to the top. I solved it by saying nothing. That seemed fine with her. She didn't seem uncomfortable at all. Just relaxed and content to be up here looking down at the people and the whole Karnival spread around her strung with lights and up over the trees to our houses, rocking the car gently back and forth, smiling, humming a tune I didn't know.

Then the wheel began turning and she laughed and I thought it was the happiest, nicest sound I'd ever heard and felt proud of myself for asking her, for making her happy and making her laugh the way she did.

As I say, the wheel was fast and up at the top almost completely silent, all the noise of the Karnival held down below as though enveloped there, and you plunged down into it and then back out of it again, the noise receding quickly, and at the top you were almost weightless in the cool breeze so that you wanted to hold on to the crossbar for a moment for fear of flying away entirely.

I looked down to her hands on the bar and that was when I saw the ring. In the moonlight it looked thin and pale. It sparkled.

I made a show of enjoying the view but mostly it was her smile and the excitement in her eyes I was enjoying, the way the wind pressed and fluttered the blouse across her breasts.

Then our ride was at its peak and the wheel turned faster, the airy sweeping glide at its most graceful and elegant and thrilling as I looked at her, her lovely open face rushing first through a frame of stars and then past the dark schoolhouse and then the pale brown tents of the Kiwanis, her hair blowing back and then forward over her brushed cheeks as we rose again, and I suddenly felt those first two or three years that she had lived and I hadn't like a terrible weighted irony, like a curse, and thought for a moment, it isn't fair. I can give her this but that's all and it's just not fair.

The feeling passed. By the time the ride was over and we waited near the top all that was left was the pleasure at how happy she looked. And how alive.

I could talk now.

"How'd you like it?"

"God, I *loved* it! You keep treating me to things, David."

"I can't believe you never rode before."

"My parents . . . I know they always meant to take us someplace. Palisades Park or somewhere. We just never got around to it, I guess."

"I heard about . . . everything. I'm sorry."

There. It was out.

She nodded. "The worst is missing them, you know? And knowing they won't be back again. Just knowing that. Sometimes you forget and it's as though they're on vacation or something and you think, gee, I wish they'd call. You miss them. You *forget* they're really gone. You forget the past six months even happened. Isn't that weird? Isn't that crazy? Then you catch yourself . . . and it's real again.

"I dream about them a lot. And they're always still alive in my dreams. We're happy."

I could see the tears well up. She smiled and shook her head.

"Don't get me started," she said.

We were on the downside now, moving, only five or six cars ahead of us. I saw the next group waiting to get on. I looked down over the bar and noticed Meg's ring again. She saw me looking.

"My mother's wedding band," she said. "Ruth doesn't like me to wear it much but my mother would have. I'm not going to lose it. I'd never lose it."

"It's pretty. It's beautiful."

She smiled. "Better than my scars?"

I flushed but that was okay, she was only kidding me. "A lot better."

The wheel moved down again. Only two more cars to go. Time moved dreamlike for me, but even at that it moved too quickly. I hated to see it end.

"How do you like it?" I asked. "Over at the Chandler's?"

She shrugged. "Okay I guess. Not like home. Not the way it was. Ruth's kind of . . . funny sometimes. But I think she means well." She paused and then said, "Woofer's a little weird."

"You can say *that* again."

We laughed. Though the comment about Ruth confused me. I remembered the reserve in her voice, the coldness that first day by the brook.

"We'll see," she said. "I suppose it takes time to get used to things, doesn't it."

We'd reached the bottom now. One of the carnies lifted the crossbar and held the car steady with his foot. I hardly noticed him. We stepped out.

"I'll tell you one thing I *don't* like," she said.

She said it almost in a whisper, like maybe she expected somebody to hear and then report to someone else—and as though we were confidants, equals, co-conspirators.

I liked that a lot. I leaned in close.

"What?" I said.

"That basement," she said. "I don't like that at all. That shelter."

Chapter Six

I knew what she meant.

In his day Willie Chandler Sr. had been very handy.

Handy and a little paranoid.

So that I guess when Khrushchev told the United Nations, “We will bury you,” Willie Sr. must have said something like the fuck you will and built himself a bomb shelter in the basement.

It was a room within a room, eight by ten feet wide and six feet high, modeled strictly according to government specifications. You went down the stairs from their kitchen, walked past the paint cans stacked beneath the stairs and the sink and then the washer and dryer, turned a corner and walked through a heavy metal bolted door—originally the door to a meat locker—and you were inside a concrete enclosure at least ten degrees colder than the rest of the place, musty-smelling and dark.

There were no electrical outlets and no light fixtures.

Willie had nailed girders to the kitchen floor beams and supported them with thick wooden posts. He had sandbagged the only window on the outside of the house and covered the inside with heavy half-inch wire-mesh screening. He had provided the requisite fire extinguisher, battery-operated radio, ax, crowbar, battery lantern, first-aid kit and bottles of water. Cartons of canned food lay stacked on a small heavy handmade hardwood table along with a Sterno stove, a travel alarm clock and an air pump for blowing up the mattresses rolled in the corner.

All this built and purchased on a milkman's salary.

He even had a pick and shovel there, for digging out after the blast.

The one thing Willie omitted and that the government recommended was a chemical toilet.

They were expensive. And he'd left before getting around to that.

Now the place was sort of ratty-looking—food supplies raided for Ruth's cooking, the extinguisher fallen off its wall mount, batteries dead in the radio and lantern, and the items themselves filthy from three solid years of grim neglect. The shelter reminded Ruth of Willie. She was not going to clean it.

* * *

We played there sometimes, but not often.

The place was scary.

It was as though he'd built a cell there—not a shelter to keep something out but a dark black hole to keep something *in*.

And in a way its central location informed the whole cellar. You'd be down there drinking a Coke talking with Ruth while she did her laundry and you'd look over your shoulder and see this evil-looking bunker sort of thing, this squat concrete wall, constantly sweating, dripping, cracked in places. As though the wall itself were old and sick and dying.

We'd go in there occasionally and scare each other.

That was what it was good for. Scaring each other. And nothing much else.

We used it sparingly.

Chapter Seven

"I'll tell you, what's missing from that goddamn Karnival's a good old-fashioned hootchie-koo!"

It was Tuesday night, the second night of Karnival and Ruth was watching Cheyenne Bodie get deputized for the umpteenth time and the town's chicken-shit mayor pinning the deputy's badge to his fringed cowhide shirt. Cheyenne looked proud and determined.

Ruth held a beer in one hand and a cigarette in the other and sat low and tired-looking in the big overstuffed chair by the fireplace, her long legs stretched out on the hassock, barefoot.

Woofer glanced up at her from the floor. "What's a hootchie-koo?"

"Hootchie-koo. Hootchie-kootchie. Dancin' girls, Ralphie. That and the freak show. When I was your age we had both. I saw a man with three arms once."

Willie Jr. looked at her. "Nah," he said.

But you could see she had him going.

"Don't contradict your mother. I did. I saw a man with three arms—one of 'em just a little bitty thing coming out of here."

She raised her arm and pointed to her armpit neatly shaved and smooth inside the dress.

"The other two were normal just like yours. I saw a two-headed cow as well, same show. 'Course that was dead."

We sat around the Zenith in an irregular circle, Woofer on the carpet next to Ruth, me and Willie and Donny on the couch, and Eddie squatting directly in front of the television so that Woofer had to shift to see around him.

Times like this you didn't have to worry about Eddie. In his house they didn't have television. He was glued to it. And if anybody could control him Ruth could.

"What else?" asked Willie Jr. "What other stuff'd you see?"

He ran his hand over his blond flattop. He was always doing that. I guess he enjoyed the feel of it though I couldn't see how he'd like the greasy waxed part up front.

"Mostly things in bottles. Stillborns. You know stillborns? In formaldehyde. Little shrunken things—goats, cats. All kinds of stuff. That's going back a *long* time. I don't remember. I do remember a man must have weighed five, six hundred pounds, though. Took three other fellas to haul him up. Fattest damn thing I ever saw or ever *want* to see."

We laughed, picturing the three guys having to help him up.

We all knew Ruth was careful of her weight.

"I tell you, carnivals were something when I was a girl."

She sighed.

You could see her face go calm and dreamy-looking then the way it did sometimes when she was looking back—way back. Not to Willie but all the way back to her childhood. I always liked watching her then. I think we all did. The lines and angles seemed to soften and for somebody's mother, she was almost beautiful.

"Ready yet?" asked Woofer. It was a big thing for him tonight, being able to go out to the Karnival this late. He was eager to get going.

"Not yet. Finish your sodas. Let me finish my beer."

She took a long deep pull on the cigarette, holding the smoke in and then letting it out all in a rush.

The only other person I knew who smoked a cigarette as hard as Ruth did was Eddie's dad. She tilted the beer can and drank.

"I wanna know about this hootchie-koo," said Willie. He leaned forward next to me on the couch, his shoulders turned inward, rounded.

As Willie got older and taller his slouch got more pronounced. Ruth said that if he kept on growing and slouching at this rate he was going to be a hunchback. A six-footer.

"Yeah," said Woofer. "What's it supposed to be? I don't get it."

Ruth laughed. "It's dancing girls, I told you. Doncha know anything? Half naked too, some of them."

She pulled the faded print dress back up to halfway over her thighs, held it there a moment, fluttered it at us, and then flapped it down again.

"Skirts up to here," she said. "And little teeny brassieres and that's all. Maybe a ruby in the belly button or something. With little dark red circles painted here, and here." She indicated her nipples, making slow circles with her fingers. Then she looked at us.

"What'd you think of *that?*"

I felt myself flush.

Woofer laughed.

Willie and Donny were watching her intently.

Eddie remained fixed on Cheyenne Bodie.

She laughed. "Well, I guess nothing like that's gonna be sponsored by the good old Kiwanis, though, is it? Not *those* boys. Hell, they'd like to. They'd love to! But they've all got *wives*. Damn hypocrites."

Ruth was always going on about the Kiwanis or the Rotary or something.

She was not a joiner.

We were used to it.

She drained her beer and stubbed out the cigarette.

She got up.

"Finish your drinks, boys," she said. "Let's go. Let's get out of here. Meg? Meg Loughlin!"

She walked into the kitchen and dropped her empty beer can in the garbage pail.

Down the hall the door to her room opened and Meg stepped out, looking a little wary at first, I thought—I guessed it was Ruth's shouting. Then her eyes settled on me and she smiled.

So that was how they were working it, I thought. Meg and Susan were in Ruth's old room. It was logical because that was the smaller of the two. But it also meant that either Ruth was bunking on the convertible sofa or with Donny and Woofer and Willie Jr. I wondered what my parents would say to *that*.

"I'm taking these boys out for a Mister Softee over at the fair, Meggie. You take care of your sister and keep yourself out of the icebox. Don't want you getting fat on us."

"Yes, ma'am."

Ruth turned to me.

"David," she said, "you know what you ought to do? You ought to go say hi to Susan. You never met and it's not polite."

"Sure. Okay."

Meg led the way down the hallway ahead of me.

Their door was to the left opposite the bathroom, the boys' room straight on. I could hear soft radio music coming from behind the door. Tommy Edwards singing "It's All In the Game." Meg opened the door and we went inside.

When you're twelve, little kids are little kids and that's about it. You're not even supposed to notice them, really. They're like bugs or birds or squirrels or somebody's roving housecat—part of the landscape but so what. Unless of course it's somebody like Woofer you can't *help* but notice.

I'd have noticed Susan though.

I knew that the girl on the bed looking up at me from her copy of *Screen Stories* was nine years old—Meg had told me that—but she looked a whole lot younger. I was glad she had the covers up so I couldn't see the casts on her hips and legs. She seemed frail enough as it was without my having to think about all those broken bones. I was aware of her wrists, though, and the long thin fingers holding the magazine.

Is this what an accident does to you? I wondered.

Except for the bright green eyes it was almost like meeting Meg's opposite. Where Meg was all health and strength and vitality, this one was a shadow. Her skin so pale under the reading lamp it looked translucent.

Donny'd said she still took pills every day for fever, antibiotics, and that she wasn't healing right, that walking was still pretty painful.

I thought of the Hans Christian Andersen story about the little mermaid whose legs had hurt her too. In the book I had the illustration even looked like Susan. The same long silky blond hair and soft delicate features, the same look of sad longtime vulnerability. Like someone cast ashore.

"You're David," she said.

I nodded and said hi.

The green eyes studied me. The eyes were intelligent. Warm too. And now she seemed both younger and older than nine.

"Meg says you're nice," she said.

I smiled.

She looked at me a moment more and smiled back at me and then went back to the magazine. On the radio Alan Freed played the Elegants' "Little Star."

Meg stood watching from the doorway. I didn't know what to say.

I walked back down the hall. The others were waiting.

I could feel Ruth's eyes on me. I looked down at the carpet.

"There you go," she said. "Now you know each other."

Chapter Eight

Two nights after Karnival a bunch of us slept out together.

The older guys on the block—Lou Morino, Glen Knott, and Harry Gray—had been in the habit for years now of camping out on warm summer nights at the old water tower in the woods behind the Little League diamond with a couple of six-packs between them and cigarettes stolen from Murphy's store.

We were all still too young for that, with the water tower all the way over on the other side of town. But that hadn't stopped us from envying them aloud and frequently until finally our parents said it would be okay if we camped out too as long as it was under supervision—meaning, in somebody's backyard. So that was what we did.

I had a tent and Tony Morino had his brother

Lou's when he wasn't using it so it was always my backyard or his.

Personally, I preferred my own. Tony's was all right—but what you wanted to do was to get back as far away from the house as possible in order to have the illusion of really being out there on your own and Tony's yard wasn't really suited to that. It tapered down over a hill with just some scrub and a field behind it. The scrub and field were boring and you were resting all night on an incline. Whereas my yard ran straight back into thick deep woods, spooky and dark at night with the shadows of elm, birch and maple trees and wild with sounds of crickets and frogs from the brook. It was flat and a lot more comfortable.

Not that we did much sleeping.

At least that night we didn't.

Since dusk we'd been lying there telling Sick Jokes and Shaddap Jokes ("Mommy, mommy! Billie just vomited into a pan on the stove!" "Shaddap and eat your stew."), the six of us laughing, crunched into a tent that was built for four—me, Donny, Willie, Tony Morino, Kenny Robertson and Eddie.

Woofer was being punished for playing with his plastic soldiers in the wire-mesh incinerator in the yard again—otherwise he might have whined long enough and loud enough to make us take him too. But Woofer had this habit. He'd hang his knights and soldiers from the mesh of the incinerator and watch their arms and legs burn slowly along with the trash, imagining God knows what, the plastic fire dripping, the soldiers curling, the black smoke pluming up.

Ruth hated it when he did that. The toys were expensive and they made a mess all over her incinerator.

There wasn't any beer but we had canteens and Thermoses full of Kool-Aid so that was all right. Eddie had half a pack of his father's Kool unfiltereds and we'd close the tent flaps and pass one around now and then. We'd wave away the smoke. Then we'd open the flaps again just in case my mom came out to check on us—though she never did.

Donny rolled over beside me and you could hear a Tasty-Cake wrapper crush beneath his bulk.

That evening when the truck came by we'd all gone out to the street to stock up.

Now, no matter who moved, something crackled.

Donny had a joke. "So this kid's in school, right? He's just a little kid, sitting at his desk and this nice old lady schoolteacher looks at him and notices he looks real sad and says, what's wrong? And he says, waaa! I didn't get no breakfast! You poor little guy, says the teacher. Well, don't worry, no big deal, she says, it's almost lunchtime. You'll get something to eat then, right? So now let's return to our geography lessons. Where's the Italian border?"

"In bed, fucking my mother, says the little kid. That's how come I didn't get no fucking breakfast!"

We laughed.

"I heard that one," said Eddie. "Or maybe I read it in *Playboy*."

"Sure," said Willie. Willie was on the other side of me over against the tent. I could smell his hair wax and, occasionally and unpleasantly, his bad teeth. "Sure," he said, "you read it in *Playboy*. Like I fucked Debra Paget. Right."

Eddie shrugged. It was dangerous to contradict him but Donny was lying between them and Donny outweighed him by fifteen pounds.

"My old man buys it," he said. "Buys it every month. So I hock it off him outa his drawer, read the jokes, check the broads, and put it back again. He never knows. No sweat."

"You better hope he never knows," said Tony.

Eddie looked at him. Tony lived across the street from him and we all knew that Tony knew that Eddie's dad beat him.

"No shit," said Eddie. There was warning in his voice.

You could almost feel Tony edge away. He was just a skinny little Italian guy but he had some status with us because he already had the downy dark beginnings of a mustache.

"You get to see *all* of 'em?" asked Kenny Robertson. "Jeez. I hear there was one with Jayne Mansfield."

"Not all of 'em," said Eddie.

He lit a cigarette so I closed the flaps again.

"I saw that one, though," he said.

"Honest?"

"Sure did."

He took a drag on the cigarette, being very Mister Cool about it. Willie sat up next to me and I could feel his big flabby belly press softly into my back. He wanted the cigarette but Eddie wasn't passing just yet.

"Biggest tits I ever seen," he said.

"Bigger than Julie London's? Bigger than June Wilkinson's?"

"Shit! Bigger than *Willie's*," he said. Then he and Donny and Tony cracked up laughing—though actually it shouldn't have been all that funny for Donny because Donny was getting them too. Small fatty pouches where the muscle should be. Kenny Robertson, I guess, was too scared to laugh. And Willie was right there beside me so I wasn't saying anything.

"Har-dee-har-har," said Willie. "So fucking funny I forgot to laugh."

"Oh that's cool," said Eddie. "What are you, in the third grade?"

"Eat me," said Willie.

"I'd have to push your mother away, spaz."

"Hey," said Kenny. "Tell us about Jayne Mansfield. You see her nips?"

"Sure you do. She's got this great body and these little juicy pointy nips and these great big tits and this great ass. But her legs are skinny."

"Fuck her legs!" said Donny.

"You fuck 'em," said Eddie. "I'll fuck the rest of her."

"You got it!" said Kenny. "God. Nips and *everything!* Amazing."

Eddie passed him the cigarette. He took a quick drag and then passed it on to Donny.

"The thing is," Kenny said, "she's a movie star. You got to wonder why she'd do that kind of thing."

"What kind of thing?" Donny asked.

"Show her tits that way in a magazine."

We thought about it.

"Well, she's not really a movie star," Donny said. "I mean, Natalie Wood's a movie star. Jayne Mansfield's just sort of in some movies."

"A starlet," said Kenny.

"Naw," said Donny. "She's too fucking old to be a starlet. Dolores Hart's a starlet. You see *Loving You*? I love that scene in the graveyard, man."

"Me too."

"That scene's with Lizabeth Scott," said Willie.

"So what?"

"I like the scene in the soda shop," said Kenny. "Where he sings and beats the shit outa the guy."

"Great," said Eddie.

"Really great," said Willie.

"Really."

"Anyway, you got to figure *Playboy*'s not just a magazine, either," said Donny. "You know, it's *Playboy*. I mean, Marilyn Monroe was in there. It's the greatest magazine ever."

"You think? Better than *Mad*?" Kenny sounded skeptical.

"Shit, yes. I mean, *Mad*'s casual. But it's just for kids, you know?"

"What about *Famous Monsters*?" asked Tony.

That was a tough one. *Famous Monsters* had just appeared and all of us were crazy for it.

"Sure," said Donny. He took a drag on the cigarette and smiled. The smile was all knowing. "Does *Famous Monsters of Filmland* show tits?" he said.

We all laughed. The logic was irrefutable.

He passed the smoke to Eddie, who took a final drag and stubbed it out on the grass, then flipped the butt into the woods.

There was one of those silences where nobody had anything to say, we were all off alone there somewhere.

Then Kenny looked at Donny. "You ever really see it?" he said.

"See what?"

"Tit."

"Real tit?"

"Yeah."

Donny laughed. "Eddie's sister."

That got another laugh because everybody had.

"I mean on a woman."

"Nah."

"Anybody?" He looked around.

"My mother," said Tony. You could tell he was shy about it.

"I walked in one time, into her bathroom, and she was putting her bra on. For a minute I saw."

"A *minute?*" Kenny was really into this.

"No. A second."

"Jeez. What was it like?"

"What do you mean what was it like? It was my mother, for chrissake! Madonn'! You little pervert."

"Hey, no offense, man."

"Yeah. Okay. None taken."

But all of us were thinking of Mrs. Morino now. She was a thick-waisted, short-legged Sicilian woman with a lot more mustache than Tony had but her breasts were pretty big. It was at once difficult and interesting and slightly repulsive to try to picture her that way.

"I'll bet Meg's are nice," said Willie.

It just hung there for a moment. But I doubt that any of us were thinking about Mrs. Morino anymore.

Donny looked at his brother.

"Meg's?"

"Yeah."

You could see the wheels turning. But Willie acted as though Donny hadn't understood. Trying to score points on him.

"Our cousin, dope. *Meg*."

Donny just looked at him. Then he said, "Hey, what time's it?"

Kenny had a watch. "Quarter to eleven."

"Great!"

And suddenly he was crawling out of the tent, and then he was standing there. Peering in, grinning.

"Come on! I got an idea!"

From my house to his all you had to do was cross the yard and go through a line of hedges and you were right behind their garage.

There was a light on in the Chandler's bathroom window and one in the kitchen and one in Meg and Susan's bedroom. By now we knew what he had in mind. I wasn't sure I liked it but I wasn't sure I didn't, either.

Obviously, it was exciting. We weren't supposed to leave the tent. If we got caught that would be the end of sleeping out and plenty of other stuff as well.

On the other hand, if we didn't get caught it was better than camping at the water tower. It was better than beer.

Once you got into the mood of the thing, it was actually kind of hard to restrain yourself from giggling.

"No ladder," whispered Eddie. "How we gonna do this?"

Donny looked around. "The birch tree," he said.

He was right. Off to the left of the yard, about fifteen feet from the house was a tall white birch bent badly by winter storms. It drooped halfway down to the scruffy grass over what was nearly the middle of the lawn.

"We can't *all* climb it," said Tony. "It'll break."

"So we'll take turns. Two at a time. Ten minutes each and the best man wins."

"Okay. Who's first?"

"Hell, it's our tree." Donny grinned. "Me and Willie're first."

I felt a little pissed at him for that. We were supposed to be best friends. But then I figured what the hell, Willie was his brother.

He sprinted across the lawn and Willie followed.

The tree forked out into two strong branches. They could lie there side by side. They had a good straight view into the bedroom and a fair one into the bathroom.

Willie kept changing position though, trying to get comfortable. It was easy to see how out of shape he was. He was awkward just handling his own weight. Whereas, for all his bulk, Donny looked like he was born in trees.

We watched them watching. We watched the house, the kitchen window, looking for Ruth, hoping not to see her.

"Me and Tony next," said Eddie. "What's the time?"

Kenny squinted at his watch. "Five minutes more."

"Shit," said Eddie. He pulled out the pack of Kools and lit one.

"Hey!" whispered Kenny. "They might see!"

"You *might* be stupid," said Eddie. "You cup it under your hand. Like this. Nobody sees."

I was trying to make out Donny's and Willie's faces, wondering if anything was going on inside. It was hard to see but I didn't think so. They just lay there like a pair of large dark tumorous growths.

I wondered if the tree would ever recover.

I hadn't been aware of the frogs or crickets but now I was, a percussive drone in the silence. All you could hear was them and Eddie pulling hard on the cigarette and exhaling and the occasional creak of the birch tree. There were fireflies in the yard blinking on and off, drifting.

"*Time,*" said Kenny.

Eddie dropped the Kool and crushed it and then he and Tony ran over to the tree. A moment later they were up and Willie and Donny were down, back with us.

The tree rested higher now.

"See anything?" I asked.

"Nothing," Willie said. It was surprising how angry he sounded. As though it were Meg's fault for not showing. As though she'd cheated him. But then Willie always was an asshole.

I looked at Donny. The light wasn't good back there but it seemed to me he had that same intent, studied look as when he'd been looking at Ruth talking about the hootchie-koo girls and what they wore and didn't wear. It was as though he were trying to figure something out and was a little depressed because he couldn't get the answer.

We stood together silently and then in a while Kenny tapped me on the shoulder.

"Time," he said.

We ran over to the tree and I slapped Tony's ankle. He slid down.

We stood there waiting for Eddie. I looked at Tony. He shrugged and shook his head, staring at the ground. Nothing. A few minutes later Eddie gave up too and slid down next to me.

"This is bullshit," he said. "Screw it. Screw her."

And they walked away.

I didn't get it. Eddie was mad now too.

I didn't let it worry me.

We went up. The climb was easy.

At the top I felt this great rush of excitement. I wanted to laugh out loud I felt so good. Something was going to happen. I knew it. Too bad for Eddie and Donny and Willie—it was going to be us. She'd be at the window any moment now and we'd see.

It didn't bother me at all that I was probably betraying Meg by spying on her. I hardly even thought of her as Meg. It was as though it wasn't really her that we were looking for. It was something more abstract than that. A real live girl and not some black-and-white photo in a magazine. A woman's body.

I was finally going to learn something.

What you had was a case of greater priority.

We settled in.

I glanced at Kenny. He was grinning.

It occurred to me to wonder why the other guys had acted so pissy.

This was fun! Even the fact that you were scared was fun. Scared that Ruth would appear suddenly on the porch, telling us to get our asses out of there. Scared that Meg would look out the bathroom window straight into your eyes.

I waited, confident.

The bathroom light went off but that didn't matter. It was the bedroom I was focused on. That's where I'd see her.

Straight-on. Naked. Flesh and blood, and someone I actually even knew a bit slightly.

I refused to even blink.

I could feel a tingling down below where I pressed against the tree.

A tune kept running around and around in my head—"Get out in that kitchen and rattle those pots and pans . . . I believe to m'soul you're the devil in nylon hose . . ." And so on.

Wild, I thought. I'm lying here in this tree. She's in there.

I waited.

* * *

The bedroom light went out.

Suddenly the house went dark.

I could have smashed something.

I could have torn that house to bits.

And now I knew exactly how the others had felt and exactly why they'd looked so mad at her, mad at Meg—because it felt like it *was* her fault, as though she was the one who'd got us up here in the first place and promised so much and then delivered nothing. And while I knew this was irrational and dumb of me that was exactly how I felt all the same.

Bitch, I thought.

And then I did feel guilty. Because that was personal.

That *was* about Meg.

And then I felt depressed.

It was as though part of me *knew*—didn't want to believe it or even think about it but knew all along.

I was never going to get that lucky. It had been bullshit from the beginning.

Just like Eddie said.

And somehow the reason for that was all wrapped up with Meg and with girls and women in general, even with Ruth and my mother somehow.

It was too big for me to grasp entirely so I suppose my mind just let it slide.

What remained was depression and a dull ache.

"Come on," I said to Kenny. He was staring at

the house, still not believing it, like he was expecting the lights to come right back on again. But he knew too. He looked at me and I could tell he knew.

All of us did.

We trooped back silently to the tent.

Inside it was Willie Jr., finally, who put the canteen down and spoke.

He said, "Maybe we could get her into The Game."

We thought about that.

And the night wound down from there.

Chapter Nine

I was in my yard trying to get the big red power mower going and sweating straight through my T-shirt already because the damn thing was worse than a motorboat to start, when I heard Ruth shout in a kind of voice I don't think I'd ever heard her use before—really furious.

"Jesus Christ!"

I dropped the cord and looked up.

It was the kind of voice my mother had been known to use when she got unhinged, which wasn't often, despite the open warfare with my father. It meant you ran for cover. But when Ruth got mad it was usually at Woofer and all she had to do then was look at him, her lips pressed tight together, her eyes narrowed down to small glittery stones, in order to shut him up or make him stop whatever he was doing. The look was completely intimidating.

We used to imitate it and laugh, Donny and Willie and I—but when Ruth was the one wearing it it was no laughing matter.

I was glad for an excuse to stop struggling with the mower so I walked around the side of our garage where you could see over into their backyard.

Ruth's wash was blowing on the clothesline. She was standing on the porch, her hands on her hips, and even if you hadn't heard the voice or what she said you could tell she was really mad.

"You stupid shit!" was what she said.

And I can tell you, that shocked me.

Sure, Ruth cursed like a sailor. That was one of the reasons we liked her. Her husband, Willie Sr., "that lovely Irish bastard" or "that idiot mick sonovabitch" and John Lentz, the town's mayor—and, we suspect, Ruth's onetime suitor—got blasted regularly.

Everybody got some now and then.

But the thing is it was always casual swearing, pretty much without real anger. It was meant to get a laugh at some poor guy's expense, and usually did.

It was just Ruth's way of describing people.

It was pretty much like our own. Our friends were all retards, scumbags, lardasses or shit-for-brains. Their mothers all ate the flies off dead camels.

This was wholly different. Shit was what she said, and shit was what she meant.

I wondered what Meg had done.

* * *

I looked up to my own porch where the back screen door was open, hoping my mother wasn't in the kitchen, that she hadn't heard her. My mother didn't approve of Ruth and I got enough grief already for spending as much time over there as I did.

I was in luck. She wasn't around.

I looked at Ruth. She hadn't said anything else and she didn't need to. Her expression said it all.

I felt kind of funny, like I was spying again, twice in two days. But of course that was exactly what I *had* to do. I wasn't about to allow her to see me watching her, exposed the way she was. It was too embarrassing. I pressed up close to the garage and peered around at her, hoping she wouldn't look over my way for any reason. And she didn't.

Their own garage blocked my view, though, so I couldn't see what the problem was. I kept waiting for Meg to show up, to see how she was taking being called a stupid shit.

And then I got another surprise.

Because it wasn't Meg.

It was Susan.

I guessed she'd been trying to help with the laundry. But it had rained last night, and it looked as though she'd dropped some of Ruth's whites on the muddy, scruffy excuse for a lawn they had because you could see the dirt stains on what she carried, a sheet or maybe a couple of pillowcases.

She was crying, really crying hard so that her whole body was shaking as she walked back toward Ruth standing rigid on the landing.

It was pathetic—this little tiny girl moving slowly along with braces on her legs and braces on her arms trying to manage just this one small pile of whites tucked under her arm that she probably shouldn't have had in the first place. I felt bad for her.

And finally, so did Ruth I guess.

Because she stepped down off the landing and took the stuff away from her and hesitated, watching her a moment as she sobbed and shook and stared down into the dirt. And then slowly you could see the tension go out of her as she raised her hand and rested it lightly, tentatively at first on Susan's shoulder, then turned and walked back to the house.

And at the very last moment just as they reached the top of the stairs Ruth looked in my direction so that I had to throw myself back fast and hard against the garage.

But all the same I'd swear to what I saw before that.

It's become a little important to me, actually, in retrospect. I try to figure it out.

Ruth's face looked very tired. Like the burst of anger was so strong it had drained her. Or maybe what I was seeing was just a little piece of something—something bigger—something that had been going on unnoticed by me for quite a while now and this was just like a kind of crescendo on a long-playing record.

But the other thing I saw was what strikes me to this day, what puzzles me.

Even at the time it made me wonder.

Just before I threw myself back, as Ruth turned looking skinny and tired with her hand on Susan's shoulder. In just that instant as she turned.

I'd swear that she was crying too.

And my question is, for whom?

Chapter Ten

The next thing was the tent worms.

It seemed to happen practically overnight. One day the trees were clean and normal and the next day they were hung with these heavy white sacks of webbing. In the bottom of the sacks you could see something vaguely dark and unhealthy-looking and if you looked closely enough you could see them moving.

"We'll burn 'em out," said Ruth.

We were standing in her yard near the birch tree, Woofer, Donny and Willie, Meg and I, and Ruth, who had on her old blue housedress with the deep pockets. It was ten o'clock in the morning and Meg had just finished her chores. There was a little smudge of dirt beneath her left eye.

"You boys gather up some sticks," she said. "Long ones, thick. And be sure to cut them green so they won't burn. Meg, get the rag bag out of the basement."

She stood squinting into the morning sunlight, surveying the damage. Virtually half the trees in their yard including the birch were already strung with sacks, some just the size of baseballs but others wide and deep as a shopping bag. The woods was full of them.

"Little bastards. They'll strip these trees in no time."

Meg went into the house and the rest of us headed for the woods to find some sticks. Donny had his hatchet so we cut some saplings and stripped them and cut them roughly in half. It didn't take long.

When we came back Ruth and Meg were in the garage soaking the rags in kerosene. We wrapped them over the saplings and Ruth tied them off with clothesline and then we soaked them again.

She handed one to each of us.

"I'll show you how it goes," she said. "Then you can do it by yourselves. Just don't set the goddamn woods on fire."

It felt incredibly adult.

Ruth trusting us with fire, with torches.

My mother never would have.

We followed her into the yard looking, I guess, like a bunch of peasants heading out after Frankenstein's monster, our unlit torches aloft. But we didn't act so adult—we acted like we were going to a party—all of us silly and excited except Meg, who was taking it very seriously. Willie got Woofer in a headlock and ground his knuckles into his crewcut, a wrestling move we'd picked up from three hundred-pound Haystacks Calhoun, famous for the Big Splash. Donny and I marched side by side behind them, pumping our torches like a couple of drum majors with batons, giggling like fools. Ruth didn't seem to mind.

When we got to the birch tree Ruth dug into her pocket and pulled out a book of safety matches.

The nest on the birch tree was a big one.

"I'll do this one," said Ruth. "You watch."

She lit the torch and held it a moment until the fire burned down and it was safe to use. It was still a pretty good blaze, though. "Be careful," she said. "You don't want to burn the tree."

She held it six inches or so below the sack.

The sack began to melt.

It didn't burn. It melted the way Styrofoam melts, fading, receding back. It was thick and multilayered but it went fast.

And suddenly all these writhing, wriggling bodies were tumbling out, fat black furry worms—smoking, crackling.

You could almost hear them scream.

There must have been hundreds in just that one nest. A layer of the sack would burn through to expose another layer and there were more in there. They just kept coming, falling to our feet like a black rain.

Then Ruth hit the mother lode.

It was as though a clot of living tar the size of a softball spilled out directly onto the torch, splitting apart as it fell.

The torch sputtered, there were so many of them, and almost seemed to go out for a moment. Then it flared again and those that had clung to it burned and fell.

"Jesus shit!" said Woofer.

Ruth looked at him.

"Sorry," he said. But his eyes were wide.

You had to admit it was incredible. I'd never seen such slaughter. The ants on the porch were nothing to this. Ants were tiny, insignificant. When you tossed the boiling water on them they just curled and died. Whereas some of these were an inch long. They twisted and writhed—they seemed to want to live. I looked at the ground. There were worms all over the place. Most of them were dead, but a lot of them weren't, and those that weren't were trying to crawl away.

"What about these guys?" I asked her.

"Forget them," she said. "They'll just die. Or the birds will get them." She laughed. "We opened the oven before they were ready. Not quite baked yet."

"They're sure baked now," said Willie.

"We could get a rock," said Woofer. "Crush 'em!"

"Listen to me when I talk. Forget them," said Ruth. She reached into her pocket again. "Here." She started handing us each books of matches.

"Remember. I want a yard left when you're through. And no going back into the woods. The woods can take care of itself."

We took them from her. All but Meg.

"I don't want them," she said.

"What?"

She held out the matches.

"I . . . I don't want them. I'll just go finish the laundry okay? This is . . . kind of . . ."

She looked down at the ground, at the black worms curled there, at the live ones crawling. Her face was pale.

"What?" said Ruth. "*Disgusting?* You offended, honey?"

"No. I just don't want . . ."

Ruth laughed. "I'll be damned. Look here boys," she said. "I'll be damned."

She was still smiling, but her face had gone really hard all of a sudden. It startled me and made me think of the other day with Susan. It was as though she'd been on some sort of hair trigger all morning with Meg and we simply hadn't noticed it. We'd been too busy, too excited.

"Look here," she said. "What we've got here is a lesson in femininity." She stepped up close. "Meg's *squeamish*. You understand how girls get squeamish, don't you boys? *Ladies* do. And Meg here is a lady. Why sure she is!"

She dropped the heavy sarcasm then and you could see the naked anger there.

"So what in the name of Jesus Christ do you suppose that makes me, Meggy? You suppose I'm not a lady? You figure ladies can't do what's necessary? Can't get rid of the goddamn pests in their goddamn garden?"

Meg looked confused. It came so fast you couldn't blame her.

"No, I . . ."

"You damn well better say no to me, honey! Because I don't need that kind of insinuation from any kid in a T-shirt can't even wipe her own face clean. You understand?"

"Yes, ma'am."

She backed away a step.

And that seemed to cool Ruth down a little. She took a breath.

"Okay," she said. "You go ahead downstairs. Go on, get back to your laundry. And call me when you're finished. I'll have something else for you."

"Yes, ma'am."

She turned and Ruth smiled.

"My boys can handle it," she said. "Can't you, boys?"

I nodded. At that moment I couldn't speak. Nobody spoke. Her dismissal of Meg was so complete with authority and a strange sense of *justice* I was really a little in awe of her.

She patted Woofer's head.

I glanced at Meg. I saw her walk back to the house, head low, wiping at her face, looking for the smudge of dirt Ruth said was there.

Ruth draped her arm across my shoulder and turned toward the elm trees in the back. I inhaled the scent of her—soap and kerosene and cigarettes and clean fresh hair.

"My boys can do it," she said to me. And her voice was very gentle again.

Chapter Eleven

By one o'clock we'd torched every nest in the Chandlers' yard, and Ruth had been right—the birds were having a field day now.

I stunk of kerosene.

I was starving and would have killed for a few White Castles just then. I settled for a bologna sandwich.

I went home.

I washed up in the kitchen and made one.

I could hear my mother in the living room ironing, humming along to the original cast album of *The Music Man*, which she and my father had bussed to New York to see last year, just before the shit hit the fan about what I could only assume was my father's latest affair. My father had plenty of opportunity for affairs and he took them. He was co-owner of a bar and restaurant called the Eagle's Nest. He met them late and he met them early.

But I guess my mother had forgotten all that for the moment and was remembering the good times now with Professor Harold Hill and company.

I hated *The Music Man*.

I shut myself in my room awhile and flipped through my dog-eared copies of *Macabre* and *Stranger Than Science* but there was nothing in there that interested me so I decided to go out again.

I walked out the back and Meg was standing on the Chandlers' back porch shaking out the living-room throw rugs. She saw me and motioned me over.

I felt a moment of awkwardness, of divided loyalty.

If Meg was on Ruth's shit list, there was probably some good reason for it.

On the other hand I still remembered that ride on the Ferris wheel and that morning by the Big Rock.

She draped the rugs carefully over the iron railing and came down off the steps across the driveway to meet me. The smudge on her face was gone but she still wore the dirty yellow shirt and Donny's old rolled-up Bermudas. There was dust in her hair.

She took me by the arm and led me silently over to the side of her house, out of sight lines from the dining room window.

"I don't get it," she said.

You could see there was something troubling her, something she'd been working on.

"Why don't they like me, David?"

That wasn't what I'd expected. "Who, the Chandlers?"

"Yes."

She just looked at me. She was serious.

"Sure they do. They like you."

"No they don't. I mean, I do everything I *can* to make them like me. I do more than my share of the work. I try to talk with them, get to know them, get them to know me, but they just don't seem to want to. It's like they *want* to not like me. Like it's better that way."

It was embarrassing. It was friends she was talking about here.

"Look," I said. "So Ruth got mad at you. I don't know why. Maybe she's having a bad day. But nobody else got mad. Willie and Woofer and Donny didn't get mad."

She shook her head. "You don't understand. Willie and Woofer and Donny *never* get mad. It's not that. Not with them. It's just that they never seem to *see* me here, either. Like I don't exist. Like I don't matter. I talk to them and they grunt and walk away. Or else when they *do* notice there's something . . . not right about it. The way they look at me. And Ruth . . ."

She'd started now and there was no stopping her.

". . . Ruth *hates* me! Me and Susan both. You don't see it. You think this was just one thing just this one time but it's not. It's all the time. I work all day for her some days and I just can't please her, nothing's right, nothing's ever the way she'd do it. I know she thinks I'm stupid, lazy, ugly . . ."

"*Ugly?*" That, at least, was obviously ridiculous.

She nodded. "I never thought I was before but now I don't even know. David, you've known these people all your life practically, right?"

"Yeah I have."

"So *why?* What did I do? I go to bed at night and it's all I can think about. We were both real happy before. You know, before we came here I used to paint. Nothing very much, just a watercolor now and then. I don't suppose I was ever too great at it. But my mother used to like them. And Susan used to like them, and my teachers. I've still got the paints and brushes but I just can't start to do one anymore. You know why? Because I know what Ruth would do, I know what she'd think. I know what she'd *say*. She'd just look at me and I'd know I was stupid and wasting my time to even try."

I shook my head. That wasn't the Ruth I knew. You could see Willie and Woofer and Donny acting strange around her—she was a girl, after all. But Ruth had always been good to us. Unlike the rest of the mothers on the block she always had plenty of time for us. Her door was always open. She handed us Cokes, sandwiches, cookies, the occasional beer. It didn't make sense and I told her so.

"Come on. Ruth wouldn't do that. Try it. Make *her* one. Make her a watercolor. I bet she'd love it. Maybe she's just not used to having girls around, you know? Maybe it just takes time. Do it. Try one for her."

She thought about it.

"I couldn't," she said. "Honest."

For a moment we just stood there. She was shaking. I knew that whatever this was all about, she wasn't kidding.

I had an idea.

"How about me, then? You could make one for me."

Without the idea in mind, without the plan, I'd never have had the nerve to ask her. But this was different.

She brightened a little.

"Would you really want one?"

"Sure I would. I'd like it a lot."

She looked at me steadily until I had to turn away. Then she smiled. "Okay. I will, David."

She seemed almost her usual self again. God! I liked it when she smiled. Then I heard the back door open.

"Meg?"

It was Ruth.

"I'd better go," she said.

She took my hand and squeezed it. I could feel the stones in her mother's wedding band. My face reddened.

"I'll do it," she said, and fled around the corner.

Chapter Twelve

She must have got right on it too because the next day it rained all day into the evening and I sat in my room reading *The Search for Bridey Murphy* and listening to the radio until I thought I'd probably kill somebody if I heard that fucking Domenico Modugno sing "Volare" one more time. And then after dinner my mother and I were sitting in the living room watching television when Meg knocked at the back door.

My mother got up. I followed her and got myself a Pepsi out of the refrigerator.

Meg was smiling, wearing a yellow slicker, her hair dripping wet.

"I can't come in," she said.

"Nonsense," said my mother.

"No, really," she said. "I just came over to give you this from Mrs. Chandler."

She handed my mother a wet brown bag with a container of milk inside. Ruth and my mother didn't exactly socialize but they were still next door neighbors and neighbors borrowed.

My mother accepted the bag and nodded. "Tell Mrs. Chandler thank you for me," she said.

"I will."

Then she dug down underneath the slicker and looked at me, and now she was really smiling.

"And this is for you," she said.

And handed me my painting.

It was wrapped with sheets of heavy opaque tracing paper taped together on both sides. You could see some of the lines and colors through it but not the shapes of things.

Before I could even say thanks or anything she said, "Bye," and waved and stepped back out into the rain and closed the door behind her.

"Well," said my mother, and she was smiling too now. "What have we here?"

"I think it's a picture," I said.

I stood there, Pepsi in one hand and Meg's painting in the other. I knew what my mother was thinking.

What my mother was thinking had the word *cute* in it.

"Aren't you going to open it?"

"Yeah, sure. Okay."

I put down the Pepsi and turned my back to her and began working on the tape. Then I lifted off the tracing paper.

I could feel my mother looking over my shoulder but I really didn't care all of a sudden.

"That's really *good*," my mother said, surprised. "That's really very good. She's really quite something, isn't she."

And it was good. I was no art critic but you didn't have to be. She'd done the drawing in ink, and some of the lines were wide and bold and some were very delicate. The colors were pale washes—only the subtle suggestions of colors but very true and lifelike with a lot of the paper showing so it gave you the impression of a bright, sunny day.

It was a picture of a boy by a flowing brook, lying on his belly across a big flat rock and looking down into the water, with trees and sky all around.

Chapter Thirteen

I took it up to The Dog House to have it framed. The Dog House was a pet shop turned hobby shop. They had beagle pups in the front window and bows and arrows, Wham-O hula hoops, model kits and a frame shop in the back, with the fish, turtles, snakes and canaries in between. The guy took a look and said, “Not bad.”

“Can I have it tomorrow?”

“You see us going crazy here?” he said. The place was empty. The 2-Guys From Harrison chain store up on Route 10 was killing him. “You can have it tonight. Come back ’round four-thirty.”

I was there by a quarter after four, fifteen minutes early, but it was ready, a nice pine frame stained mahogany. He wrapped it in brown paper.

It fit perfectly into one of the two rear baskets on my bike.

By the time I got home it was almost dinnertime so I had to wait through the pot roast and green beans and mashed potatoes with gravy. Then I had to take the garbage out.

Then I went over.

The television was blaring the theme from *Father Knows Best*, my least favorite TV show, and down the stairs for the billionth time came Kathy and Bud and Betty, beaming. I could smell the franks and beans and sauerkraut. Ruth was in her chair with her feet up on the hassock. Donny and Willie sprawled together on the couch. Woofer lay on his belly so close to the TV set you had to wonder about his hearing. Susan sat watching from a straight-back chair in the dining room and Meg was out doing the dishes.

Susan smiled at me. Donny just waved and turned back to watch TV.

"Jeez," I said. "Don't anybody get up or nothing."

"Watcha got there, sport?" said Donny.

I held up the painting wrapped in brown paper.

"Those Mario Lanza records you wanted."

He laughed. "Creep."

And now Ruth was looking at me.

I decided to jump right in.

I heard the water shut off in the kitchen. I turned and Meg was watching me, wiping her hands on her apron. I gave her a smile and my guess is she knew right away what I was doing.

"Ruth?"

"Yeah? Ralphie, turn the TV down. That's it. What's up, Davy?"

I walked over to her. I glanced over my shoulder

at Meg. She was coming toward me through the dining room. She was shaking her head. Her mouth was forming a silent "no."

That was okay. It was just shyness. Ruth would see the painting and she'd get over it.

"Ruth," I said. "This is from Meg."

I held it out to her.

She smiled first at me and then at Meg and took it from me. Woofer had *Father Knows Best* turned low now so you could hear the crinkling of the stiff brown paper as she unwrapped it. The paper fell away. She looked at the painting.

"Meg!" she said. "Where'd you get the money to buy this?"

You could tell she admired it. I laughed.

"It costs just the framing," I said. "She *painted* it for you."

"She did? Meg did?"

I nodded.

Donny, Woofer and Willie all crowded around to see.

Susan slipped off her chair. "It's beautiful!" she said.

I glanced at Meg again still standing anxious and hopeful looking in the dining room.

Ruth stared at the painting. It seemed like she stared a long time.

Then she said, "No, she didn't. Not for me. Don't kid me. She painted it for *you*, Davy."

She smiled. The smile was a little funny somehow. And now I was getting anxious too.

"Look here. A boy on a rock. Of course it's for you."

She handed it back to me.

"I don't want it," she said.

I felt confused. That Ruth might refuse it had never even occurred to me. For a moment I didn't know what to do. I stood there holding it, looking down at it. It was a beautiful painting.

I tried to explain.

"But it's really *meant* for you, Ruth. Honest. See, we talked about it. And Meg wanted to do one for you but she was so . . ."

"David."

It was Meg, stopping me. And now I was even more confused, because her voice was stern with warning.

It made me almost angry. Here I was in the middle of this damn thing and Meg wouldn't let me get myself out of it.

Ruth just smiled again. Then looked at Willie and Woofer and Donny.

"Take a lesson, boys. Remember this. It's important. All you got to do any time is be nice to a woman—and she'll do all kinds of good things for you. Now Davy was nice to Meg and got himself a painting. Nice painting. That *is* what you got, isn't it, Davy? I mean that's *all* you got? I know you're a little young but you never know."

I laughed, blushing. "Come on, Ruth."

"Well, I'm telling you you *do* never know. Girls are plain easy. That's their problem. Promise 'em a little something and you can have whatever you want half the time. I know what I'm saying. Look at your father. Look at Willie Sr. He was gonna own his own company when we married. Fleet of milk trucks. Start with one and work his way on up. I was gonna help him with the books just like I did back on Howard Avenue during the war. *Ran* that plant during the war. We were gonna be richer than my folks were when I was a kid in Morristown, and that was pretty rich, I'll tell you. But you know what I got? Nothing. Not a damned thing. Just you three poppin' out one, two, three, and that lovely Irish bastard's off to God knows where. So I get three hungry mouths to feed, and now I've got two more.

"I tell you, girls are dumb. Girls are *easy*. Suckers straight on down the line."

She walked past me to Meg. She put her arm around her shoulders and then she turned to the rest of us.

"You take this painting now," she said. "I know you made it for David here and don't you try to tell me any different. But what I want to know is, what are you gonna *get* out of it? What do you think this boy's going to give you? Now Davy's a nice boy. Better than most I'd say. Definitely better. But darlin'—he's not gonna give you nothing! If you think he will you got another thing coming.

"So I'm just saying I hope that painting's all you been giving him and all you will give him, and this is for your own good I'm telling you. Because you already got what men want right down here and it ain't your goddamn *artwork*."

I could see Meg's face begin to tremble, and I knew she was trying not to cry. But unexpected as all this was I was trying not to laugh. Donny too. The whole thing was weird and maybe it was partly the tension, but what Ruth had said about the artwork was *funny*.

Her arm tightened around Meg's shoulders.

"And if you *give* them what they want, then you're nothing but a slut, honey. You know what a slut is? Do you, Susan? Of course you don't. You're too young. Well, a slut's somebody who'll spread her legs for a man, it's that simple. So they can weasel their way inside. Woofer, you quit your goddamn grinning.

"Anybody who's a slut deserves a thrashing. Anybody in this town would agree with me. So I just warn you, honey, any slutting around this house will mean your ass is grass and Ruth's the lawn mower."

She released Meg and walked into the kitchen. She opened the refrigerator door.

"Now," she said. "Who wants a beer?"

She gestured toward the painting.

"Kind of pale-looking thing, anyway," she said, "doncha think?" and reached for the six-pack.

Chapter Fourteen

Two beers was all it took me in those days and I went home lazy and high, with the usual promise not to breathe a word to my parents, which wasn't necessary. I'd sooner have chopped off a finger.

Once Ruth finished her lecture, the rest of the evening had been pretty uneventful. Meg went into the bathroom for a while and when she came out again it was as though nothing had happened. Her eyes were dry. Her face an unreadable blank. We watched *Danny Thomas* and drank our beers and then at one point during a commercial I made plans to go bowling Saturday with Willie and Donny. I tried to catch Meg's eye but she wouldn't look at me. When the beers were done I went home.

I hung the painting next to the mirror in my room.

But there was a feeling of strangeness that

wouldn't leave me. I'd never heard anyone use the word *slut* before but I knew what it meant. I'd known since cribbing *Peyton Place* from my mother. I wondered if Eddie's sister Denise was still too young to qualify. I remembered her naked, bound to a tree, her thick smooth tender nipples. Crying, laughing—sometimes both together. I remembered the folded flesh between her legs.

I thought about Meg.

I lay in bed and thought how easy it was to hurt a person. It didn't have to be physical. All you had to do was take a good hard kick at something they cared about.

I could too if I wanted.

People were vulnerable.

I thought about my parents and what they were doing and how they kept kicking at each other. So regularly now that, being in the middle as I was, I had contrived not to care about either of them.

Little things, mostly, but they added up.

I couldn't sleep. My parents were in the next room, my father snoring. I got up and went into the kitchen for a Coke. Then I went into the living room and sat on the couch. I didn't turn the lights on.

It was well after midnight.

The night was warm. There was no breeze. As usual my parents had left the windows open.

Through the screen I could see directly into the Chandlers' living room. Their lights were still burning. Their windows were open too and I heard voices. I couldn't make out much of what was being said but I knew who was speaking.

Willie. Ruth. Then Meg. Then Donny. Even Woofer was still up—you could hear his voice high and shrill as a girl's, laughing.

The others were all yelling about something.

". . . for a *boy!*" I heard Ruth say. Then she faded out again into a mixed jumble of sounds and voices all together.

I saw Meg move back into the frame of the living-room window. She was pointing, yelling, her whole body rigid and shaking with anger.

"You will *not!*" I heard her say.

Then Ruth said something low and out of my hearing range but it came out like a growl, you could get that much, and you could see Meg sort of collapse all of a sudden, you could watch her fold. And then she was crying.

And a hand shot out and slapped her.

It slapped her so hard she fell back out of frame and I couldn't see her anymore.

Willie moved forward.

He started to follow her. Slowly.

Like he was stalking her.

"That's it!" I heard Ruth say. Meaning, I think, that Willie should let her alone.

There was a moment where I guess nobody moved.

Then bodies came and went for a while, drifting by the window, everybody looking sullen and angry, Willie and Woofer and Donny and Ruth and Meg picking up things from the floor or rearranging the chairs or whatever and slowly moving away. I heard no more voices, no talking. The only one I didn't see was Susan.

I sat watching.

The lights went off. You could see a dim glow from the bedrooms and that was all. Then even that was gone and the house was black as ours was.

Chapter Fifteen

That Saturday at the alleys Kenny Robertson missed his seven pin for an easy spare in the tenth frame, finishing with a 107. Kenny was skinny and had a tendency to throw every pound he had into the ball and throw it wild. He came back mopping his brow with his father's lucky handkerchief, which hadn't been too lucky for him at all that day.

He sat between me and Willie behind the score-card. We watched Donny line up on his usual spot to the left of the second arrow.

"You think any more about it?" he asked Willie. "About getting Meg into The Game?"

Willie smiled. I guess he was feeling good. He was probably going to break 150 and that didn't happen often. He shook his head.

"We got our own Game now," he said.

III

Chapter Sixteen

Those nights I'd sleep at the Chandlers', once we got tired of fooling around and Woofer was asleep, we'd talk.

It was mostly Donny and I. Willie never had much to say and what he did say was never too smart. But Donny was bright enough and, as I said, the closest I had to a best friend, so we'd talk—about school and girls, the kids on *American Bandstand*, the endless mysteries of sex, what the rock 'n' roll tunes we heard on the radio *really* meant and so on, until long into the night.

We talked about wishes, hopes, even nightmares sometimes.

It was always Donny who initiated these talks and always I who finished them. At some point long past exhaustion I'd lean over the top of my bunk and say something like, see what I mean? and he'd be asleep, leaving me alone at the mercy of my thoughts, uncomfortable and unspent, sometimes till dawn. It took time for me to cut deep enough into whatever it was I felt and then once I did I couldn't bear to give up the taste of it.

I'm still that way.

The dialogue is solo now. I don't talk. No matter who's in bed with me I never do. My thoughts slip off into nightmares sometimes but I don't share them. I have become now what I only began to be then—completely self-protective.

It started, I suppose, with my mother coming into my room when I was seven. I was asleep. "I'm leaving your dad," she said, waking me. "But I don't want you to worry. I'll take you with me. I won't leave you. Not ever." And I know that from seven to fourteen I waited, prepared myself, *became* myself who was separate from each of them.

That, I guess, was how it started.

But between seven and thirteen Ruth happened, and Meg and Susan happened. Without them that conversation with my mother might even have been good for me. It might only have saved me from shock and confusion once the time came. Because kids are resilient. They bounce back to confidence and sharing.

I wasn't able to. And that's due to what happened after, to what I did and didn't do.

My first wife, Evelyn, calls me sometimes, wakes me up at night.

"Are the children all right?" she asks me. Her voice is terrified.

We had no kids together, Evelyn and I.

She'd been in and out of institutions a number of times, suffering bouts of acute depression and anxiety but still it's uncanny, this fixation of hers.

Because I never told her. Not any of this, never.

So how could she know?

Do I talk in my sleep? Did I confess to her one night? Or is she simply sensing something hidden in me—about the only real reason we never did have children. About why I never allowed us to.

Her calls are like nightbirds flying screeching around my head. I keep waiting for them to return. When they do I'm taken by surprise.

It's frightening.

Are the children all right?

I've long since learned not to ruffle her. Yes, Evelyn, I tell her. Sure. They're fine. Go back to sleep now, I say.

But the children are not fine.

They will never be.

Chapter Seventeen

I knocked on the back screen door.

Nobody answered.

I opened it and walked inside.

I heard them laughing right away. It was coming from one of the bedrooms. Meg's was a kind of high-pitched squealing sound, Woofer's a hysterical giggle. Willie Jr's. and Donny's were lower, more masculine-sounding.

I wasn't supposed to be there—I was being punished. I'd been working on a model of a B-52, a Christmas present from my father, and I couldn't get one of the wheels on right. So I tried about three or four times and then hauled off and kicked it to pieces against the bedroom door. My mother came in and it was a whole big scene and I was grounded.

My mother was out shopping now. For a moment at least, I was free.

I headed for the bedrooms.

They had Meg up against the bedroom wall in a corner by the window.

Donny turned around.

"Hey, David! She's *ticklish!* Meg's ticklish!"

And then it was like there was this prearranged signal because they all went at her at once, going for her ribs while she twisted and tried to push them away and then doubled over, elbows down to cover her ribs, laughing, her long red ponytail swinging.

"Get her!"

"I got her!"

"*Get* her, Willie!"

I looked over and there was Susan sitting on the bed, and she was laughing too.

"Owww!"

I heard a slap. I looked up.

Meg's hand was covering her breast and Woofer had his own hand up to his face where the redness was spreading and you could see he was going to cry. Willie and Donny stood away.

"What the hell!"

Donny was mad. It was fine if he belted Woofer but he didn't like it if anybody else did.

"You bitch!" said Willie.

He took an awkward open-handed swing at the top of her head. She moved easily out of its way. He didn't try again.

"What'd you have to do that for?"

"You saw what he did!"

"He didn't do nothin'."

"He pinched me."

"So what."

Woofer was crying now. "I'm *telling!*" he howled.

"Go ahead," said Meg.

"You won't like it if I do," said Woofer.

"I don't care *what* you do. I don't care what any of you do." She pushed Willie aside and walked between them past me down the hall into the living room. I heard the front door slam.

"Little bitch," said Willie. He turned to Susan. "Your sister's a goddamn bitch."

Susan said nothing. He moved toward her though and I saw her flinch.

"You see that?"

"I wasn't looking," I said.

Woofer was sniveling. There was snot running all down his chin.

"She *bit* me!" he yelled. Then he ran past me too.

"I'm telling Ma," said Willie.

"Yeah. Me too," said Donny. "She can't get away with that."

"We were just foolin' around, for chrissakes."

Donny nodded.

"She really whacked him."

"Well, Woofer touched her tit."

"So what. He didn't mean to."

"You could get a shiner like that."

"He could still get one."

"Bitch."

There was all this nervous energy in the room.

Willie and Donny were pacing like pent-up bulls. Susan slid off the bed. Her braces made a sharp metallic clatter.

"Where you going?" said Donny.

"I want to see Meg," she said quietly.

"Screw Meg. You stay here. You saw what she did, didn't you?"

Susan nodded.

"All right then. You know she's gonna get punished, right?"

He sounded very reasonable, like an older brother explaining something very patiently to a not-too-bright sister. She nodded again.

"So you want to side with her and get punished too? You want your privileges taken away?"

"No."

"Then you stay right here, okay?"

"All right."

"Right in this room."

"All right."

"Let's find Ma," he said to Willie.

I followed them out of the bedroom through the dining room and out the back door.

Ruth was around back of the garage, weeding her patch of tomatoes. The dress she wore was old and faded and much too big for her, cinched tight at the middle. The scoop neck hung open wide.

She never wore a bra. I stood over her and I could see her breasts almost to the nipple. They were small and pale and they trembled as she worked. I kept glancing away, afraid she'd notice, but my eyes were like a compass needle and her breasts were due north.

"Meg hit Woofer," said Willie.

"She did?" She didn't seem concerned. She just kept weeding.

"Slapped him," said Donny.

"Why?"

"We were just fooling around."

"Everybody was tickling her," said Willie. "So she hauls off and clobbers him in the face. Just like that."

She tugged out a patch of weeds. The breasts shook. They had gooseflesh on them. I was fascinated. She looked at me and my eyes got to hers just in time.

"You too, Davy?"

"Huh?"

"You tickling Meg too?"

"No. I just came in."

She smiled. "I'm not accusing you."

She got to her knees and then stood up and pulled off the dirty work gloves.

"Where's she now?"

"Don't know," said Donny. "She ran out the door."

"How about Susan?"

"She's in the bedroom."

"She saw all this?"

"Yeah."

"Okay."

She marched across the lawn toward the house and we followed. At the porch she wiped her thin bony hands over her hips. She pulled off the scarf that bound her short brown hair and shook it free.

I figured I had maybe twenty minutes before my mother came home from shopping so I went inside.

We followed her into the bedroom. Susan sat right where we left her on the bed looking at a magazine, open to a picture of Liz and Eddie Fisher on one page facing across to Debbie Reynolds on the other. Eddie and Liz looked happy, smiling. Debbie looked sour.

"Susan? Where's Meg?"

"I don't know, ma'am. She left."

Ruth sat down next to her on the bed. She patted her hand.

"Now I'm told you saw what happened here. That right?"

"Yes, ma'am. Woofer touched Meg and Meg hit him."

"Touched her?"

Susan nodded and placed her hand over her skinny little chest like she was pledging allegiance to the flag. "Here," she said.

Ruth just stared for a moment.

Then she said, "And did you try to stop her?"

"Stop Meg you mean?"

"Yes. From hitting Ralphie."

Susan looked bewildered. "I couldn't. It was too fast, Mrs. Chandler. Woofer touched her and then right away Meg hit him."

"You should have tried, honey." She patted her hand again. "Meg's your sister."

"Yes, ma'am."

"You hit somebody in the face and it can do all kinds of things. You could miss and break an eardrum, poke out an eye. That's dangerous behavior."

"Yes, Mrs. Chandler."

"Ruth. I told you. Ruth."

"Yes, Ruth."

"And you know what it means to be in connivance with somebody who does that kind of thing?"

She shook her head.

"It means you're guilty too, even though maybe you didn't *do* anything in particular. You're sort of a fellow traveler. You understand me?"

"I don't know."

Ruth sighed. "Let me explain to you. You love your sister, right?"

Susan nodded.

"And *because* you love her, you'd forgive her something like this, wouldn't you? Like hitting Ralphie?"

"She didn't mean to hurt him. She just got mad!"

"Of course she did. So you'd forgive her, am I right?"

"Uh-huh."

Ruth smiled. "Well now you see that's just plain *wrong*, honey! That's just what puts you in connivance with her. What she did wasn't right, it's bad behavior, and you forgiving her just because you love her, that's not right either. You got to stop this sympathizin', Suzie. It doesn't matter that Meg's your sister. Right's right. You got to remember that if you want to get along in life. Now you just slip over the side of the bed here, pull up your dress and slide down your drawers."

Susan stared at her. Wide-eyed, frozen.

Ruth got off the bed. She unbuckled her belt.

"C'mon, hon'," she said. "It's for your own good. I got to teach you about connivance. You see, Meg's not here for her share. So you got to get it for both of you. Your share's for not saying, hey, cut that out, Meg—sister or no sister. Right's right. Her share's for doing it in the first place. So you come on over here now. Don't make me drag you."

Susan just stared. It was as though she *couldn't* move.

"Okay," said Ruth. "Disobedience is another thing."

She reached over and firmly—though not what you'd call roughly—took Susan by the arm and slid her off the bed. Susan began to cry. The leg braces clattered. Ruth turned her around so she faced the bed and leaned her over. Then she pulled up the back of her frilled red dress and tucked it into her waistband.

Willie snorted, laughing. Ruth shot him a look.

She pulled down the little white cotton panties, down over the braces around her ankles.

"We'll give you five for conniving, ten for Meg. And five for disobeying. Twenty."

Susan was really crying now. I could hear her. I watched the stream of tears roll down across her cheek. I felt suddenly shamed and started to move back through the doorway. Some impulse from Donny told me that maybe he wanted to do the same. But Ruth must have seen us.

"You stay put, boys. Girls just cry. There's nothing you can do about it. But this is for her own good and you being here's a part of it and I want you to stay."

The belt was thin fabric, not leather. So maybe it wouldn't hurt too bad, I thought.

She doubled it over and raised it above her head. It whistled down.

Smack.

Susan gasped and began crying in earnest, loudly.

Her behind was as pale as Ruth's breasts had been, covered with a fine thin platinum down. And now it trembled too. I could see a red spot rise high on her left cheek near the dimple.

I looked at Ruth as she raised the belt again. Her lips were pressed tight together. Otherwise she was expressionless, concentrating.

The belt fell again and Susan howled.

A third time and then a fourth, in rapid succession.

Her ass was splotchy red now.

A fifth.

She seemed to be almost gagging on mucus and tears, her breath coming in gulps.

Ruth was swinging wider. We had to back away.

I counted. Six. Seven. Eight, nine, ten.

Susan's legs were twitching. Her knuckles white where she gripped the bedspread.

I'd never heard such crying.

Run, I thought. Jesus! I'd damn well run.

But then of course she couldn't run. She might just as well have been chained there.

And that made me think of The Game.

Here was Ruth, I thought, playing The Game.

I'll be goddamned. And even though I winced every time the belt came down I just couldn't get over it. The idea was amazing to me. An adult. *An adult* was playing The Game. It wasn't the same exactly but it was close enough.

And all of a sudden it didn't feel so forbidden anymore. The guilt seemed to fall away. But the excitement of it remained. I could feel my fingernails dig deep into the palms of my hands.

I kept count. Eleven. Twelve. Thirteen.

There were tiny beads of perspiration across Ruth's upper lip and forehead. Her strokes were mechanical. *Fourteen. Fifteen.* Her arm went up. Beneath the beltless, shapeless dress I could see her belly heave.

"Wow!"

Woofer slipped into the room between me and Donny.

Sixteen.

He was staring at Susan's red, twisted face. "Wow," he said again.

And I knew he was thinking what I was thinking—what we all were thinking.

Punishments were private. At my house they were at least. At everybody's house, as far as I knew.

This wasn't punishment. This was The Game.

Seventeen. Eighteen.

Susan fell to the floor.

Ruth bent over her.

She was sobbing, her whole frail body twitching now, head buried between her arms, her knees drawn up as tight to her chest as the casts permitted.

Ruth was breathing heavily. She pulled up Susan's panties. She lifted her up and slid her back on the bed, lying her on her side and smoothing the dress down over her legs.

"All right," she said softly. "That'll do. You just rest now. You owe me two."

And then we all just stood a moment, listening to the muffled sobbing.

I heard a car pull in next door.

"Shit!" I said. "My mother!"

I raced through the living room, out the door to the side of their house and peered through the hedges. My mother was pulled in all the way to the garage. She had the back of the station wagon open and was bent over lifting out bags marked A&P.

I dashed across the driveway to our front door and ran up the stairs to my room. I opened a magazine.

I heard the back door open.

"David! Come on down here and help me with the groceries!"

It slammed shut.

I went out to the car. My mother was frowning. She handed me one bag after another.

"The place was absolutely mobbed," she said. "What have you been doing?"

"Nothing. Reading."

As I turned to go back inside I saw Meg across the street from the Chandlers' standing by the trees in front of Zorns' house.

She was staring at the Chandlers' and chewing on a blade of grass, looking thoughtful, as though she were trying to decide about something.

She didn't seem to see me.

I wondered what she knew.

I took the bags inside.

Then later I went out to the garage to get the garden hose and I saw them in the yard, just Meg and Susan, sitting in the tall splotchy grass beyond the birch tree.

Meg was brushing Susan's hair. Long smooth strokes of the brush that were firm and even but delicate too, as though the hair could bruise if you didn't get it right. Her other hand caressed it from below and under, stroking with just the tips of the fingers, lifting it and letting it gently fall.

Susan was smiling. Not a big smile but you could see her pleasure, how Meg was soothing her.

And for a moment I realized how connected the two of them were, how alone and special in that connection. I almost envied them.

I didn't disturb them.

I found the garden hose. Coming out of the garage the breeze had shifted and I could hear Meg humming. It was very soft, like a lullaby. "Goodnight Irene." A song my mother used to sing on long nighttime car trips when I was little.

Goodnight, Irene, goodnight, Irene, I'll see you in my dreams.

I caught myself humming it all day. And every time I did I'd see Meg and Susan sitting in the grass together and feel the sun on my face and the stroke of the brush and the soft smooth hands.

Chapter Eighteen

"David, have you got any money?"

I felt around in my pockets and came up with a crinkled dollar bill and thirty-five cents in change. We were walking over to the playground, Meg and I. There was going to be a game there in a little while. I had my left-handed fielder's mitt and an old black-taped ball.

I showed her the money.

"Would you loan it to me?"

"*All* of it?"

"I'm hungry," she said.

"Yeah?"

"I want to go over to Cozy Snacks for a sandwich."

"For a *sandwich?*"

I laughed. "Why doncha just steal a couple of candy bars? The counter's easy there."

I'd done it myself on plenty of occasions. Most of us did. The best was just to walk up to whatever you wanted and take it and then walk right out again. Nothing furtive and no hesitations. The place was always busy. There was nothing to it. And nobody had any use for Mr. Holly, the old guy who ran the place, so there wasn't any guilt involved.

But Meg just frowned. "I don't steal," she said.

Well jeez, I thought, meet Miss Priss.

I felt a little contempt for her. *Everybody* stole. It was part of being a kid.

"Just loan me the money, will you?" she said. "I'll pay you back. I promise."

I couldn't stay mad at her.

"Okay. Sure," I said. I dumped it into her hand. "But what do you want a sandwich for? Make one at Ruth's."

"I can't."

"How come?"

"I'm not supposed to."

"Why?"

"I'm not supposed to eat yet."

We crossed the street. I looked left and right and then I looked at her. She had that masked look. Like there was something she wasn't telling. Plus she was blushing.

"I don't get it."

Kenny and Eddie and Lou Marino were already on the diamond tossing a ball around. Denise was standing behind the backstop watching them. But nobody saw us yet. I could tell Meg wanted to go but I just stared at her.

"Ruth says I'm fat," she said finally.

I laughed.

"Well?" she said.

"Well what?"

"Am I?"

"What? Fat?" I knew she was serious but I still had to laugh. " 'Course not. She's kidding you."

She turned abruptly. "Some joke," she said. "You just *try* going without dinner *and* breakfast *and* lunch for a day."

Then she stopped and turned back to me. "Thanks," she said.

And then she walked away.

Chapter Nineteen

The ball game dissolved about an hour after it started. By that time most of the kids on the block were there, not just Kenny and Eddie and Denise and Lou Morino but Willie, Donny, Tony Morino and even Glen Knott and Harry Gray, who showed up because Lou was playing. With the older kids there it was a good fast game—until Eddie hit his hard line drive down the third-base line and started running.

Everybody but Eddie knew it was foul. But there was no telling Eddie that. He rounded the bases while Kenny went to chase the ball. And then there was the usual argument. Fuck you and fuck you and no, fuck *you*.

The only difference was that this time Eddie picked up his bat and went after Lou Morino.

Lou was bigger and older than Eddie but Eddie

had the bat, and the upshot was that rather than risk a broken nose or a concussion, he stalked off the field in one direction taking Harry and Glen along with him while Eddie stalked off the other way.

The rest of us played catch.

That was what we were doing when Meg came by again.

She dropped some change into my hand and I put it in my pocket.

"I owe you eighty-five cents," she said.

"Okay."

I noticed that her hair was just a little oily, like she hadn't washed it that morning. She still looked nice though.

"Want to do something?" she said.

"What?"

I looked around. I guess I was afraid the others would hear.

"I don't know. Go down by the brook?"

Donny threw me the ball. I pegged it at Willie. As usual he slumped after it too slowly and missed.

"Never mind," said Meg. "You're too busy."

She was irritated or hurt or something. She started to walk away.

"No. Hey. Wait."

I couldn't ask her to play. It was hardball and she had no glove.

"Okay, sure. We'll go down to the brook. Hang on a minute."

There was only one way to do this gracefully. I had to ask the others.

"Hey guys! Want to go down to the brook? Catch some crayfish or something? It's hot here."

Actually the brook didn't sound bad to me. It *was* hot.

"Sure. I'll go," said Donny. Willie shrugged and nodded.

"Me too," said Denise.

Great, I thought. Denise. Now all we need is Woofer.

"I'm gonna go get some lunch," said Kenny. "Maybe I'll meet you down there."

"Okay."

Tony vacillated and then decided he was hungry too. So that left just us five.

"Let's stop at the house," said Donny. "Get some jars for the crayfish and a Thermos of Kool-Aid."

We went in through the back door and you could hear the washing machine going in the basement.

"Donny? That you?"

"Yeah, Ma."

He turned to Meg. "Get the Kool-Aid, will ya? I'll go down after the jars and see what she wants."

I sat with Willie and Denise at the kitchen table. There were toast crumbs on it and I brushed them onto the floor. There was also an ashtray crammed with cigarette butts. I looked through the butts but there was nothing big enough to crib for later.

Meg had the Thermos out and was carefully pouring lime Kool-Aid into it from Ruth's big pitcher when they came upstairs.

Willie had two peanut butter jars and a stack of tin cans with him. Ruth was wiping her hands on her faded apron. She smiled at us and then looked over at Meg in the kitchen.

"What are you doing?" she said.

"Just pouring out some Kool-Aid."

She dug into the pocket of her apron and took out a pack of Tareytons and lit one.

"Thought I said stay out of the kitchen."

"Donny wanted some Kool-Aid. It was Donny's idea."

"I don't care whose idea it was."

She blew out some smoke and started coughing. It was a bad cough, right up from the lungs, and she couldn't even talk for a moment.

"It's only Kool-Aid," said Meg. "I'm not eating."

Ruth nodded. "Question is," she said, taking another drag of the cigarette, "question is, what did you sneak before I got here?"

Meg finished pouring and put down the pitcher. "Nothing," she sighed. "I didn't *sneak* anything."

Ruth nodded again. "Come here," she said.

Meg just stood there.

"I said come over here."

She walked over.

"Open your mouth and let me smell your breath."

"What?"

Beside me Denise began to giggle.

"Don't sass me. Open your mouth."

"Ruth . . ."

"Open it."

"No!"

"What's that? What'd you say?"

"You don't have any right to . . ."

"I got all the right in the world. Open it."

"No!"

"I said open it, liar."

"I'm not a liar."

"Well I know you're a slut so I guess you're a liar too. Open it!"

"No."

"Open your mouth!"

"No!"

"I'm telling you to."

"I won't."

"Oh yes you will. If I have to get these boys to pry it open you will."

Willie snorted, laughing. Donny was still standing in the doorway holding the cans and jars. He looked embarrassed.

"Open your *mouth*, slut."

That made Denise giggle again.

Meg looked Ruth straight in the eye. She took a breath.

And for a moment she suddenly managed an adult, almost stunning dignity.

"I told you, Ruth," she said. "I said no."

Even Denise shut up then.

We were astonished.

We'd never seen anything like it before.

Kids were powerless. Almost by definition. Kids were supposed to *endure* humiliation, or run away from it. If you protested, it had to be oblique. You ran into your room and slammed the door. You screamed and yelled. You brooded through dinner. You acted out—or broke things accidentally on purpose. You were sullen, silent. You screwed up in school. And that was about it. All the guns in your arsenal. But what you did *not* do was you did not stand up to an adult and say go fuck yourself in so many words. You did not simply stand there and calmly say no. We were still too young for that. So that now it was pretty amazing.

Ruth smiled and stubbed out her cigarette in the cluttered ashtray.

"I guess I'll go get Susan," she said. "I expect she's in her room."

And then it was her turn to stare Meg down.

It lasted a moment, the two of them facing off like gunfighters.

Then Meg's composure shattered.

"You leave my sister *out* of this! You leave her alone!"

Her hands were balled up into fists, white at the knuckles. And I knew that she knew, then, about the beating the other day.

I wondered if there had been other times, other beatings.

But in a way we were relieved. This was more like it. More like what we were used to.

Ruth just shrugged. "No need for you to get all upset about it, Meggy. I just want to ask her what she knows about you raiding the icebox in between meals. If you won't do what I ask, then I guess she'd be the one to know."

"She wasn't even *with* us!"

"I'm sure she's heard you, honey. I'm sure the neighbors have heard you. Anyhow, sisters know, don't they? Sorta instinctive, really."

She turned toward the bedroom. "Susan?"

Meg reached out and grabbed her arm. And it was like she was a whole other girl now, scared, helpless, desperate.

"God *damn* you!" she said.

You knew right away it was a mistake.

Ruth whirled and smacked her.

"You touch me? You *touch* me, dammit? You *hold* with me?"

She slapped her again as Meg backed away, and again as she stumbled against the refrigerator, off balance, and fell to her knees. Ruth leaned over and gripped her jaw, pulling on it hard.

"Now you open your goddamn mouth, you hear me? Or I'll kick the living shit out of you and your precious little sister! You hear me? Willie? Donny?"

Willie got up and went to her. Donny looked confused.

"Hold her."

I felt frozen. Everything was happening so fast. I was aware of Denise sitting next to me, goggle-eyed.

"I said hold her."

Willie got out of his seat and took her right arm and I guess Ruth was hurting her where she held tight to her jaw because she didn't resist. Donny put his jars and cans on the table and took hold of her left. Two of the cans rolled off the table and clattered to the floor.

"Now *open*, tramp."

And then Meg did fight, trying to get to her feet, bucking and rolling against them, but they had her tight. Willie was enjoying himself, that was obvious. But Donny looked grim. Ruth had both hands on her now, trying to pry her jaws apart.

Meg bit her.

Ruth yelled and stumbled back. Meg squirmed to her feet. Willie twisted her arm behind her back and yanked it up. She yelled and doubled over and tried to pull away, shaking her left arm hard to get it away from Donny in a kind of simultaneous panic and she almost made it, Donny's grip was uncertain enough, she almost got it free.

Then Ruth stepped forward again.

For an instant she just stood there, studying her, looking I guess for an opening. Then she balled up a fist and hit her in the stomach exactly the way a man would hit a man, and nearly as hard. What you heard was like somebody punching a basketball.

Meg fell, choking, and gasped for breath.

Donny let her go.

"Jesus!" whispered Denise beside me.

Ruth stepped back.

"You want to fight?" she said. "Okay. Fight."

Meg shook her head.

"You don't want to fight? No?"

She shook her head.

Willie looked at his mother.

"Too bad," he said quietly.

He still had her arm. And now he started twisting. She doubled over.

"Willie's right," said Ruth. "It is too bad. Come on, Meg honey, *fight*. Fight him."

Willie twisted. She jumped with the pain and gasped and shook her head a third time.

"Well I guess she just won't do it," said Ruth. "This girl don't want to do *anything* I say today."

She shook the hand Meg had bitten and examined it. From where I sat it was just a red spot. Meg hadn't broken the skin or anything.

"Let her go," said Ruth.

He dropped her arm. Meg slumped forward. She was crying.

I didn't like to watch. I glanced away.

I saw Susan standing in the hall, holding on to the wall, looking frightened, staring around the corner. Eyes riveted on her sister.

"I gotta go," I said in a voice that sounded strangely thick to me.

"What about the brook?" said Willie. Sounding disappointed, the big ass. Like nothing had happened at all.

"Later," I said. "I gotta go now."

I was aware of Ruth watching me.

I got up. I didn't want to go by Meg for some reason. Instead I walked past Susan to the front door. She didn't seem to notice me.

"David," said Ruth. Her voice was very calm.

"Yes?"

"This is what you'd call a domestic dispute," she said.

"Just between us here. You saw what you saw. But it's nobody's business but ours. You know? You understand?"

I hesitated, then nodded.

"Good boy," she said. "I knew you were. I knew you'd understand."

I walked outside. It was a hot, muggy day. Inside it had been cooler.

I walked back to the woods, cutting away from the path to the brook and into the deeper woods behind the Morino house.

It was cooler there. It smelled of pine and earth.

I kept seeing Meg slumped over, crying. And then I'd see her standing in front of Ruth looking her coolly in the eye saying I told you I said no. For some reason these alternated with remembering an argument with my mother earlier that week. You're just like your father, she'd said. I'd responded furiously. Not nearly as well as Meg had. I'd lost it. I'd raged. I'd hated her. I thought about that now in a detached kind of way and then I thought about all this other stuff today.

It had been an amazing morning.

But it was as though everything canceled everything.

I walked through the woods.

I didn't feel a thing.

Chapter Twenty

You could get from my house to Cozy Snacks through the woods by crossing the brook at the Big Rock and then walking along the far bank past two old houses and a construction site, and I was coming home that way the next day with a Three Musketeers, some red licorice and some Fleer's Double Bubble—which, thinking of Meg, I'd actually paid for—in a paper bag when I heard Meg scream.

I knew it was her. It was just a scream. It could have been anybody's. But I knew.

I got quiet. I moved along the bank.

She was standing on the Big Rock. Willie and Woofer must have surprised her there with her hand in the water because her sleeve was rolled up and the brook water beaded her forearm and you could see the long livid scar like a worm pulsing up through her skin.

They were pelting her with the cans from the cellar, and Woofer's aim, at least, was good.

But then Willie was aiming for the head.

A harder target. He always went wide.

While Woofer hit her first on her bare knee and then, when she turned, in the center of the back.

She turned again and saw them pick up the glass peanut butter jars. Woofer fired.

Glass shattered at her feet, sprayed her legs.

It would have hurt her bad to get hit with one of those.

There was nowhere for her to go except into the brook. She couldn't have scaled the high bank beside me, at least not in time. So that was what she did.

She went into the water.

The brook was running fast that day and the bottom was covered with mossy stones. I saw her trip and fall almost immediately while another jar smashed on a rock nearby. She hauled herself up, gasping and wet to the shoulders, and tried to run. She got four steps and fell again.

Willie and Woofer were howling, laughing so hard they forgot to throw their jars any more.

She got up and this time kept her footing and splashed downstream.

When she turned the corner there was good heavy thicket to cover her.

It was over.

Amazingly nobody had seen me. They still didn't. I felt like a ghost.

I watched them gather up their few remaining cans and jars. Then they walked off laughing down the path to their house. I could hear them all the way, voices gradually fading.

Assholes, I thought. There's glass all over now. We can't go wading. Not at least until it floods again.

I crossed carefully across the Rock to the other side.

Chapter Twenty-One

Meg fought back on the Fourth of July.

It was dusk, a warm night gracefully fading to dark, and there were hundreds of us out there on blankets in Memorial Field in front of the high school waiting for the fireworks to start.

Donny and I sat with my parents—I'd invited him over for dinner that night—and they sat with their friends the Hendersons, who lived two blocks away.

The Hendersons were Catholic and childless, which right away meant that something was wrong, though nobody seemed to know what it was exactly. Mr. Henderson was big and outdoorsy and given to plaid and corduroy, what you'd call a man's man, kind of fun. He raised beagles in his backyard and let us shoot his BB guns sometimes when we went over. Mrs. Henderson was thin, blond, pug-nosed, and pretty.

Donny once said he couldn't see the problem. He'd have fucked her in a minute.

From where we sat we could see Willie, Woofer, Meg, Susan and Ruth across the field sitting next to the Morino family.

The entire town was there.

If you could walk or drive or crawl, on the Fourth of July you came to the fireworks. Apart from the Memorial Day Parade it was our one big spectacle of the year.

And pro forma the cops were there. Nobody really expected any trouble. The town was still at that stage where everybody knew everybody, or knew somebody else who did. You went out and left your door open all day in case somebody came by and you weren't there.

The cops were family friends, most of them. My dad knew them from the bar or from the VFW.

Mostly they were just making sure that nobody threw cherry bombs too near the blankets. Standing around waiting for the show like the rest of us.

Donny and I listened to Mr. Henderson, who was talking about the beagles' new litter and drank iced tea from the Thermos and belched out pot roast fumes at one another, laughing. My mother always made pot roast with a lot of onions in it. It drove my father crazy but it was just the way we liked it. In half an hour we'd be farting.

The public address system blared John Philip Sousa.

A quarter-moon was up over the high school building.

In the dim gray light you could see little kids chasing each other through the crowd. People were lighting sparklers. Behind us a full pack of two-inchers went off like machine-gun fire.

We decided to get some ice cream.

The Good Humor truck was doing a bang-up business, kids wading in four deep. We gradually pushed our way through without getting stepped on. I got a Brown Cow and Donny got a Fudgesicle and we hauled ourselves back out again.

Then we saw Meg by the side of the truck, talking to Mr. Jennings.

And it stopped us dead in our tracks.

Because Mr. Jennings was also *Officer* Jennings. He was a cop.

And there was something in the way she was acting, gesturing with her hands, leaning forward sort of *into* him, so that we knew right away what she was saying.

It was scary, shocking.

We stood there rooted to the spot.

Meg was telling. Betraying Ruth. Betraying Donny and everybody.

She was facing away from us.

For a moment we just stared at her and then as if on cue we looked at one another.

Then we went over. Eating our ice creams. Very casual. We stood right beside her off to one side.

Mr. Jennings glanced at us for a second but then looked off in the general direction of Ruth and

Willie and the others, and then, nodding, listening carefully, looked attentively back to Meg.

We worked studiously at the ice creams. We looked around.

"Well, that's her right, I guess," he said.

"*No,*" said Meg. "You don't understand."

But then we couldn't hear the rest of it.

Mr. Jennings smiled and shrugged. He put a big freckled hand on her shoulder.

"Listen," he said. "For all I know maybe your parents would've felt exactly the same. Who's to say? You've got to think of Miz Chandler as your mom now, don't you?"

She shook her head.

And then he became aware of us, I think, really aware of Donny and me and who we were for the first time and what we might mean in terms of the conversation they were having there. You could see his face change. But Meg was still talking, arguing.

He watched us over her shoulder; looked at us long and hard.

Then he took her arm.

"Let's walk," he said.

I saw her glance nervously in Ruth's direction but it was getting hard to see by now, pretty much full dark with only the moon and stars and the occasional sparkler to see by, so there wasn't much chance that Ruth had noticed them together. From where I stood the crowd was already a shapeless mass like scrub and cactus studding a prairie. I knew where they were sitting but I couldn't make them out or my parents and the Hendersons either.

But you knew perfectly well why she was scared. I felt scared myself. What she was doing felt exciting and forbidden, exactly like trying to see her through the windows from the birch tree.

Mr. Jennings turned his back to us and gently moved her away.

"Shit" whispered Donny.

I heard a whoosh. The sky exploded. Bright white puffballs popped and showered down.

Oooooooo, went the crowd.

And in the ghostly white light of the aftershock I looked at him. I saw confusion and worry.

He had always been the reluctant one with Meg. He still was now.

"What are you going to do?" I asked him.

He shook his head.

"He won't believe her," he said. "He won't do *nothin'*. Cops talk but they never do anything to you."

It was like something Ruth had said to us once. Cops talk but they never *do*.

He repeated it now as we walked back to our blankets like an article of faith. Like it *had* to be.

Almost like a prayer.

Chapter Twenty-Two

The prowl car pulled in around eight the following evening. I saw Mr. Jennings walk up the steps and knock and Ruth let him in. Then I waited, watching out my living room window. Something turning over and over in my stomach.

My parents were at a birthday party at the Knights of Columbus and my sitter was Linda Cotton, eighteen and freckled and, I thought, cute, though nothing compared to Meg. At seventy-five cents an hour she couldn't have cared less what I was doing so long as it was quiet and didn't interfere with her watching *The Adventures of Ellery Queen* on the TV.

We had an agreement, Linda and I. I wouldn't tell about her boyfriend Steve coming over or the two of them necking on the sofa all night and I could do pretty much whatever I wanted on condition that I was home in bed before my parents returned. She knew I was getting too old for sitters anyhow.

So I waited until the prowl car pulled away again and then I went next door. It was about quarter to nine.

They were sitting in the living room and dining room. All of them. It was quiet and nobody moved and I got the feeling it had been that way for a long time.

Everybody was staring at Meg. Even Susan was.

I had the strangest feeling.

Later, during the Sixties, I would realize what it was. I would open a letter from the Selective Service System and read the card inside that told me my status had now been changed to 1A.

It was a sense of *escalation*.

That the stakes were higher now.

I stood in the doorway. It was Ruth who acknowledged me.

"Hello, David," she said quietly. "Sit down. Join us." Then she sighed. "Somebody get me a beer, will you?"

Willie got up in the dining room and went into the kitchen, got a beer for her and one for himself, opened them and handed one to her. Then he sat down again.

Ruth lit a cigarette.

I looked at Meg sitting in a folding chair in front of the blank gray eye of the television. She looked scared but determined. I thought of Gary Cooper walking out onto the silent street at the end of *High Noon*.

"Well now," said Ruth. "Well now."

She sipped the beer, smoked the cigarette.

Woofer squirmed on the couch.

I almost turned and went out again.

Then Donny got up in the dining room. He walked over to Meg. He stood there in front of her.

"You brought a *cop* here after my mom," he said. "After my *mother*."

Meg looked up at him. Her face relaxed a little. It was Donny, after all. Reluctant Donny.

"I'm sorry," she said. "I just had to be sure it wouldn't . . ."

His hand shot up and slashed across her face.

"Shut up! Shut up, *you!*"

His hand was poised in front of her, ready, trembling.

It looked like it was all he could do not to hit her again and a whole lot harder this time.

She stared at him, aghast.

"Sit down," Ruth said quietly.

It was like he hadn't heard her.

"Sit down!"

He pulled himself away. His about-face was practically military. He stalked back into the dining room.

Then there was a silence again.

Finally Ruth leaned forward. "What I want to know is this. What did you think, Meggy? What went through your mind?"

Meg didn't answer.

Ruth started coughing. That deep, hacking cough she had. Then she got control.

"What I mean to say is, did you think he was gonna take you away or something? You and Susan? Get you out of here?

"Well I'll tell you it's not gonna happen. He's not gonna take you anywhere, girly. Because he doesn't *care to*. If he'd cared to he'd have done it on the spot back at the fireworks and he didn't, did he?

"So what's left? What'd you have in mind?

"You think maybe I'd be scared of him?"

Meg just sat there, arms folded, with that determined look in her eyes.

Ruth smiled, sipped her beer.

And she looked determined too in her way.

"Problem is," she said, "what do we do now? There's nothing about that man or any other man that scares me, Meggy. If you didn't know that before, then I sure hope you know it now. But I can't have you running to the cops every ten, twenty minutes either. So the question is, what now?

"I'd send you someplace if there was someplace to send you. Believe me I would. Damned if I need some stupid little whore out ruinin' my reputation. And God knows they don't pay me enough to bother trying to correct you. Hell, with what they pay it's a wonder I can even feed you!"

She sighed. "I guess I got to think about this," she said. Then she got to her feet and walked into the kitchen. She opened the refrigerator.

"You get to your room. Susie too. And stay there."

She reached for a beer and then laughed.

"Before Donny gets to thinking he might come over and smack you again."

She opened the can of Budweiser.

Meg took her sister's arm and led her into the bedroom.

"You too, David," said Ruth. "You better get on home. Sorry. But I got some difficult thinking to do."

"That's okay."

"You want a Coke or something for the road?"

I smiled. For the road. I was right next door.

"No, that's okay."

"Want me to sneak you a beer?"

She had that old mischievous twinkle in her eye. The tension dissolved. I laughed.

"That'd be cool."

She tossed me one. I caught it.

"Thanks," I said.

"Don't mention it," she said and this time all of us laughed, because *don't mention it* was a code between us.

It was always what she said to us kids when she was letting us do something our parents wouldn't want us to do or let us do in our own houses. *Don't mention it.*

"I won't," I said.

I stuffed the can into my shirt and went outside.

When I got back to my house Linda was curled up in front of the TV set watching Ed Byrnes comb his hair during the opening credits of *77 Sunset Strip*. She looked sort of glum. I guessed that Steve wasn't showing up tonight.

" 'Night," I said and went up to my room.

I drank the beer and thought of Meg. I wondered if I should try to help her somehow. There was a conflict here. I was still attracted to Meg and liked her but Donny and Ruth were much older friends. I wondered if she really even *needed* helping. Kids got slapped, after all. Kids got punched around. I wondered where this was going.

What do we do now? said Ruth.

I stared at Meg's watercolor on my wall and began to wonder about that too.

Chapter Twenty-Three

What Ruth decided was that, from then on, Meg was never allowed to leave the house alone. Either she was with her, or Donny or Willie. Mostly she didn't leave at all. So that I never had a chance to ask Meg what she wanted done, *if* she wanted something done, never mind deciding whether I'd actually do it or not.

It was out of my hands. Or so I thought.

That was a relief to me.

If I felt that anything was lost—Meg's confidence, or even just her company—I was never all that aware of it. I knew that things had taken a pretty unusual turn next door and I guess I was looking for some distance from it for a while, to sort things out for myself.

So I saw less than usual of the Chandlers for the next few days and that was a relief too. I hung around with Tony and Kenny and Denise and Cheryl, and even with Eddie now and then when it felt safe.

The street was buzzing with news of what was happening over there. Sooner or later every conversation came back to the Chandlers. What made it so incredible was that Meg had gotten the police involved. *That* was the revolutionary act, the one we couldn't get over. Could you imagine turning in an adult—especially an adult who might just as well have been your mother—to the cops? It was practically unthinkable.

Yet it was also fraught with potential. You could see Eddie in particular stewing over the idea. Daydreaming about his father I guessed. A thoughtful Eddie was not something we were used to either. It added to the strangeness.

But apart from the business with the cops, all anybody really knew—including me—was that people were getting punished a lot over there for seemingly little reason, but that was nothing new except that it was happening at the Chandlers', which we'd all considered safe haven. That and the fact that Willie and Donny were participating. But even that didn't strike us as too odd.

We had The Game as precedent.

No, mostly it was the cops. And it was Eddie who, after a while, had the final word on that subject.

"Well, it didn't get her *shit* though, did it," he said. Thoughtful Eddie.

But it was true. And strangely enough, in the course of the week that followed our feelings slowly changed toward Meg as a result of that.

From admiration at the sheer all-or-nothing boldness of the act, at the very *concept* of challenging Ruth's authority so completely and publicly, we drifted toward a kind of vague contempt for her. How could she be so dumb as to think a cop was going to side with a kid against an adult, anyway? How could she fail to realize it was only going to make things worse? How could she have been so naive, so trusting, so God-and-apple-pie stupid?

The policeman is your friend. Horseshit. None of us would have done it. We knew better.

You could actually almost resent her for it. It was as though in failing with Mr. Jennings she had thrown in all our faces the very fact of just how powerless we were as kids. Being "just a kid" took on a whole new depth of meaning, of ominous threat, that maybe we knew was there all along but we'd never had to think about before. Shit, they could dump us in a river if they wanted to. We were *just kids*. We were property. We *belonged* to our parents, body and soul. It meant we were doomed in the face of any real danger from the adult world and that meant hopelessness, and humiliation and anger.

It was as though in failing herself Meg had failed us as well.

So we turned that anger outward. Toward Meg.

I did too. Over just that couple of days I flicked a slow mental switch. I stopped worrying. I turned off on her entirely.

Fuck it, I thought. Let it go where it goes.

Chapter Twenty-Four

Where it went was to the basement.

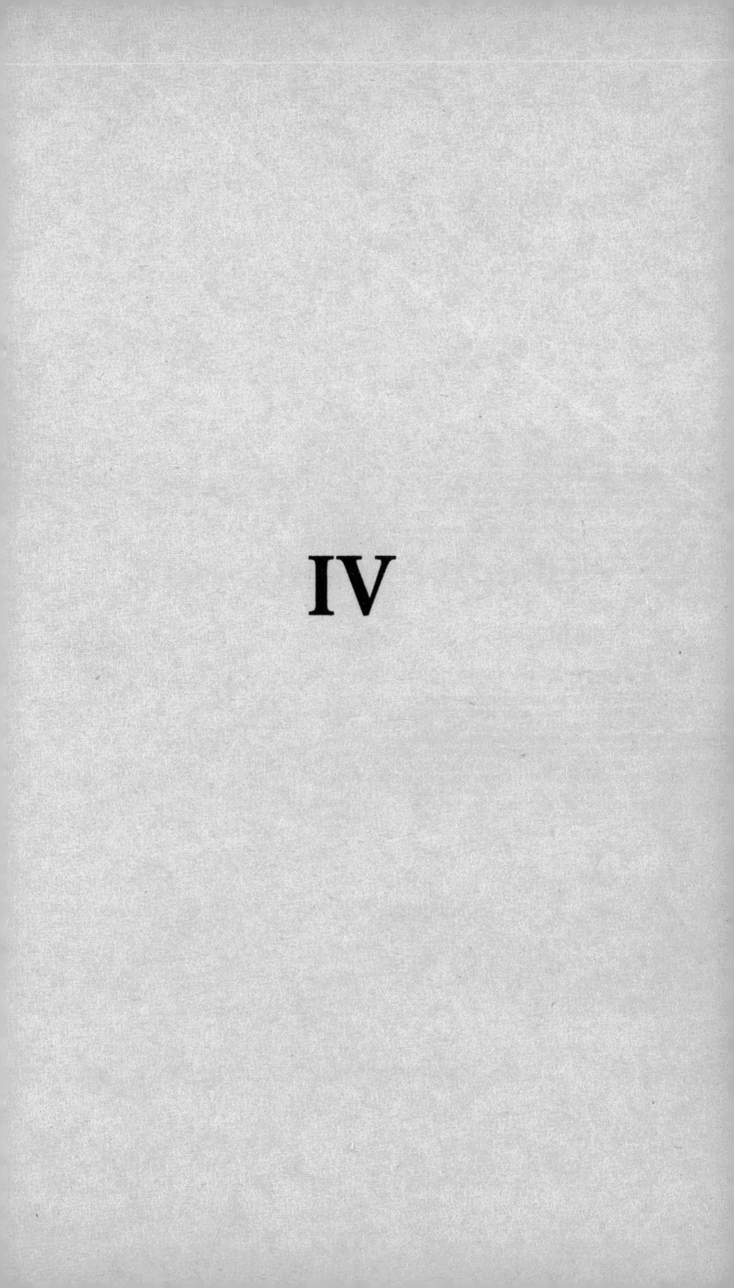

IV

Chapter Twenty-Five

The day I finally did go over and knock on the door nobody answered, but standing on the porch I was aware of two things. One was Susan crying in her room loud enough to hear her through the screen. The other was downstairs. A scuffling. Furniture scraping roughly across the floor. Muffled voices. Grunts, groans. A whole rancid danger in the air.

The shit, as they say, was hitting the fan.

It's amazing to me now how eager I was to get down there.

I took the stairs two at a time and turned the corner. I knew where they were.

At the doorway to the shelter Ruth stood watching. She smiled and moved aside to let me by.

"She tried to run away," she said. "But Willie stopped her."

They were stopping her now all right, all of them, Willie and Woofer and Donny all together, going at her like a tackle dummy against the concrete wall, taking turns, smashing into her stomach. She was already long past arguing about it. All you heard was the whoosh of breath as Donny hit her and drove her tightly folded arms into her belly. Her mouth was set, grim. A hard concentration in her eyes.

And for a moment she was the heroine again. Battling the odds.

But just for a moment. Because suddenly it was clear to me again that all she could do was take it, powerless. And lose.

And I remember thinking *at least it's not me*.

If I wanted to I could even join them.

For that moment, thinking that, I had power.

I've asked myself since, *when did it happen? when was I, yes, corrupted?* and I keep coming back to exactly this moment, these thoughts.

That sense of power.

It didn't occur to me to consider that this was only a power granted to me by Ruth, and perhaps only temporary. At the time it was quite real enough. As I watched, the distance between Meg and me seemed suddenly huge, insurmountable. It was not that my sympathies toward her stopped. But for the first time I saw her as essentially other than me. She was vulnerable. I wasn't. My position was favored here. Hers was as low as it could be.

Was this inevitable, maybe? I remembered her asking me, *why do they hate me?* and I didn't believe it then, I didn't have any answer for her. Had I missed something? Was there maybe some flaw in her I hadn't seen that predetermined all of this? For the first time I felt that maybe Meg's separation from us might be justified.

I wanted to feel it was justified.

I say that now in deepest shame.

Because it seems to me now that so much of this was strictly personal, part of the nature of the world as I saw it. I've tried to think that it was all the fault of my parents' warfare, of the cold blank calm I developed in the center of their constant hurricane. But I don't quite believe that anymore. I doubt I ever did entirely. My parents loved me, in many ways better than I deserved—however they felt about one another. And I knew that. For almost anyone that would have been enough to eliminate any appetite for this whatsoever.

No. The truth is that it was me. That I'd been waiting for this, or something like this, to happen all along. It was as though something starkly elemental were at my back, sweeping through me, releasing and becoming me, some wild black wind of my own making on that beautiful bright sunny day.

And I ask myself: Whom did I hate? Whom and what did I fear?

In the basement, with Ruth, I began to learn that anger, hate, fear and loneliness are all one button awaiting the touch of just a single finger to set them blazing toward destruction.

And I learned that they can taste like winning.

* * *

I watched Willie step back. For once he didn't look clumsy. His shoulder caught her squarely in the stomach, lifted her off her feet.

I suppose her only hope was that one of them would miss and smash his head against the wall. But nobody was going to. She was tiring. There was nowhere to maneuver, nowhere to go. Nothing to do but take it till she fell. And that would be soon now.

Woofer got a running start. She had to bend her knees in order not to take it in the groin.

"Cry, goddammit!" Willie yelled. Like the others he was breathing hard. He turned to me.

"She won't *cry*," he said.

"She don't care," said Woofer.

"She'll cry," said Willie. "I'll make her."

"Too much pride," said Ruth behind me. "Pride goeth before a fall. You ought to all remember that. Pride falls."

Donny rammed at her.

Football was his game. Her head snapped back against the cinder block. Her arms fell open. The look in her eyes was glazed now.

She slid a few inches down the wall.

Then she stopped and held there.

Ruth sighed.

"That'll be enough for now, boys," she said. "You're not going to get her to cry. Not this time."

She held out her arm, beckoning.

"Come on."

You could see they weren't done yet. But Ruth sounded bored and final.

Then Willie muttered something about stupid whores, and one by one they filed past us.

I was last to leave. It was hard to take my eyes away.

That this could happen.

I watched her slide down the wall to squat on the cold concrete floor.

I'm not sure she was ever aware of me.

"Let's go," said Ruth.

She closed the metal door and bolted it shut behind me.

Meg was left in there in the dark. Behind the door to a meat locker. We went upstairs and poured some Cokes. Ruth got out cheddar cheese and crackers. We sat around the dining room table.

I could still hear Susan crying in the bedroom, softer now. Then Willie got up and turned on the television and *Truth or Consequences* came on and you couldn't hear her anymore.

We watched for a while.

Ruth had a women's magazine open in front of her on the table. She was smoking a Tareyton, flipping through the magazine, drinking from her Coke bottle.

She came to a photo—a lipstick ad—and stopped.

"I don't see it," she said. "The woman's ordinary. You see it?"

She held up the magazine.

Willie looked and shrugged and bit into a cracker. But I thought the woman was pretty. About Ruth's age, maybe a little younger, but pretty.

Ruth shook her head.

"I see her everywhere I look," she said, "I swear it. *Everywhere.* Name's Suzy Parker. Big model. And I just don't see it. A redhead. Maybe that's it. Men like the redheads. But hell, Meg's got red hair. And Meg's hair's prettier than that, doncha think?"

I looked at the picture again. I agreed with her.

"I just don't see it," she said, frowning. "Meg's definitely prettier than that. A whole lot prettier."

"Sure she is," said Donny.

"World's crazy," said Ruth. "It just don't make any sense to me at all."

She cut a slice of cheese and placed it on a cracker.

Chapter Twenty-Six

"Get your mom to let you sleep over at my house tonight," said Donny. "There's something I want to talk to you about."

We were standing at the bridge on Maple skimming stones down into the water. The brook was clear and sluggish.

"What's wrong with talking now?"

"Nothing."

But he didn't say what was on his mind.

I don't know why I resisted the idea of sleeping over. Maybe it was knowing I'd get more involved with them somehow. Or maybe it was just that I knew what my mom would say—there were girls at the Chandlers' these days, and staying over there would not seem so clear-cut to her anymore.

She should only know, I thought.

"Willie wants to talk to you too," said Donny.

"*Willie* does?"

"Yeah."

I laughed. The notion of Willie having something on his mind worth actually speaking about.

Actually it was intriguing.

"Well in that case I guess I'll just have to, then, won't I," I said.

Donny laughed too, and skimmed a long one three skips down across the dappling bands of sunlight.

Chapter Twenty-Seven

My mother wasn't happy.

"I don't think so," she said.

"Mom, I sleep there *all* the time."

"Not lately you don't."

"You mean since Meg and Susan?"

"That's right."

"Look. It's no big deal. It's the same as before. The guys get the bunk beds and Meg and Susan are in Ruth's room."

"Mrs. Chandler's room."

"Right. Mrs. Chandler's room."

"So where is Mrs. Chandler?"

"On the couch. On the pullout in the living room. What's the big deal?"

"You know what's the big deal."

"No, I don't."

"Yes you do."

"No I *don't*."

"What?" said my father, walking into the kitchen from the living room. "What big deal is that?"

"He wants to stay over there again," said my mother. She was snapping green beans into a colander.

"What? Over there?"

"Yes."

"So let him." He sat down at the kitchen table and opened up his newspaper.

"Robert, there are two young girls there now."

"So?"

She sighed. "Please," she said. "Please don't be dense, Robert."

"Dense, hell," said my father. "Let him. Is there any coffee?"

"Yes," she said. She sighed again and brushed her hands off on her apron.

I got up and got to the coffeepot ahead of her and turned on the flame beneath it. She looked at me and then went back to the beans.

"Thanks, Dad," I said.

"I didn't say you could go," said my mother.

I smiled. "You didn't say I couldn't, either."

She looked at my father and shook her head. "Dammit, Robert," she said.

"Right," said my father. And then he read his paper.

Chapter Twenty-Eight

"We told her about The Game," said Donny.

"Who?"

"Ruth. My mom. Who else, shit-for-brains?"

Donny was alone in the kitchen when I came in, making a peanut butter sandwich that I guess was dinner that night.

There were smears of peanut butter and grape jelly and bread crumbs on the counter. Just for fun I counted the sets of silverware in the drawer. There were still only five.

"You *told* her?"

He nodded. "Woofer did."

He took a bite of the sandwich and sat down at the dining room table. I sat across from him. There was a half-inch cigarette burn in the wood I hadn't seen before.

"Jesus. What'd she say?"

"Nothin'. It was weird. It was like she *knew*, you know?"

"Knew? Knew what?"

"Everything. Like it was no sweat. Like she figured we were doing it all along. Like every kid did."

"You're kidding."

"No. I swear."

"Bullshit."

"I'm telling you. All she wanted to know was who was with us so I told her."

"You *told* her? Me? Eddie? *Everybody?*"

"Like I said she didn't care. Hey. Would you please not blow your cool on this, Davy? It didn't bother her."

"Denise? You told her about Denise too?"

"Yeah. Everything."

"You said she was *naked?*"

I couldn't believe it. I'd always thought that Willie was the stupid one. I watched him eat the sandwich. He smiled at me and shook his head.

"I'm telling you. You don't have to worry about it," he said.

"Donny."

"Really."

"Donny."

"Yes, Davy."

"Are you *nuts?*"

"No, Davy."

"Do you realize for a goddamn second what would happen to me if . . ."

"Nothing's going to happen to you, for God's sake. Will you stop being such a friggin' queer about it? It's my mom, for God's sake. Remember?"

"Oh that makes me feel just fine. Your mom knows we tie naked little girls to trees. Great."

He sighed. "David, if I'd known you were gonna be such an amazing retard about it I wouldn't of told you."

"*I'm* the retard, right?"

"Yeah." He was pissed now. He popped the last gooey corner of the sandwich into his mouth. He stood up.

"Look, jerk. What do you think is going on in the shelter right now? Right this minute?"

I just looked at him. How did I know? Who cared?

Then it dawned on me. Meg was there.

"No," I said.

"Yes," he said. He went to the refrigerator for a Coke.

"Bullshit."

He laughed. "Will you stop saying bullshit? Look, don't believe me. Go take a look. Hell, I just came up for a sandwich."

I ran downstairs. I could hear him laughing behind me.

It was getting dark outside so the basement lights were on, naked bulbs over the washer/dryer and under the stairs and over the sump pump in the corner.

Willie was standing behind Ruth at the door to the shelter.

They both had flashlights in their hands.

Ruth lit hers and waved it at me once like a cop at a roadblock.

"Here's Davy," she said.

Willie gave me a glance. *Who gives a shit.*

My mouth was open. It felt dry. I licked my lips. I nodded to Ruth and looked around the corner through the doorway.

And it was hard to comprehend at first—I guess because maybe it was out of context, and probably because it was Meg, and definitely because Ruth was there. It felt dreamlike—or like some game you play on Halloween when everyone is in costume and nobody's quite recognizable themselves even though you know who they are. Then Donny came downstairs and slapped his hand down on my shoulder. He offered me the Coke.

"See?" he said. "I told you."

I did see.

They'd taken ten-penny nails and driven them into the beams Willie Sr. had lain along the ceiling—two nails, about three feet apart.

They'd cut two lengths of clothesline and tied Meg's wrists and looped a line over each of the nails and then run the lines down to the legs of the heavy worktable, tying them off down there rather than up at the nail so that they could be adjusted, tightened, just by untying each one and pulling it around the loop and then tying it tighter again.

Meg was standing on a small pile of books—three thick red volumes of the World Book Encyclopedia.

She was gagged and blindfolded.

Her feet were bare. Her shorts and short-sleeve blouse were dirty. In the space between the two, stretched out as she was, you could see her navel.

Meg was an inny.

Woofer paced around in front of her running the beam of his flashlight up and down her body.

There was a bruise just under the blindfold on her left cheek.

Susan sat on a carton of canned vegetables, watching. A blue strand of ribbon made a bow in her hair.

Off in the corner I could see a pile of blankets and an air mattress. I realized Meg had been sleeping there. I wondered for how long.

"We're all here," said Ruth.

A dim amber light bled in from the rest of the basement but mostly it was just Woofer's beam in there and the shadows moved erratically along with him when he moved, making things look strange and fluid and ghostly. The wire mesh over the single high window seemed to shift back and forth by subtle inches. The two four-by-four wooden posts supporting the ceiling slid across the room at odd angles. The ax, pick, crowbar and shovel stacked in the corner opposite Meg's bed appeared to switch positions with one another, looming and shrinking as you watched, shapeshifting.

The fallen fire extinguisher crawled across the floor.

But it was Meg's own shadow that dominated the room—head back, arms wide apart, swaying. It was an image straight out of all our horror comics, out of *The Black Cat* with Lugosi and Karloff, out of *Famous Monsters of Filmland*, out of every cheap twenty-five cent paperback historical thriller about the Inquisition ever written. Most of which I figured we'd collected.

It was easy to imagine torchlight, strange instruments and processions, braziers full of hot coals.

I shivered. Not at the chill but at the potential.

"The Game is she's got to tell," said Woofer.

"Okay. Tell what?" Ruth asked.

"Tell anything. Something secret."

Ruth nodded, smiling. "Sounds right. Only how's she going to do that with the gag on?"

"You don't *want* her to tell right away, Mom," said Willie. "Anyway, you always know when they're ready."

"You sure? You want to tell, Meggy?" said Ruth. "You ready?"

"She's *not* ready," insisted Woofer. But he needn't have bothered. Meg didn't make a sound.

"So now what?" Ruth asked.

Willie pushed off from the doorjamb where he was leaning and ambled into the room.

"Now we take a book away," he said.

He bent over, pulled out the middle one and stepped back.

The ropes were tighter now.

Willie and Woofer both had their flashlights on. Ruth's was still at her side, unlit.

I could see some red around Meg's wrists from the pull of the ropes. Her back arched slightly. The short-sleeve shirt rode up. She was only just able to stand with her feet down flat on the two remaining books and I could already see the strain in her calves and thighs. She went up on her toes for a moment to take the pressure off her wrists and then sank down again.

Willie switched off his flashlight. It was spookier that way.

Meg just hung there, swaying slightly.

"Confess," said Woofer. Then he laughed. "No. Don't," he said.

"Do another book," said Donny.

I glanced at Susan to see how she was taking this. She was sitting with her hands folded in the lap of her dress and her face looked very serious and she was staring intently at Meg but there was no way to read what she was thinking or feeling at all.

Willie bent down and pulled out the book.

She was up on the balls of her feet now.

Still she made no sound.

The muscles of her legs defined themselves sharply against her skin.

"Let's see how long she can go like that," said Donny. "It's gonna hurt after a while."

"Nah," said Woofer. "It's still too easy. Let's do the last one. Get 'er up on her tiptoes."

"I want to watch her a while. See what happens."

But the fact was that nothing was happening. Meg seemed determined to tough this out. And she was strong.

"Don't you want to give her a chance to confess? Isn't that the idea?" asked Ruth.

"Nah," said Woofer. "Still too soon. C'mon.

This is no good. Take the other book, Will."

Willie did.

And then Meg did make some kind of sound behind the gag, just once, a sort of tiny exhaled groan as all at once just breathing became harder. Her blouse pulled up to right beneath her breasts and I could see her belly rise and fall in an irregular labored rhythm against her rib cage. Her head fell back for a moment and then came forward again.

Her balance was precarious. She began to sway.

Her face flushed. Her muscles strained with tension.

We watched, silent.

She was beautiful.

The vocal sounds that accompanied her breathing were coming more frequently now as the strain increased. She couldn't help it. Her legs began to tremble. First the calves and then the thighs.

A thin sheen of sweat formed over her ribs, glistened on her thighs.

"We should strip her," Donny said.

The words just hung there for a moment, suspended as Meg was suspended, tipping a balance that was every bit as precarious.

Suddenly it was me who felt dizzy.

"Yeah," said Woofer.

Meg had heard. She shook her head. There was indignation, anger and fear there. Sounds came from behind the gag. *No. No. No.*

"Shut up," said Willie.

She started trying to jump, pulling on the ropes, trying to throw them off the nails, squirming. But all she was doing was hurting herself, chafing her wrists.

She didn't seem to care. She wasn't going to let it happen.

She kept trying.

No. No.

Willie walked over and thumped her on the head with the book.

She slumped back, stunned.

I looked at Susan. Her hands were still clasped together in her lap but the knuckles were white now. She looked directly at her sister, not at us. Her teeth were biting hard and steadily at her lower lip.

I couldn't watch her.

I cleared my throat and found something like a voice.

"Hey, uh . . . guys . . . listen, I don't really think . . ."

Woofer whirled on me.

"We've got *permission!*" he screamed. "We do! I say we take off her clothes! I say strip her!"

We looked at Ruth.

She stood leaning in the doorway, her arms folded close into her belly.

There was something keyed tight about her, like she was angry or doing some hard thinking. Her lips pressed together in a characteristic straight thin line.

Her eyes never left Meg's body.

Then finally she shrugged.

"That's The Game, isn't it?" she said.

Compared with the rest of the house and even

the basement it was cool down there but now, suddenly, it didn't feel cool. Instead there was a growing filmy closeness in the room, a sense of filling up, a thickening, a slow electric heat that seemed to rise from each of us filling and charging the air, surrounding us, isolating us, yet somehow mingling us all together too. You could see it in the way Willie stood leaning forward, the World Book clutched in his hand. In the way Woofer edged closer, the beam of his flashlight less erratic now, lingering, caressing Meg's face, her legs, her stomach. I could feel it from Donny and Ruth beside me, seeping in and over and through me like some sweet poison, a quiet knowledge shared.

We were going to do this. We were going to do this thing.

Ruth lit a cigarette and threw the match on the floor.

"Go ahead," she said.

Her smoke curled into the shelter.

"Who gets to do it?" said Woofer.

"I do," said Donny.

He stepped past me. Both Woofer and Willie had their flashlights on her now. I could see Donny dig into his pocket and bring out the pocketknife he always carried there. He turned to Ruth.

"You care about the clothes, Ma?" he asked.

She looked at him.

"I won't have to do the shorts or anything," he said. "But . . ."

He was right. The only way he was going to get

the blouse off her was to rip or cut it off.

"No," said Ruth. "I don't care."

"Let's see what she's got," said Willie.

Woofer laughed.

Donny approached her, folding out the blade.

"Don't start anything," he said. "I won't hurt you. But if you start something we'll just have to hit you again. You know? It's stupid."

He unbuttoned the blouse carefully, pulling it away from her body as though shy of touching her. His face was red. His fingers were awkward. He was trembling.

She started to struggle but then I guess thought better of it.

Unbuttoned, the blouse hung shapeless over her. I could see she wore a white cotton bra underneath. For some reason that surprised me. Ruth never wore a bra. I guess I'd assumed Meg wouldn't either.

Donny reached over with the penknife and cut through the left sleeve up to the neckline. He had to saw through the seam. But he'd kept the blade sharp. The blouse fell away behind her.

Meg began to cry.

He walked over to the other side and cut through the right sleeve the same way. Then he jerked the seam apart, a quick tearing sound. Then he stepped back.

"Shorts," said Willie.

You could hear her crying softly and trying to say something behind the gag. *No. Please.*

"Don't kick," said Donny.

The shorts zipped halfway down the side. He unzipped them and tugged them down over her hips, adjusting the thin white panties upward as he did so, then slid the shorts down over her legs to the floor. The leg muscles jerked and trembled.

He stepped away from her again and looked at her.

We all did.

We'd seen Meg wearing just as little I suppose. She had a two-piece bathing suit. Everybody did that year. Even little kids. And we'd seen her wearing that.

But this was different. A bra and panties were private and only other girls were supposed to see them and the only other girls in the room were Ruth and Susan. And Ruth was allowing this. Encouraging it. The thought was too large to consider for long.

Besides, here was Meg right in front of us. In front of our very eyes. The senses overwhelmed all thought, all consideration.

"You confess yet, Meggy?" Ruth's voice was soft. She shook her head yes. An enthusiastic *yes*.

"No she don't," said Willie. "No way." A sheen of greasy sweat rolled off his flattop down across his forehead. He wiped it off.

We all were sweating now. Meg most of all. Droplets glistened in her armpits, in her navel, across her belly.

"Do the rest," said Willie. "Then maybe we'll let her confess."

Woofer giggled. "Right after we let her do the hoochykoo," he said.

Donny stepped forward. He cut the right strap of her bra and then the left. Meg's breasts slid upward slightly, straining free of the cups.

He could have unsnapped it from the back then but instead he walked around in front of her. He slid the blade beneath the thin white band between the cups and started sawing.

Meg was sobbing.

It must have hurt to cry like that because every time her body moved the ropes were there, pulling at her.

The knife was sharp but it took a little while. Then there was a tiny pop and the bra fell away. Her breasts were bare.

They were whiter than the rest of her, pale and perfect and lovely. They shuddered with her crying. The nipples were pinkish brown and—to me—startlingly long, almost flat at the tips. Tiny plateaus of flesh. A form I'd never seen before and wanted instantly to touch.

I'd stepped farther into the room. Ruth was completely behind me now.

I could hear myself breathing.

Donny knelt in front of her and reached up. For a moment it looked like adoration, like worship.

Then his fingers hooked into the panties and drew them down over her hips, down her legs. He took his time.

Then that was another shock.

Meg's hair.

A small tuft of pale blond-orange down in which droplets of sweat gleamed.

I saw tiny freckles on her upper thighs.

I saw the small fold of flesh half hidden between her legs.

I studied her. Her breasts. How would they feel to touch?

Her flesh was unimaginable to me. The hair between her legs. I knew it would be soft. Softer than mine. I wanted to touch her. Her body would be hot. It trembled uncontrollably.

Her belly, her thighs, her strong pale white ass.

The stew of sex ripened, thickened in me.

The room reeked of sex.

I felt a hard weight between my legs. I moved forward, fascinated. I stepped past Susan. I saw Woofer's face, pale and bloodless as he watched. I saw Willie's eyes riveted to that tuft of down.

Meg had stopped crying now.

I turned to glance at Ruth. And she'd moved forward too, was standing inside the doorway now. I saw her left hand move against her right breast, the fingers gently closing, and then fall away.

Donny knelt beneath her, looking up.

"Confess," he said.

Her body began to spasm.

I could smell her sweat.

She nodded. She had to nod.

It was surrender.

"Get the ropes," he said to Willie.

Willie went to the table and untied the ropes, let out some slack until her feet came down flat on the bare cement floor, then tied them off again.

Her head fell forward with relief.

Donny stood up and removed the gag. I realized it was Ruth's yellow kerchief. Then she opened her mouth and he pulled out the rag they'd wadded up and stuffed in there. He threw the rag on the floor and put the kerchief in the back pocket of his jeans. A corner hung out slightly. For a moment he looked like a farmer.

"Could you . . . ? My arms . . ." she said. "My shoulders . . . they hurt."

"No," said Donny. "That's it. That's all you get."

"Confess," said Woofer.

"Tell us how you play with yourself," said Willie. "I bet you put your finger in, doncha?"

"No. Tell us about the syph." Woofer laughed.

"Yeah, the clap," said Willie, grinning.

"Cry," said Woofer.

"I already did cry," said Meg. And you could see she'd got a little bit of the old tough defiance back now that she wasn't hurting quite so much anymore.

Woofer just shrugged. "So cry again," he said.

Meg said nothing.

I noticed that her nipples had gone softer now, a smooth silky-looking shiny pink.

God! She was beautiful.

It was as though she read my mind.

"Is David here?" she said.

Willie and Donny looked at me. I couldn't answer.

"He's here," said Willie.

"David . . ." she said. But then I guess she couldn't finish. She didn't need to, though. I knew by the way she said it.

She didn't want me there.

I knew why too. And knowing why shamed me

just as she'd shamed me before. But I couldn't leave. The others were there. Besides, I didn't want to. I wanted to see. I needed to see. Shame looked square in the face of desire and looked away again.

"And Susan?"

"Yeah. Her too," said Donny.

"Oh God."

"Screw that," said Woofer. "Who cares about Susan? Where's the confession?"

And now Meg sounded weary and adult. "Confession's stupid," she said. "There's no confession."

It stopped us.

"We could haul you right on up again," said Willie.

"I know that."

"We could *whip* you," said Woofer.

Meg shook her head. "Please. Just leave me alone. Leave me be. There's no confession."

And the thing was that nobody really expected that.

For a moment we all just stood around waiting for somebody to say something, something that would convince her to play The Game the way it was supposed to be played. Or force her. Or maybe for Willie to haul her back again like he'd said. Anything that would keep it going further.

But in just those few moments something was gone. To get it back we'd have to start all over again. I think we all knew it. The sweet heady feeling of danger had suddenly slipped away. It had gone as soon as she started talking.

That was the key.

Talking, it was Meg again. Not some beautiful naked victim, but Meg. A person with a mind, a voice to express her mind, and maybe even rights of her own.

Taking the gag off was a mistake.

It left us feeling sullen and angry and frustrated. So we stood there.

It was Ruth who broke the silence.

"We could do that," she said.

"Do what?" asked Willie.

"Do what she says. Leave her alone. Let her think about it awhile. That seems fine to me."

We thought about it.

"Yeah," said Woofer. "Leave her alone. In the dark. Just *hanging* there."

It was one way, I thought, to start over.

Willie shrugged.

Donny looked at Meg. I could see he didn't want to leave. He looked at her hard.

He raised his hand. Slowly, hesitantly, he moved it toward her breasts.

And suddenly it was like I was part of him. I could feel my own hand there, the fingers nearly touching her. I could almost feel the slick moist heat of her skin.

"Unh-unh," said Ruth. "*No.*"

Donny looked at her. Then he stopped. Just inches from her breast.

I took a breath.

"Don't you touch that girl," said Ruth. "I don't want any of you touching her."

He dropped his hand.

"Girl like her," said Ruth, "isn't even clean. You keep your hands off her. You hear?"

We heard.

"Yeah, Ma," Donny said.

She turned to go. She stomped out her cigarette butt on the floor and waved to us. "C'mon," she said. "But first you better gag her again."

I looked at Donny, who was looking at the rag on the floor.

"It's dirty," he said.

"Not that dirty," said Ruth. "I don't want her screaming at us all night. Put it in."

Then she turned to Meg.

"You want to think about one thing, girl," she said. "Well, two things exactly. First that it could be your little sister and not you hanging there. And second that *I know* some of the things you've done wrong. And I'm interested to hear them. So maybe this confessing isn't such a kid's game after all. I can hear it from the one of you or I can hear it from the other. You think about that," she said, and turned and walked away.

We listened to her climb the stairs.

Donny gagged her.

He could have touched her then but he didn't.

It was like Ruth was still in the room, watching. A presence that was a whole lot more than the lingering smell of her smoke in the air yet just as insubstantial. Like Ruth was a ghost who haunted us, her sons and me. Who'd haunt us forever if we pushed or disobeyed her.

And I think I realized then the sharp razor edge she'd honed to her permission.

The show was Ruth's and Ruth's only.

The Game was nonexistent.

And by that reckoning it was not just Meg but all of us stripped and naked, hanging there.

Chapter Twenty-Nine

Lying in bed, we were haunted by Meg. We couldn't sleep.

Time would pass in total silence in the warm dark and then somebody'd say something, how she looked when Willie took the last book away, what it must feel like to stand there so long with your hands tied over your head, whether it hurt, what it was like to finally see a girl's naked body, and we'd talk about that a while until moments later we got quiet again as each of us wrapped himself up in his own little cocoon of thought and dreams.

But there was only one object to these dreams. Meg. Meg as we'd left her.

And finally we had to see her again.

Donny'd no sooner suggested it than we saw the risks involved. Ruth had told us to leave her alone.

The house was small and sounds carried, and Ruth slept one thin door away, in Susan's room—*was Susan lying awake like us? thinking of her sister?*—directly above the shelter. If Ruth awoke and caught us the unthinkable might happen—she might exclude us all in the future.

We already knew there'd be a future.

But the images we remembered were too strong. It was almost as though we needed confirmation to believe we'd really been there. Meg's nudity and accessibility were like a siren's song. They absolutely beckoned.

We had to risk it.

The night was moonless, black.

Donny and I climbed off the top bunks. Willie and Woofer slid out beneath.

Ruth's door was closed.

We tiptoed past. For once Woofer resisted the urge to giggle.

Willie lifted one of the flashlights off the kitchen table and Donny eased open the cellar door.

The stairs squeaked. There was nothing to do about it except pray and hope for luck.

The shelter door squeaked too but not so badly. We opened it and went inside, standing barefoot on the cold concrete floor the same as she was—and there was Meg, exactly as we remembered as though no time at all had passed, exactly as we'd pictured her.

Well, not quite.

Her hands were white, splotched with red and

blue. And even in the flashlight's thin uneven light you could see how pale her body was. She was all gooseflesh, nipples puckered up brown and tight.

She heard us come in and made a soft whiny sound.

"Quiet," whispered Donny.

She obeyed.

We watched her. It was like standing in front of some sort of shrine—or like watching some strange exotic animal in a zoo.

Like both at once.

And I wonder now if anything would have been different had she not been so pretty, had her body not been young and healthy and strong but ugly, fat, flabby. Possibly not. Possibly it would have happened anyway. The inevitable punishment of the outsider.

But it seems to me more likely that it was precisely *because* she was beautiful and strong, and we were not, that Ruth and the rest of us had done this to her. To make a sort of judgment on that beauty, on what it meant and didn't mean to us.

"I bet she'd like some water," said Woofer.

She shook her head. *Yes*. Oh yes please.

"If we give her water we got to take off the gag," said Willie.

"So what? She won't make noise."

He stepped forward.

"You won't make any noise, will ya, Meg? We can't wake Mom."

No. She shook her head firmly side to side. You could tell she wanted that water a lot.

"You trust her?" Willie said.

Donny shrugged. "If she makes any noise then she gets in trouble too. She's not stupid. So give it to her. Why not?"

"I'll get it," said Woofer.

There was a sink beside the washer/dryer. Woofer turned it on and we could hear it lightly running behind us. He was being unusually quiet about it.

Unusually nice, too, for Woofer.

Willie untied the gag just as he'd done earlier and pulled the dirty wad of rag out of her mouth. She moaned and began to work her jaw side to side.

Woofer came back with an old glass fruit jar full of water.

"I found it by the paint cans," he said. "It don't smell too bad."

Donny took it from him and tilted it to Meg's lips. She drank hungrily, making small glad noises in her throat every time she swallowed. She drained the jar in no time.

"Oh God," she said. "Oh God. Thank you."

And it was a weird feeling. Like everything was forgiven. Like she was really *grateful* to us.

It was amazing in a way. That just one jar of water could do that.

I thought again how helpless she was.

And I wondered if the others were feeling what I was feeling—this overwhelming, almost dizzying need to touch her. To put my hands on her. To see exactly what she *felt like*. Breasts, buttocks, thighs. That blond-red curly tuft between her legs.

Exactly what we weren't supposed to do.

It made me feel like fainting. The push and pull. It was that strong.

"Want some more?" said Woofer.

"Could I? Please?"

He ran out to the sink and then back again with another jarful. He gave it to Donny and she drank that too.

"Thanks. Thank you."

She licked her lips. They were chapped, dry, split in places.

"Do you . . . do you think you could . . . ? The ropes . . . they hurt me a lot."

And you could see they did. Even though her feet were flat on the floor she was still stretched tight.

Willie looked at Donny.

Then they both looked back at me.

I felt confused for a moment. Why should they care what I thought? It was like there was something they were looking for from me and they weren't sure that they'd find it.

Anyway, I nodded.

"I guess we could," said Donny. "A little. On one condition though."

"Anything. What?"

"You have to promise not to fight."

"Fight?"

"You have to promise not to make any noise or anything and you have to promise not to fight and not to tell anybody later on. Tell anybody *anytime*."

"Tell what?"

"That we touched you."

And there it was.

It was what we'd all been dreaming about in that bedroom upstairs. I shouldn't have been surprised. But I was. I could hardly breathe. I felt like everybody in the room could hear my heartbeat.

"Touched me?" said Meg.

Donny blushed deeply. "You know."

"Oh my God," she said. She shook her head. "Oh Jesus. Come on."

She sighed. Then thought for a moment.

"No," she said.

"We wouldn't hurt you or anything," said Donny. "Just touch."

"No."

Like she'd weighed and considered it and simply couldn't see her way clear to do that no matter what happened and that was her final say on the matter.

"Honest. We wouldn't."

"No. You're not doing that to me. Any of you."

She was mad now. But so was Donny.

"*We could do it to you anyway, jerk-off*. Who's gonna stop us?"

"I am."

"How?"

"Well you'll only do it to me once goddamn you, and only one of you. Because I won't just tell. I'll scream."

And there wasn't any question but that she meant it. She'd scream. She didn't care.

She had us.

"Okay," said Donny. "Fine. Then we leave the

ropes the way they are. We put the gag back on and that's that."

You could see she was close to tears. But she wasn't giving in to him. Not on this. Her voice was bitter.

"All right," she said. "Gag me. Do it. Leave. Get out of here!"

"We will."

He nodded to Willie and Willie stepped forward with the rag and scarf.

"Open up," he said.

For a moment she hesitated. Then she opened her mouth. He put the rag in and tied the scarf around it. He tied it tighter than he had to, tighter than before.

"We still got a deal," said Donny. "You got some water. But we were never here. You understand me?"

She nodded. It was hard to be naked and hanging there and proud at the same time but she managed it.

You couldn't help admiring her.

"Good," he said. He turned to leave.

I had an idea.

I reached out and touched his arm as he passed and stopped him.

"Donny?"

"Yeah?"

"Look. Let's give her some slack. Just a little. All we have to do is push the worktable up an inch or two. Ruth won't notice. I mean, look at her. You want to dislocate a shoulder or something? Morning's a long way off, you know what I mean?"

I said this in a voice loud enough so that she could hear.

He shrugged. "We gave her a choice. She wasn't interested."

"I know that," I said. And here I leaned forward and smiled at him and whispered. "But she might be *grateful*," I said. "You know? She might remember. Next time."

We pushed the table.

Actually we sort of lifted and pushed it so as not to make much noise and with the three of us and Woofer it wasn't too hard. And when we were done she had maybe an inch of slack, just enough to give her a bend at the elbow. It was more than she'd had in a very long while.

"See you," I whispered as I closed the door.

And in the dark I think she nodded.

I was a conspirator now, I thought. In two ways. On both sides.

I was working both sides from the middle.

What a great idea.

I was proud of myself.

I felt smart and virtuous and excited. I'd helped her. One day would come the payoff. One day, I knew, she'd let me touch her. It would come to that. Maybe not the others—but me.

She'd *let* me.

So "See you, Meg," I whispered.

Like she'd thank me.

I was out of my mind. I was crazy.

Chapter Thirty

In the morning we came down and Ruth had untied her and brought her a change of clothes along with a cup of hot tea and some unbuttered white toast and she was drinking and eating that sitting cross-legged on the air mattress when we arrived.

Clothed, freed, with the gag and blindfold gone, there wasn't much mystery left in her. She looked pale, haggard. Tired and distinctly grumpy. It was hard to remember the proud Meg or the suffering Meg of the day before.

You could see she was having trouble swallowing.

Ruth stood over her acting like a mother.

"Eat your toast," she said.

Meg looked up at her and then down at the paper plate in her lap.

We could hear the television upstairs—some game show. Willie shuffled his feet.

It was raining outside and we could hear that too.

She took a bite of the crust and then chewed forever until it must have been as thin as spit before swallowing.

Ruth sighed. It was as though watching Meg chew was this great big trial for her. She put her hands on her hips and with her legs apart she looked like George Reeves in the opening credits of *Superman*.

"Go on. Have some more," she said.

Meg shook her head. "It's too . . . I can't. My mouth is so dry. Could I just wait? Have it later? I'll drink the tea."

"I'm not wasting food, Meg. Food's expensive. I made that toast for you."

"I . . . I know. Only . . ."

"What do you want me to do? Throw it out?"

"No. Couldn't you just leave it here? I'll have it in a while."

"It'll be hard by then. You should eat it now. While it's fresh. It'll bring bugs. Roaches. Ants. I'm not having bugs in my house."

Which was kind of funny because there already were a couple of flies buzzing around in there.

"I'll eat it real soon, Ruth. I promise."

Ruth seemed to think about it. She adjusted her stance, brought her feet together, folded her arms across her breasts.

"Meg honey," she said, "I want you to try to eat it now. It's good for you."

"I know it is. Only it's hard for me now. I'll drink the tea, okay?"

She raised the mug to her lips.

"It's not supposed to be easy," said Ruth. "Nobody said it was easy." She laughed. "You're a woman, Meg. That's hard—not easy."

Meg looked up at her and nodded and drank steadily at the tea.

Donny and Woofer and Willie and I stood in our pajamas and watched from the doorway.

I was getting a little hungry myself. But neither Ruth nor Meg had acknowledged us.

Ruth watched her and Meg kept her eyes on Ruth and drank, small careful sips because the tea was still steamy hot, and we could hear the wind and rain outside and then the sump pump kicking in for a while and stopping, and still Meg drank and Ruth just stared.

And then Meg looked down for a moment, breathing in the warm fragrant steam from the tea, enjoying it.

And Ruth exploded.

She whacked the mug from her hands. It shattered against the whitewashed cinder-block wall. Tea running down, the color of urine.

"Eat it!"

She stabbed her finger at the toast. It had slipped halfway off the paper plate.

Meg held up her hands.

"Okay! All right! I will! I'll eat it right away! All right?"

Ruth leaned down to her so that they were almost nose to nose and Meg couldn't have taken a bite then if she'd wanted to—not without pushing the toast up into Ruth's face. Which wouldn't have been a good idea. Because Ruth was burning mad.

"You fucked up Willie's wall," she said. "God-damn you, you broke my mug. You think mugs come cheap? You think tea's *cheap?*"

"I'm sorry." She picked up the toast but Ruth was still leaning in close. "I'll eat. All right? Ruth?"

"You fucking better."

"I'm going to."

"You fucked up Willie's wall."

"I'm sorry."

"Who's going to clean it? Who's going to clean that wall?"

"I will. I'm sorry, Ruth. Really."

"Fuck you, sister. You know who's going to clean it?"

Meg didn't answer. You could see she didn't know what to say. Ruth just seemed to get madder and madder and nothing could calm her.

"*Do* you?"

"N . . . on."

Ruth stood up straight and bellowed.

"*Su-san!* Su-san! You come down here!"

Meg tried to stand. Ruth pushed her down again. And this time the toast did fall off the plate to the floor.

Meg reached down to pick it up and got hold of the piece she'd been eating. But Ruth's brown loafer came down on the other one.

"Forget it!" she said. "You don't want to eat, you don't need to eat."

She grabbed the paper plate. The remaining piece of toast went flying.

"You think I should *cook* for you? You little bitch. You little ingrate!"

Susan came hobbling down the stairs. You could hear her way before you saw her.

"Susan, you get in here!"

"Yes, Mrs. Chandler."

We made way for her. She went past Woofer and he bowed and giggled.

"Shut up," said Donny.

But she did look pretty dignified for a little girl, neatly dressed already and very careful how she walked and very serious-looking.

"Over to the table," said Ruth.

She did as she was told.

"Turn around."

She turned to face the table. Ruth glanced at Meg, and then slipped off her belt.

"Here's how we clean the wall," she said. "We clean the wall by cleaning the slate."

She turned to us.

"One of you boys come over here and pull up her dress and get rid of them panties."

It was the first thing she'd said to us all morning.

Meg started to get up again but Ruth pushed her down hard a second time.

"We're gonna make a rule," she said. "You disobey, you wise-mouth me, you sass me, *anything* like that, missy—and she pays for it. She gets the thrashing. And you get to watch. We'll try that. And if that doesn't work then we'll try something else."

She turned to Susan.

"You think that's fair, Suzie? That you should pay for your trash sister? For what she does?"

Susan was crying quietly.

"N . . . noooo," she moaned.

" 'Course not. I never said it was. Ralphie, you get over here and bare this girl's little butt for me. You other boys get hold of Meg, just in case she gets mean or stupid enough to walk into the line of fire here.

"She gives you any trouble, smack her. And careful where you touch her. She's probably got crabs or something. God only knows where that cunt has been before we got her."

"Crabs?" said Woofer. "Real *crabs?*"

"Never mind," said Ruth. "Just do what I told you to do. You got all your life to learn about whores and crab lice."

And it went just like before, except that Meg was there. Except that the reasoning was crazy.

But by then we were used to that.

Woofer pulled her pants down over the casts and nobody even had to hold her this time while Ruth gave her twenty, fast, with no letup, while she screamed and howled as her ass got redder and redder in that close little room that Willie Sr. had built to withstand the Atomic Bomb—and at first Meg struggled when she heard the howling and crying and the sound of the belt coming down but Willie took her arm and twisted it behind her back, pressed her facedown into the air mattress so that she had all she could do to breathe, never mind helping, tears running down not just Susan's face but hers too and splotching the dirty mattress while Donny and I stood watching and listening in our wrinkled pajamas.

* * *

When it was over Ruth stood back and slipped her belt through her belt loops and Susan bent over with difficulty, braces chattering, and pulled up her panties, then smoothed the back of the dress down over her.

Willie let go of Meg and stepped away.

As Susan turned toward us, Meg lifted her head off the mattress and I watched their glances meet. I saw something pass between them. Something that seemed suddenly placid behind the tears, sad and oddly tranquil.

It unnerved me. I wondered if they weren't stronger than all of us after all.

And I was aware that once again this thing had escalated somehow.

Then Meg's eyes shifted to Ruth and I saw how.

Her eyes were savage.

Ruth saw it too and took an involuntary step back away from her. Her own eyes narrowed and ranged the room. They fixed on the corner where the pick, ax, crowbar and shovel stood propped together like a little steel family of destruction.

Ruth smiled. "I think Meg's pissed at us, boys," she said.

Meg said nothing.

"Well, we all know that won't get her anywhere at all. But let's just pick up that stuff over there so she's not too tempted. She's maybe just dumb enough to try. So get 'em. And lock the door behind you when you leave.

"By the way, Meggy," she said. "You just passed on lunch and dinner. Have a real nice day."

She turned and left the room.

We watched her go. Her walk was a little unsteady, I thought, almost like she'd been drinking though I knew that wasn't so.

"You want to tie her up again?" Woofer asked Willie.

"*Try it,*" said Meg.

Willie snorted. "That's real cool, Meg," he said. "Act tough. We could do it whenever we want to and you know it. And Susan's here. Remember that."

Meg glared at him. He shrugged.

"Maybe later, Woof," said Willie, and he went and got the ax and shovel. Woofer took the pick and the crowbar and followed him.

And then there was a discussion as to where to put it all now that it was outside the protection of the shelter. The basement flooded sometimes so there was a danger of rusting. Woofer wanted to hang them from the ceiling support beams. Donny suggested they nail them to the wall. Willie said fuck it, put 'em by the boiler. *Let* 'em rust. Donny won and they went looking through Willie Sr.'s old World War II footlocker by the dryer, which served as a toolbox now, for hammer and nails.

I looked at Meg. I had to brace myself to do so. I guess I was expecting hate. Half dreading and half hoping it'd be there because then, at least, I'd know where I stood with her and with the rest of them. I could already see that playing the middle was going to be tough. But there wasn't any hate that I could see. Her eyes were steady. Sort of neutral.

"You could run away," I said softly. "I could maybe help you."

She smiled but it wasn't pretty.

"And what would you want for that, David?" she said. "Got any ideas?"

And for a moment she did sound a little like the tramp Ruth said she was.

"No. Nothing," I said. But she'd got me. I was blushing.

"Really?"

"Honest. Really. Nothing. I mean, I don't know where you could go but at least you could get away."

She nodded and looked at Susan. And then her tone of voice was totally different, very matter-of-fact, incredibly reasonable and very adult again.

"*I* could," she said. "But *she* can't."

And suddenly Susan was crying again. She stood looking at Meg for a moment and then hobbled over and kissed her on the lips and on the cheek and then on the lips again.

"We'll do *something*," she said. "Meg? We'll do something. All right?"

"Okay," said Meg. "All right."

She looked at me.

They hugged and when they were finished Susan came over to me standing by the door and took my hand.

And together we locked her in again.

Chapter Thirty-One

Then, as if to negate my offer of help, I stayed away.

Under the circumstances it was the best I could do.

Images haunted me.

Meg laughing on the Ferris wheel, lying on the Rock by the brook. Working in the garden in her shorts and halter with a big straw hat over her head. Running bases, fast, over at the playground. But most of all Meg naked in the heat of her own exertions, vulnerable and open to me.

On the other side I saw Willie's and Donny's tackle dummy.

I saw a mouth crushed into an air mattress for being unable to swallow a piece of toast.

The images were contradictory. They confused me.

So trying to decide what to do, if anything, and

with the excuse of a rainy, ugly week to live through, I stayed away.

I saw Donny twice that week. The others I didn't see at all.

The first time I saw him I was emptying the garbage and he ran out into the gray afternoon drizzle with a sweatshirt pulled over his head.

"Guess what," he said. "No water tonight."

It had been raining for three days.

"Huh?"

"*Meg*, dummy. Ruth's not letting her have any water tonight. Not until tomorrow morning."

"How come?"

He smiled. "Long story," he said. "Tell you about it later."

Then he ran back into the house.

The second time was a couple of days later. The weather had cleared and I was climbing onto my four-speed on the way to the store for my mother. Donny came riding up the driveway behind me on his old beat-up Schwinn.

"Where you going?"

"Over to the store. My mom needs milk and shit. You?"

"Up to Eddie's. There's a game on up at the water tower later. Braves versus Bucks. Want us to wait for you?"

"Nah." It was Little League and didn't interest me.

Donny shook his head.

"I gotta get outta here," he said. "This stuff is driving me crazy. You know what they got me doin' now?"

"What."

"Throwin' her shit pan out in back of the yard! You believe that?"

"I don't get it. Why?"

"She's not allowed upstairs at all anymore. No toilet privileges, nothin'. So the stupid little fuck tries to hold it. But even *she's* got to piss and shit sometime and now I got the goddamn detail! You believe it? What the hell's the matter with Woofer?" He shrugged. "But Mom says it's got to be one of us older guys."

"Why?"

"How the hell do I know?"

He pushed off.

"Hey, you sure you don't want us to wait up for you?"

"Nah. Not today."

"Okay. See ya then. Stop over, huh?"

"Okay, I will."

I didn't, though. Not then.

It seemed so foreign to me. I couldn't even imagine her going to the bathroom, much less using a pan that somebody would have to dump in back of the yard. What if I went over there and they hadn't cleaned up yet that day? What if I had to smell her piss and shit down there? The whole thing disgusted me. *She* disgusted me. That wasn't Meg. That was somebody else.

It became yet another strange new image to trouble me. And the problem was there was nobody to talk to, nobody to sort things out with.

If you talked to the kids on the block it was clear that everybody had some notion of what was happening over there—some vague and others pretty specific. But nobody had any *opinions* about it. It was as though what was happening were a storm or a sunset, some force of nature, something that just happened sometimes. And there was no point discussing summer showers.

I knew enough to be aware that, if you were a boy, you were expected to bring some matters to your father.

So I took a shot at that.

Now that I was older I was supposed to put in some time at the Eagle's Nest now and then, helping to stock and clean up and whatnot, and I was working on the grill in the kitchen with a whetstone and some soda water, pushing the grease into the side troughs with the whetstone as the grill slowly cooled and the soda water loosened the grease—drudge work of the kind I'd seen Meg do a thousand times—when finally I just started talking.

My father was making shrimp salad, crumbling bits of bread in to make it stretch further.

There was a liquor delivery coming in and through the windowed partition between bar and kitchen we could see Hodie, my dad's day shift bartender, ticking off the cartons on an order sheet and arguing with the delivery man over a couple cases of vodka. It was the house brand and evidently the guy had shorted him. Hodie was mad. Hodie was a rail-thin Georgia cracker with a temper volatile enough to have kept him in the brig throughout half the war. The delivery man was sweating.

My father watched, amused. Except to Hodie, two cases was no big deal. Just so long as my father wasn't paying for something he wasn't getting. But maybe it was Hodie's anger that got me started.

"Dad," I said. "Did you ever see a guy hit a girl?"

My father shrugged.

"Sure," he said. "I guess so. Kids. Drunks. I've seen a few. Why?"

"You figure it's ever . . . okay . . . to do that?"

"Okay? You mean justified?"

"Yeah."

He laughed. "That's a tough one," he said. "A woman can really tick you off sometimes. I'd say in general, no. I mean, you got to have better ways to deal with a woman than that. You have to respect the fact that the woman's the weaker of the species. It's like being a bully, you know?"

He wiped his hands on his apron. Then he smiled.

"Only thing is," he said, "I've got to say I've seen 'em deserve it now and then. You work in a bar, you see that kind of thing. A woman gets too much to drink, gets abusive, loud, maybe even takes a poke at the guy she's with. Now what's he supposed to do? Just sit there? So he whacks her one. Now, you've got to break up that kind of thing straightaway.

"See, it's like the exception that proves the rule. You should never hit a woman, never—and God forbid I ever catch you doing it. Because if I do you've had it. But sometimes there's nothing else you *can* do. You get pushed that far. You see? It works both ways."

I was sweating. It was as much the conversation as the work but with the work there I had an excuse.

My father had begun on the tuna salad. There was crumbled bread in that too, and pickle relish. In the next room Hodie had run the guy back to his truck to search for the missing vodka.

I tried to make sense of what he was saying: it was never okay but then sometimes it was.

You get pushed that far.

That got stuck in my mind. Had Meg pushed Ruth too hard at some point? Done something I hadn't seen?

Was this a *never* or a *sometimes* situation?

"Why d'you ask?" said my father.

"I don't know," I said. "Some of us were talking."

He nodded. "Well, best bet's to keep your hands to yourself. Men *or* women. That's how you stay out of trouble."

"Yes, sir."

I poured some more soda water on the grill and watched it sizzle.

"People say Eddie's dad beats up on Mrs. Crocker, though. On Denise and Eddie too."

My father frowned. "Yes. I know."

"You mean it's true."

"I didn't say it was true."

"But it is, right?"

He sighed. "Listen," he said. "I don't know why you're all of a sudden so interested. But you're old enough to know, to understand I guess . . . it's like I said before. Sometimes you get pushed, a man *feels* pushed, and he does . . . what he knows he shouldn't ought to do."

And he was right. I *was* old enough to understand. And I heard a subtext there. Distinct as the echoes of Hodie yelling at the delivery man outside.

At some point and for some reason, my father had hit my mother.

And then I even half remembered it. Waking up out of a deep sleep. The crash of furniture. Yelling. And a slap.

A long time ago.

I felt a sudden shock of anger toward him. I looked at his bulk and thought about my mother. And then slowly the coldness set in, the sense of isolation and of safety.

And it occurred to me that my mother was the one to talk to about all this. She'd know how it felt, what it meant.

But I couldn't then. Not even if she'd been there right that minute. I didn't try.

I watched my father finish the salads and wipe his hands again on the white cotton apron we used to joke about getting condemned by the Board of Health and then start slicing salami on the electric meat slicer he'd just bought and was so proud of and I pushed the grease into the trough until the grill was shiny clean.

And nothing whatever was solved.

And soon I went back again.

Chapter Thirty-Two

What brought me back was that single unstoppable image of Meg's body.

It sparked a thousand fantasies, day and night. Some of them tender, some violent—some ridiculous.

I'd be lying in bed at night with the transistor radio hidden under the pillow playing Danny and the Juniors' "At the Hop," and I'd close my eyes and there would be Meg jitterbugging with some unseen partner, the only girl at Teen's Canteen dancing in a pair of white bobby sox rolled down at the top and nothing else. Comfortable with her nudity as though she'd just bought the emperor's new clothes.

Or we'd be playing Monopoly sitting across from one another and I'd hit Boardwalk or Marvin

Gardens and she'd stand up and sigh and step out of her thin white cotton panties.

But more often the song on the radio would be something like "Twilight Time" by the Platters and Meg would be naked in my arms in the deep blue Technicolor starlight and we'd kiss.

Or the game would be The Game—and there was nothing funny about it at all.

I felt nervous and jumpy.

I felt like I *had* to go over. Just as I was afraid of what I'd find when I did.

Even my mother noticed it. I'd catch her watching me, lips pursed, wondering, as I leapt up from the dinner table spilling the water glass or lurched into the kitchen for a Coke.

Perhaps that was one reason I never spoke to her. Or maybe it was just that she was my mother, and a woman.

But I did go over.

And when I did, things had changed again.

I let myself in and the first thing I heard was Ruth coughing, then talking in a low voice, and I realized it had to be Meg she was speaking to. She had that tone she would never have used to any of the rest of us, like she was a teacher talking to a little girl, instructing. I went downstairs.

They'd rigged up the work light, strung the cable from the outlet over the washer to a hook in one of Willie Sr.'s crossbeams. The caged bulb dangled, brightly glaring.

Ruth was sitting in a folding chair, part of the old card-table set they kept down there, sitting with her back to me, smoking. Cigarette butts littered the floor like she'd been there a while.

The boys were nowhere around.

Meg was standing in front of her in a frilly yellow dress, not the sort of dress you'd picture her wearing at all, and I guessed it was Ruth's, and old, and could see it was none too clean. It had short puffy sleeves and a full pleated skirt, so that her arms and legs were bare.

Ruth was wearing a blue-green version of something similar, but plainer, less flounce and frills.

Above the cigarette smoke I could smell camphor. Mothballs.

Ruth kept talking.

You might have thought they were sisters at first, roughly the same weight though Ruth was taller and skinnier, both of them with hair that was slightly oily now and both of them wearing these old smelly dresses like they were trying things on for a party.

Except that Ruth just sat there smoking.

While Meg was up against one of Willie's four-by-four support posts, arms tied tightly around it behind her back, feet tied too.

She had the gag on but no blindfold.

"When I was a girl like you," Ruth was saying, "I did, I searched for God. I went to every church in town. Baptist, Lutheran, Episcopal, Methodist. You name it. I even went to the novenas over at Saint Matties, sat up in the balcony where the organ was.

"That was before I *knew*, see, what women were. And you know who taught me? My mom did."

" 'Course, she didn't know she was teaching me,

not the way I'm teaching you. It was more what I saw.

"Now I want you to know and understand that they gave me everything, my parents did—everything a girl could wish for, that's what I had. Except for college of course, but girls didn't go in for college much in those days anyhow. But my daddy, rest his soul, he worked hard for a living and my momma and me, we had it all. Not like Willie did me."

She lit a new Tareyton from the butt of the old one and tossed the butt to the floor. And I guessed she hadn't noticed me behind her or else she didn't care because even though Meg was looking right at me with a strange sort of expression on her face, and even though I'd made the usual noise coming down the rickety old stairs, she didn't turn or stop talking, not even to light the cigarette. She talked right through the smoke.

"But my daddy *drank* like Willie," she said, "and I'd hear him. Him coming in nights and straight for the bed and mount my mother like a mare. I'd hear 'em huffin' and puffin' up in there, my mother no-no-no-ing and the occasional odd slap now and then and that was just like Willie too. Because we women repeat the same mistakes as our mothers made giving in all the time to a man. I had that weakness too and that's how come I got all these boys he left me with to starve with. Can't work the way I did, back there during the war. The men get all the jobs now. And I've got kids to raise.

"Oh, Willie sends the checks but it's not enough.

You know that. You see that. Your checks don't do much good either.

"Can you see what I'm saying to you? You got the Curse. And I don't mean your period. You got it worse even than I ever did. I can smell it on you, Meggy! You'll be doing just what my mother and I did with some asshole of an Irishman beatin' up on you and fuckin' you and making you like it, makin' you *love* it, and then wham, he's up and gone.

"That fucking. That's the thing. That warm wet pussy of yours. That's the Curse, you know? Curse of Eve. That's the weakness. That's where they got us.

"I tell you. A woman's nothing but a slut and an animal. You got to see that, you got to remember. Just used and screwed and punished. Nothing but a stupid loser slut with a hole in her and that's all she'll *ever* be.

"Only thing I can do for you is what I'm doing. I can sort of try to *burn* it outta you."

She lit a match.

"See?"

She tossed it at Meg's yellow dress. It died reaching her and fell smoking to the floor. She lit another.

"*See?*"

She leaned in farther this time and tossed it and when the match hit the dress it was still burning. It lodged between the pleats. Meg squirmed against the four-by-four and shook it off.

"Strong young healthy girl like you—you think you smell so fresh and good. But to me you smell like burning. Like hot cunt. You got the Curse and the weakness. You've got it, Meggy."

There was a small black spot on her dress where the match had been. Meg was looking at me, making sounds behind the gag.

Ruth dropped her cigarette and shifted her foot to grind it out.

She got off the chair, leaned down and struck another match. The room seemed suddenly thick with sulfur.

She held it to the hem of the dress.

"See?" she said. "I'd think you'd be grateful."

Meg squirmed, struggling hard against the ropes. The hem charred brown and black but did not flare.

The match burned low. Ruth shook it out and dropped it.

Then she lit another.

She held it low to the hem, the same place she'd already burned. There was a feeling about her like some strange mad scientist performing an experiment in a movie.

The scorched dress smelled like ironing.

Meg struggled. Ruth just took her dress in hand and applied the match until it began to burn, then dropped it back against Meg's leg.

I watched the thin line of flame start crawling.

Spreading.

It was like Woofer with his soldiers in the incinerator. Only this was for real. Meg's high muffled squealing made it real.

It was halfway up her thigh now.

I started to move, to bat the flames out with my hands. Then Ruth reached over and doused her dress with the Coke she'd had sitting beside her on the floor.

She looked at me, laughing.

Meg slumped with relief.

I guess I looked pretty scared. Because Ruth kept laughing. And I realized that part of her must have been aware I was there behind her all along. But she didn't care. My eavesdropping didn't matter. Nothing mattered but her concentration on the lesson she was giving Meg. It was there in her eyes, something I'd never seen before.

I've seen it since.

Too frequently.

In the eyes of my first wife, after her second nervous breakdown. In the eyes of some of her companions at the "rest home." One of whom, I'm told, murdered his wife and infant children with a pair of garden shears.

It's a cold, stark emptiness that has no laughter in it. No compassion, and no mercy. It's feral. Like the eyes of a hunting animal.

Like the eyes of snakes.

That was Ruth.

"What do you think?" she said. "Think she'll listen?"

"I don't know," I said.

"You want to play cards?"

"Cards?"

"Crazy Eights or something."

"Sure. I guess." Anything, I thought. Anything you want to do.

"Just till the boys come home," she said.

We went upstairs and played and I don't think we said ten words to each other the whole game.

I drank a lot of Cokes. She smoked a lot of cigarettes.

She won.

Chapter Thirty-Three

It turned out that Donny, Willie, and Woofer had been to a matinee of *How to Make a Monster*. That would have pissed me off ordinarily because just a few months ago we'd seen a double bill together of *I Was a Teenage Werewolf* and *I Was a Teenage Frankenstein* and this was a kind of sequel, with the same monsters, and they were supposed to wait for me or at least remind me. But they said it wasn't as good as the first two anyway and I was still thinking about what I'd seen below, and as Ruth and I got to the last couple of hands the subject came round to Meg.

"She stinks," said Woofer. "She's dirty. We ought to wash her."

I hadn't noticed any stink.

Just camphor, smoke and sulfur.

And Woofer was one to talk.

"Good idea," said Donny. "It's been a while. I bet she'd like it."

"Who cares what she likes?" said Willie.

Ruth just listened.

"We'd have to let her come upstairs," said Donny. "She could try to run away."

"Come on. Where's she gonna go?" said Woofer. "Where's she gonna run to? Anyway we could tie her."

"I guess."

"And we could get Susan."

"I guess so."

"Where is she?"

"Susan's in her room," said Ruth. "I think she hides from me."

"Nah," said Donny. "She reads all the time."

"She hides. I think she hides."

Ruth's eyes still looked strange and glittery to me, and I guess to the others too. Because nobody contradicted her any further.

"How about it, Ma?" said Woofer. "Can we?"

Our card game was over but Ruth still sat there shuffling the deck. Then she nodded.

"She could use it I suppose," she said dully.

"We'll have to strip her," said Willie.

"*I'll* do that," Ruth said. "You boys remember."

"Yeah," said Woofer. "We remember. No touching."

"That's right."

I looked at Willie and Donny. Willie was scowling. He had his hands in his pockets. He shuffled his feet, shoulders hunched.

What a retard, I thought.

But Donny looked thoughtful, like a full-grown man with a purpose and a job to do now and he was considering the best and most efficient way to go about it.

Woofer smiled brightly.

"Okay," he said. "Let's get her!"

We trooped downstairs, Ruth trailing a ways behind.

Donny untied her, legs first and then the hands, gave her a moment to massage her wrists and then tied them back together again in front of her. He took off the gag and put it in his pocket.

Nobody mentioned the burns or Coke stains on her dress. Though they had to be the first thing you noticed.

She licked her lips.

"A drink?" she asked.

"In a minute," said Donny. "We're going upstairs."

"We are?"

"Yeah."

She didn't ask why.

Holding onto the rope, Donny led her upstairs, with Woofer ahead of him and Willie and I directly in back. Again Ruth lagged behind.

I was very aware of her back there. There was something wrong with her—that I was sure of. She seemed tired, distant, not wholly *there*. Her footsteps on the stairs seemed lighter than ours were, lighter than they should be, barely a whisper—though she moved slowly and with difficulty, like she'd gained twenty pounds. I didn't know much about mental problems then but I knew what I was watching wasn't entirely normal. She bothered me.

When we got upstairs Donny sat Meg down at the dining room table and got her a glass of water from the kitchen sink.

It was the first I'd noticed the sink. It was piled high with dirty dishes, more than they could have used in just one day. More like two or three days' worth was stuffed in there.

And seeing that made me notice other things, made me look around a bit.

I was not a kid who noticed dust. Who did? But I noticed how dusty and dirty the place was now, most visibly on the end tables in the living room behind me where you could see the streaks of hand prints across the surface. There were toast crumbs on the table in front of Meg. The ashtray beside her looked as if it hadn't been cleaned in decades. I saw two wooden matches lying on the throw rug in the hall next to a piece of paper that looked like the crumpled-up top of a cigarette pack, casually discarded.

I had the strangest feeling. Of something winding down. Disintegrating slowly.

Meg finished her glass of water and asked for another. *Please*, she said.

"Don't worry," said Willie. "You'll get water."

Meg looked puzzled.

"We're gonna wash you," he said.

"What?"

"The boys thought it would be nice if you had a shower," said Ruth. "You'd like that wouldn't you."

Meg hesitated. You could see why. That wasn't exactly the way Willie had put it. Willie had said we're gonna wash you.

"Y-yes," she said.

"Very thoughtful of them too," said Ruth. "I'm glad you're glad."

It was like she was talking to herself, almost mumbling.

Donny and I exchanged a look. I could see he was a little nervous about her.

"Think I'll have a beer," said Ruth.

She got up and went to the kitchen.

"Anybody join me?"

Nobody seemed to want any. That in itself was unusual. She peered into the refrigerator. She looked around. Then she closed it again.

"None left," she said, shuffling back to the dining room. "Why didn't somebody buy beer?"

"Mom," said Donny. "We can't. We're kids. They don't *let* us buy beer."

Ruth chuckled. "Right," she said.

Then she turned around again. "I'll have a scotch instead."

She dug into the cabinet and came up with a bottle. She walked back into the dining room, picked up Meg's water glass and poured herself about two inches of the stuff.

"We gonna do this or not?" said Willie.

Ruth drank. "Sure we are," she said.

Meg looked from one of us to the other. "I don't understand," she said. "Do what? I thought I was . . . I thought you were letting me have a shower."

"We are," said Donny.

"We have to supervise, though," said Ruth.

She took another drink and the liquor seemed to strike a sudden fire in back of her eyes.

"Make sure you get clean," she said.

Meg understood her then.

"I don't want it," she said.

"Don't *matter* what you want," said Willie. "What matters is what we want."

"You stink," said Woofer. "You need a shower."

"It's decided already," said Donny.

She looked at Ruth. Ruth hunched over her drink watching her like a tired old bird of prey.

"Why can't you just . . . give me . . . a little *privacy?*"

Ruth laughed. "I'd have thought you'd have about had it with privacy, down there all day."

"That's not what I mean. I mean . . ."

"I know what you mean. And the answer is we can't trust you. Can't trust you one way, can't trust you another. You'll go in there, throw a little water on yourself, and that's not clean."

"No I wouldn't. I swear I wouldn't. I'd *kill* for a shower."

Ruth shrugged. "Well then. You got one. And you don't have to kill for it, do you?"

"Please."

Ruth waved her away. "Get outta that dress now, before you get me mad."

Meg looked at each of us one at a time and then I guess she figured that a supervised shower was better than no shower at all because she sighed.

"My hands," she said.

"Right," said Ruth. "Unzip her, Donny. Then undo her hands. Then do 'em up again."

"Me?"

"Yeah."

I was a little surprised too. I guess she'd decided to relax on the no touching rule.

Meg stood up and so did Donny. The dress unzipped to halfway down her back. He untied her. Then he went behind her again to slip the dress off her shoulders.

"Can I have a towel please, at least?"

Ruth smiled. "You're not wet yet," she said. She nodded to Donny.

Meg closed her eyes and stood very still and rigid while Donny took the frilly short sleeves and dragged them down over her arms and bared her breasts and then her hips and thighs, and then it lay at her feet. She stepped out of it. Her eyes were still shut tight. It was as though if she couldn't see us then we couldn't see her.

"Tie her again," said Ruth.

I realized I was holding my breath.

Donny walked around in front of her. She put her hands together for him and Donny started to tie them.

"No," said Ruth. "Put them behind her this time."

Meg's eyes flashed open.

"*Behind* me! How am I going to wash if . . . ?"

Ruth stood up. "Goddammit! Don't you sass me, girl! If I say behind you then it's behind you and if I say stuff 'em up your ass then you'll do that too! Don't you sass me! You hear? Goddammit! Goddamn you!

"*I'll* wash you—that's how! Now do as I say. Fast!"

And you could see that Meg was scared but she didn't resist as Donny took her arms behind her and tied them at the wrists. She'd closed her eyes again. Only this time there were little pools of wet around them.

"All right, head her in," said Ruth.

Donny marched her down the narrow hallway to the bathroom. We followed. The bathroom was small but all of us crowded inside. Woofer sat on the hamper. Willie leaned against the sink. I stood next to him.

In the hall opposite the bathroom there was a closet, and Ruth was rummaging around in there. She came out with a pair of yellow rubber gloves.

She put them on. They went all the way up to her elbows.

She leaned over and turned on the tap in the bathtub.

The tap marked "H" for hot.

That tap only.

She let it run awhile.

She tested it with her hand, letting it run down over the rubber glove.

Her mouth was a grim straight line.

The water ran hard and steaming. Pounded against the drain. Then she threw the setting to "Shower" and closed the clear plastic curtain.

The steam billowed up.

Meg's eyes were still shut. Tears streaked down her face.

The steam threw a mist over all of us now.

Suddenly Meg felt it. And knew what it meant.

She opened her eyes and threw herself back, frightened, screaming, but Donny already had one arm and Ruth grabbed the other. She fought them, bucking and twisting, screaming *no no*. And she was strong. She was still strong.

Ruth lost her grip.

"God damn you!" she bellowed. "You want me to get your sister? You want me to get your precious Susan? You want her in here instead? *Burning*?"

Meg whirled on her. Suddenly furious. Wild. Insane.

"Yes!" she screamed. "Yes! You bitch! Get Susan! Get her! I don't give a *damn* anymore!"

Ruth looked at her, eyes narrowed. Then she looked at Willie. She shrugged.

"Get her," she said mildly.

He didn't have to.

I turned as he passed me and then saw him stop because Susan was there already, watching us, standing in the hall. And she was crying too.

Meg saw her too.

And she crumbled.

"Noooooo," she cried. "Noooooo. Pleeease . . ."

And for a moment we stood silent in the warm heavy mist listening to the scalding stream and to her sobbing. Knowing what would happen. Knowing how it would be.

Then Ruth threw the curtain aside.

"Get her in," she said to Donny. "And be careful of yourself."

I watched them put her in and Ruth adjust the shower nozzle to send the scorching spray up slowly over her legs and thighs and belly and finally up over her breasts to shatter across her nipples while her arms strained desperately to break free behind her and everywhere the water hit went suddenly red, red, the color of pain—and at last I couldn't stand the screaming.

And I ran.

V

Chapter Thirty-Four

But only once.
I didn't run again.

After that day I was like an addict, and my drug was *knowing*. Knowing what was possible. Knowing how far it could go. Where they'd dare to take it all.

It was always *they*. I stood outside, or felt I did. From both Meg and Susan on the one side and the Chandlers on the other. I'd participated in nothing directly. I'd watched. Never touched. And that was all. As long as I maintained that stance I could imagine I was, if not exactly blameless, not exactly culpable either.

It was like sitting in a movie. Sometimes it was a scary movie, sure—where you worried whether the hero and heroine were going to make it through all right. But just that. Just a movie. You'd get up when it was over properly scared and excited and walk out of the dark and leave it all behind.

And then sometimes it was more like the kind of movies that came along later in the Sixties—foreign movies, mostly—where the dominant feeling you had was of inhabiting some fascinating, hypnotic density of obscure illusion, of layers and layers of meaning that in the end indicated a total absence of meaning, where actors with cardboard faces moved passively through surreal nightmare landscapes, empty of emotions, adrift.

Like me.

Of course we wrote and directed these mind-films of ours as well as watched them. So I suppose it was inevitable that we add to our cast of characters.

I suppose it was also inevitable that Eddie Crocker be our first audition.

It was a bright sunny morning toward the end of July, three weeks into Meg's captivity, when I first went over and found him there.

In the few days since the shower they'd let her keep her clothes on—there were blisters and they were allowing them to heal—and they were treating her pretty well all told, feeding her soup and sandwiches, giving her water when she wanted it. Ruth had even put sheets over the air mattress and swept the cigarette butts off the floor. And it was tough to say whether Willie did more complaining about his latest toothache or about how boring things had gotten.

With Eddie, that changed.

She still had her clothes on when I got there—a pair of faded jeans and a blouse—but they had her bound and gagged again, lying on her stomach over the worktable, each arm tied to one of the legs of the table, feet tied together on the floor.

Eddie had one of his Keds off and was pounding her ass.

Then he'd quit for a while and Willie'd work on her back, legs, and rear with a leather belt. They hit her hard. Eddie especially.

Woofer and Donny stood watching.

I watched too. But only briefly.

I didn't like him there.

Eddie was too much into it.

It was far too easy to picture him walking down the street that day grinning at us with the blacksnake between his teeth, flinging it over and over at us until the snake lay dead in the street.

This was the kid who would bite the head off a frog.

This was the kid who would just as soon hit you in the head with a rock or whack you in the balls with a stick as look at you.

Eddie was passionate.

It was hot that day and the sweat rolled off him, streamed out of his close-cut carrot-red hair and down across his forehead. As usual he had his shirt off so we could see his great physique and the smell of his sweat rolled off him too.

He smelled salty and sticky-sweet, like old bad meat.

I didn't stay.

I went upstairs.

Susan was putting together a jigsaw puzzle on the kitchen table. There was a half-empty glass of milk beside her.

The television, for once, was silent. You could hear the slaps and laughter from below.

I asked for Ruth.

Ruth, Susan said, was lying in the bedroom. One of her headaches. She'd been having them a lot lately.

So we sat there saying nothing. I got myself a Budweiser from the fridge. Susan was doing pretty well on the puzzle. She had more than half of it done. The picture was called "Fur Traders Descending the Missouri," by George Caleb Bingham and showed a grim gnarly old man in a funny pointed cap and a dreamy-faced teenager in a canoe paddling downstream at sunset, a black cat sitting tethered to the prow. She had the edges in and the cat and the canoe and most of the man and boy. There was only the sky and the river and some of the trees left now.

I watched her fit a piece into the river. I sipped the beer.

"So how you doin'?" I asked.

She didn't look up. "Fine," she said.

I heard laughter from the shelter.

She tried another piece. It didn't fit.

"That bother you?" I said. I meant the sounds.

"Yes," she said. But she didn't say it as though it did. It was just a fact of life.

"A lot?"

"Uh-huh."

I nodded. There was nothing much to say then after that. I watched her and drank the beer. Pretty soon she had the boy completed and was working on the trees.

"I can't *make* them stop, y'know?" I said.

"I know."

"Eddie's there. For one thing."

"I know."

I finished the beer.

"I would if I could," I said. I wondered if it was true. So did she.

"Yes?" she said.

And for the first time she looked up at me, eyes very mature and thoughtful. A lot like her sister's.

" 'Course I would."

She went back to the puzzle again, frowning.

"Maybe they'll get tired," I said, realizing as soon as I said it how lame that sounded. Susan didn't answer.

But then a moment later the sounds did stop and I heard footsteps come up the stairs.

It was Eddie and Willie. Both of them flushed, shirts open. Willie's middle a fat, dead-white ugly roll. They ignored us and went to the refrigerator. I watched them crack a Coke for Willie and a Bud for Eddie and then push things around looking for something to eat. I guess there wasn't much because they closed it again.

"You gotta give it to her," Eddie was saying. "She don't cry much. She ain't chicken."

If I had felt detached from all this, Eddie was in

another realm entirely. Eddie's voice was like ice. It was Willie who was fat and ugly but it was Eddie who disgusted me.

Willie laughed. "That's 'cause she's all cried out," he said. "You should've seen her after her scrubbin' the other day."

"Yeah. I guess. You think we should bring something down for Donny and Woofer?"

"They didn't ask for nothin'. They want it, let 'em get it."

"I wish you had some food, man," said Eddie.

And they started to walk back down. They continued to ignore us. That was fine with me. I watched them disappear down the stairwell.

"So what are you gonna do?" said Eddie. I felt his voice drift up at me like a wisp of toxic smoke. "Kill her?"

I froze.

"Nah," said Willie.

And then he said something else but the sound of their footsteps on the stairs drowned it out for us.

Kill her? I felt the words slide along my spine. *Somebody walking over my grave*, my mother would say.

Leave it to Eddie, I thought. Leave it to him.

To state the obvious.

I'd wondered how far it could go, how it could end. Wondered it obscurely, like a mathematical problem.

And here was the unimaginable quietly imagined, two kids discussing it, a Coke and a beer in hand.

I thought of Ruth lying in the bedroom with her sick headache.

I thought of how they were down there all alone with her now—with Eddie with them.

It could happen. Yes it could.

It could happen fast. Almost by accident.

It didn't occur to me to wonder why I still equated Ruth with supervision. I just did.

She was still an adult, wasn't she?

Adults couldn't let that happen, could they?

I looked at Susan. If she'd heard what Eddie'd said she gave no sign. She worked on the puzzle.

Hands trembling, afraid to listen and just as scared not to, I worked with her.

Chapter Thirty-Five

Eddie was there every day after that for about a week. On the second day his sister Denise came too. Together they force-fed her crackers, which she couldn't really eat because the gag had been on overnight again and they'd denied her water. Eddie got mad and smacked her across the mouth with an aluminum curtain rod, bending the rod and leaving a broad red welt across her cheek, cutting her lower lip.

The rest of the day they played tackle dummy again.

Ruth was hardly ever there. Her headaches came more and more frequently now. She complained about her skin itching, particularly her face and hands. It seemed to me she'd lost weight. A fever blister appeared on her lip and stayed for days.

Even with the TV on you could always hear her coughing upstairs, deep down into her lungs.

With Ruth not around the prohibition against touching Meg disappeared.

Denise was the one who started it. Denise liked to pinch. She had strong fingers for a girl her age. She would take Meg's flesh and twist it, commanding her to cry. Most of the time Meg wouldn't cry. That made Denise try harder. Her favorite targets were Meg's breasts—you could tell because she saved them for last.

And then, usually, Meg would cry.

Willie liked to drape her over the table, pull down her pants and smack her bottom.

Woofer's thing was insects. He'd put a spider or a thousand-legger on her belly and watch her cringe.

It was Donny who surprised me. Whenever he thought that no one was looking he'd run his hands across her breasts or squeeze them slightly or feel her between her legs. I saw him plenty of times but I never let on.

He did it gently, like a lover. And once when the gag was off I even saw him kiss her. It was an awkward kiss but sort of tender and strangely chaste when you consider that he had her there to do anything he wanted to her.

Then Eddie came in laughing one day with a dog turd in a plastic cup and they held her down over the table while Woofer pinched her nostrils until she had to open her mouth to breathe and Eddie slipped it in. And that was the last time anybody kissed her.

* * *

On Friday that week I had been working in the yard all afternoon until about four o'clock, and when I went over I could hear the radio blaring from the back-door landing, so I went down and saw that the group had expanded again.

Word had gotten around.

Not only were Eddie and Denise there but Harry Gray, Lou and Tony Morino, Glenn Knott and even Kenny Robertson—a dozen people crowded into that tiny shelter counting Meg and me—and Ruth was standing in the doorway watching, smiling as they shouldered and elbowed her back and forth between them like a human pinball caught between a dozen human flippers.

Her hands were tied behind her.

There were beer cans and Cokes on the floor. Cigarette smoke hung over the room in thick gray drifting clouds. At some point the radio played an old Jerry Lee Lewis tune, "Breathless," and everybody laughed and started singing.

It ended with Meg on the floor, bruised and sobbing. We trooped upstairs for refreshments.

My movie kept rolling.

Kids came and went after that all that following week. Usually they did nothing but watch, but I remember Glen Knott and Harry Gray making her into what they called a "sandwich" one day—when Ruth wasn't around—rubbing against her from front and back while she hung from the lines suspended from the nails in the beams across the ceiling. I remember Tony Morino bringing Woofer half a dozen garden slugs to put all over her body.

But unless it hurt, Meg was usually quiet now. After the dogshit incident it was hard to humiliate her. And not much could scare her. She seemed resigned. As though maybe all she had to do was wait and maybe we'd all get bored by this eventually and it would pass. She rarely rebelled. If she did we'd just call in Susan. But most of the time it didn't come to that. She'd climb out of or into her clothes pretty much on command now. *Out of* only when we knew Ruth wasn't going to be around or if Ruth herself suggested it, which wasn't very often.

And much of the time we just sat there around the worktable, playing cards or Clue and drinking Cokes or looking through magazines, talking, and it was like Meg wasn't even there at all except that we'd say something to mock or shame her now and then. Abuse that was casual and ordinary. Her presence compelled us in much the same passive way a trophy did—she was the centerpiece of our clubhouse. We spent most of our time there. It was the middle of summer but we were all getting pasty from sitting in the cellar. Meg just sat or stood there bound and silent, and mostly we asked nothing of her. Then maybe somebody would get an idea—a new way to use her—and try it out.

But basically it looked like maybe she was right. Maybe we'd just get bored one day and stop coming. Ruth seemed preoccupied with herself and her various physical ailments—preoccupied, strange and distant. And without her to feed the flames our attentions toward Meg got more and more sporadic, less intense.

It occurred to me too that we were well into August now. In September we all started school again. Willie, Donny, and I were leaving for our first term at a brand new junior high, Mount Holly, completed just this summer, and Meg would be starting at the high school. It would *have* to end by then. It only stood to reason. You could keep a person chained out of sight through summer vacation and no one would notice necessarily. But keeping a kid out of school was something else.

So by September it would be over, one way or another.

So maybe she was right, I thought. Maybe all she needed to do was wait.

Then I'd think about what Eddie'd said. And worry that she was real wrong indeed.

It was Eddie who finished the clubhouse.

He did it by upping the ante again.

There were two incidents. The first one happened on a rainy, ugly day, the kind of day that starts out gray and never gets beyond the color of cream of mushroom soup before fading to black again.

Eddie had stolen two six-packs from his father and brought them along and he and Denise and Tony Morino chugged a few while Willie, Woofer, Donny and I went at ours more slowly. Soon the three of them were drunk and the six-packs gone and Willie went upstairs for more. Which was when Eddie decided he had to piss. Which gave him an idea. He whispered it around.

When Willie came back he and Tony Morino took Meg down onto the floor and laid her on her back and tied her arms tightly to the legs of the table. Denise grabbed hold of her feet. They spread some newspapers under her head.

Then Eddie pissed in her face.

If Meg had not been tied to the table I think she'd have tried to kill him.

But instead people were laughing while she struggled and finally she slumped back down and lay there.

Then Donny got to thinking that Ruth wasn't going to like it much. They'd better clean things up. So they got Meg to her feet and tied her arms behind her back and held her, and Woofer picked up the papers and brought them outside to the incinerator while Donny ran some water in the big cement sink they had in the cellar for draining out the water from the washer. He dumped in a lot of Tide. Then he came back and he and Tony and Willie marched her out of the shelter into the basement proper over to the sink.

They pushed her head down into the soapy water and held her under, laughing, while Willie scrubbed her hair. In a moment or two she was struggling. When they let her up she had to gasp for air.

But she was clean.

Then Eddie got another idea.

We had to rinse her, he said.

He let out the water, drained it, and ran the rinse

water straight-out hot, just as Ruth had done in the shower.

Then, alone, he dunked her under.

When he let her up to the surface again her face was lobster red and she was shrieking, and Eddie's hand was so red you had to wonder how he'd held it there.

But now she was rinsed.

Cleaned and rinsed. And wouldn't Ruth be pleased about that?

Ruth was furious.

All the next day she kept cold compresses over Meg's eyes. There was serious fear for her sight. Her eyes were so puffy she could hardly open them, and they kept oozing liquid a whole lot thicker than anybody's tears ought to be. Her face looked splotched and horrible, like she'd contracted a mammoth case of poison ivy. But it was the eyes that worried everybody.

We kept her on the air mattress. We fed her.

Wisely, Eddie stayed away.

And the next day she was better. And the next day better still.

And the third day Eddie came back again.

I wasn't there that day—my father had me over at the Eagle's Nest—but I heard about it fast enough.

It seemed that Ruth was upstairs lying down and they figured she was asleep, napping through another headache. Woofer, Donny and Willie were playing Crazy Eights when Eddie and Denise walked in.

Eddie wanted to take off her clothes again, just

to look he said, and everybody agreed. He was quiet, calm. Drinking a Coke.

They stripped her and gagged her and tied her faceup across the worktable, only this time they tied each of her feet to one of the table legs as well. Eddie's idea. He wanted to spread her. They left her awhile while the game of cards went on and Eddie finished his Coke.

Then Eddie tried to put the Coke bottle up inside her.

I guess they were all so amazed and involved with what he was doing that they didn't hear Ruth come down behind them because when she walked through the door there was Eddie with the lip of the green Coke bottle already inside her and everybody crowded around.

Ruth took one look and started screaming how nobody was supposed to touch her, *nobody*, she was dirty, she had *diseases*, and Eddie and Denise got the hell out of there, fast, leaving her to rail at Woofer and Willie and Donny.

And the rest of this I got from Donny.

And Donny said he was scared.

Because Ruth went really bonkers.

She raged around the room tearing at things and jabbering crazy stuff about how she never *got out* anymore, not to a movie or dinner or dancing or parties, all she ever did was sit here minding these goddamn fucking *kids*, cleaning, ironing, making lunch and breakfast, how she was getting old in there, *old*, her good years gone, her body gone all to hell on her—all the time slamming at the walls and the wire-mesh screen over the window and the worktable, kicking Eddie's Coke bottle until it smashed against the wall.

And then she said something like *and you! you!* to Meg and stared at her furious like it was her fault that Ruth's body was going and she couldn't go out anymore and called her a whore and a slut and no-good fucking trash—and then hauled off and kicked her, twice, between her legs.

And now she had bruises there. Terrible bruises.

Luckily, said Donny, Ruth had been wearing slippers.

I could picture it.

I had a dream that night, the night he told me.

I was home watching television and the fights were on, Sugar Ray Robinson against some big ungainly nameless faceless white guy, and my father was asleep next to me snoring in the overstuffed chair while I sat watching from the couch, and aside from the light from the TV set it was dark in the house and I was tired, very tired—and then things switched and I was suddenly actually *at* the fights, I was ringside, with people cheering around me, and Sugar Ray was wading in at the guy in that way he had, moving like a tank, flat-footed, swinging. It was exciting.

So I was cheering for Sugar Ray and I looked around for my father to see if he was cheering too but he was dead asleep in the seat beside me just as he'd been on the couch, sinking slowly to the floor. "Wake up," my mother said, nudging him. I guess she'd been there all along but I hadn't seen her there. "Wake up," she said.

But he didn't. And I looked back to the ring and instead of Sugar Ray it was Meg inside the ring, Meg as I'd first seen her standing by the brook that day in shorts and a pale sleeveless blouse, her pony-tail red as flame swinging back and forth behind her as she pounded at the guy, pounded him. And I stood up, cheering, screaming.

"*Meg! Meg! Meg!*"

I woke up crying. My pillow soaked with tears.

I felt confused. Why should I be crying? *I wasn't feeling anything*.

I went to my parents' room.

They had separate beds now. They'd had them for years. As in the dream, my father was snoring. My mother slept silently beside him.

I walked to my mother's bed and stood there watching her, a dainty little dark-haired woman who looked younger at that moment, sleeping, than I think I'd ever seen her.

The room smelled thick with their sleep, the musty odor of breathing.

I wanted to wake her. I wanted to tell her. Everything.

She was the only one I *could* tell.

"Mom?" I said. Yet I said it very quietly, part of me still too scared or too unwilling to risk disturbing her. Tears were rolling down my cheeks. My nose was running. I sniffled. The sniffling sounded louder to me than my voice did calling her.

"Mom?"

She shifted, moaning slightly.

I had only to try one more time, I thought, in order to wake her.

And then I thought of Meg, alone in the long dark night of the shelter, lying there. Hurting.

Then I saw the dream.

I felt something clutch at me.

I couldn't breathe. I felt a sudden dizzying, rising horror.

The room went black. I felt myself exploding.

And I knew my part in this.

My dull, careless betrayal.

My evil.

I felt the sob come at me huge and involuntary as a scream. It *felt* like a scream. I covered my mouth and ran stumbling from the room, fell huddled to my knees in the hall outside their door. I sat there shaking, crying. I couldn't stop crying.

I sat there a very long time.

They didn't waken.

When I got to my feet it was nearly morning.

I went to my room. Through the window from my bed I watched the night turn deepest black and then a rich dark blue.

My thoughts spun round and round, diving through me like the morning sparrows flying off the eaves.

I sat and knew myself entirely and calmly watched the sunrise.

Chapter Thirty-Six

It helped that for now at least the others were excluded. I needed to talk to her. I had to convince her I'd finally help.

I'd get her to run away with or without Susan. I couldn't see that Susan was in so much danger anyhow. Nothing had happened to her so far except some spankings, at least nothing I'd seen. It was Meg who was in trouble. By now, I thought, she's got to have realized that.

It was both easier and harder than I expected.

Harder because I found out I was excluded too.

"My mom doesn't want *anybody* around," said Donny. We were biking over to the Community Pool, our first day there in weeks. It was hot with no breeze and three blocks from our street we were sweating.

"How come? I didn't do anything. Why me?"

We rode along a downslope. We coasted awhile.

"It's not that. You hear what Tony Morino did?"

"What."

"He told his mother."

"What?"

"Yeah. The little shit. His brother, Louie, let us onto it. I mean, not everything. I guess he *couldn't* tell her everything. But enough. Told her we had Meg in the cellar. Told her Ruth called her a whore and a slut and beat up on her."

"Jesus. What'd she say?"

Donny laughed. "Lucky for us the Morinos are real strict Catholics. His mom said she probably deserved it, she's probably loose or something. She said parents have a right and Ruth's her mother now. So you know what we did?"

"What?"

"Me and Willie pretended we didn't know. We got Tony to come along with us out to Bleeker's Farm, the woods back there. He doesn't know the place at all. We got him lost and then we ditched him back in the swamps. Took him two and a half hours to find his way out and get home and by then it was dark. But you know the best part about it? His mom beat the crap out of him for missing dinner and coming home full of swamp muck and shit. His *mom!*"

We laughed. We pulled into the newly poured driveway by the Recreation building and parked our bikes at the bike stand and walked across the sticky, sweet-smelling tarmac to the pool.

We showed our plastic badges at the gate. The

pool was crowded. Little kids kicking and splashing in the shallows like a school of piranha. The baby pool full of moms and dads guiding along their infants, pudgy fingers clutching duckies-and-dragons inner tubes. There were long impatient lines at the diving boards and refreshment stand. Yellowjackets in every trashcan swarming through ice-cream wrappers and soda.

The screaming and splashing and yelling while everybody ran around the fenced-in grass and concrete was deafening. The lifeguard's whistle seemed to shriek about every thirty seconds. We threw off our towels and went over to the eight-foot section and sat with our legs dangling down in the chlorine-smelling water.

"So what's that got to do with me?" I asked him.

He shrugged. "I dunno," he said. "My mom's all worried now. That somebody's going to tell."

"Me? Jeez, I won't tell," I said. Picturing myself in the dark, standing over my sleeping mother. "You know I won't tell."

"I know. Ruth's just weird these days."

I couldn't push it further. Donny wasn't as stupid as his brother. He knew me. He'd know if I was pushing and wonder.

So I waited. We splashed with our feet.

"Look" he said, "I'll talk to her, all right? It's bullshit. You been comin' over our house for how many years now?"

"A lot."

"So screw it. I'll talk to her. Let's get wet."

We slipped into the pool.

* * *

The part that was easy was convincing Meg to go.

There was a reason for that.

For one last time, I told myself, I was going to have to stand and watch, waiting for the moment I could speak. And then I'd convince her. I even had a plan in mind.

And then it would be over.

I'd have to pretend I was with them no matter what—that it didn't matter. One last time.

Yet it almost didn't happen.

Because that one last time was nearly enough to push us both over the edge. That last time was horrible.

Chapter Thirty-Seven

"It's okay," Donny told me the following day. "My mom says it's okay to come."

"Come where?" said my mother.

She was standing behind me at the kitchen counter, chopping onions. Donny stood on the porch behind the screen. With me in the way he hadn't noticed her.

The kitchen reeked of onions.

"Where are you going?" she said.

I looked at him. He thought fast.

"We're gonna try to get up to Sparta next Saturday, Mrs. Moran. Soft of a family picnic. We thought maybe David could come too. Would that be all right?"

"I don't see why not," said my mother, smiling. Donny was unfailingly polite to her without being obnoxious about it and she liked him for that though she had no use at all, really, for the rest of the family.

"Great! Thanks, Mrs. Moran. See you later, David," he said.

So in a little while I went over.

Ruth was back into The Game.

She looked terrible. There were sores on her face and you knew she'd been scratching them because two were already scabbed over. Her hair was oily, limp, flecked with dandruff. The thin cotton shift looked as though she'd been sleeping in it for days. And now I was sure she'd lost weight. You could see it in her face—the hollows under the eyes, the skin pulled tight across the cheekbones.

She was smoking as usual, sitting in a folding chair facing Meg. There was a half-eaten tuna sandwich on a paper plate beside her and she was using it as an ashtray. Two Tareyton butts poked up out of the sagging wet white bread.

She was watching attentively, leaning forward in the chair, eyes narrowed. And I thought of the way she looked when she was watching her game shows on TV, shows like *Twenty-One*. Charles Van Doren, the English teacher from Columbia, had just been called a cheat for winning $129,000 on the show the week before. Ruth had been inconsolable. As though she was cheated too.

But she watched Meg now with the same thoughtful intensity as when Van Doren was in his soundproof booth.

Playing along.

While Woofer poked Meg with his pocketknife.

They had hung her from the ceiling again, and she was up on her toes, straining, volumes of the World Book scattered at her feet. She was naked. She was dirty, she was bruised. Her skin had a pallor now beneath the sheen of sweat. But none of that mattered. It should have, but it didn't. The magic—the small cruel magic of seeing her that way—hovering over me for a moment like a spell.

She was all I knew of sex. And all I knew of cruelty. For a moment I felt it flood me like a heady wine. I was with them again.

And then I looked at Woofer.

A pint-sized version of me, or what I could be, with a knife in his hand.

No wonder Ruth was concentrating.

They all were, Willie and Donny too, nobody saying a word, because a knife wasn't a strap or a belt or a stream of hot water, knives could hurt you seriously, permanently, and Woofer was small enough to only just barely understand that, to know that death and injury could happen but not to sense the consequences. They were skating thin ice and they knew it. Yet they let it go. They wanted it to happen. They were educating.

I didn't need the lessons.

So far there wasn't any blood but I knew there was every chance that there would be, it was just a matter of time. Even behind the gag and blindfold you could see that Meg was terrified. Her chest and stomach heaved with fitful breathing. The scar on her arm stood out like jagged lightning.

He poked her in the belly. On her toes the way she was, there was no way she could back away from him. She just jerked against the ropes convulsively. Woofer giggled and poked her below the navel.

Ruth looked at me and nodded a greeting and lit another Tareyton. I recognized Meg's mother's wedding band fitting loose on her ring finger.

Woofer slid the blade over Meg's ribcage and poked her armpit. He did it so fast and so recklessly I kept looking for a line of blood along her ribs. But that time she was lucky. I saw something else though.

"What's that?"

"What's what?" said Ruth distractedly.

"On her leg there."

"There was a red two-inch wedge-shaped mark on her thigh, just above the knee.

She puffed the Tareyton. She didn't answer.

Willie did. "Mom was ironing," he said. "She gave us some shit so Mom heaved the iron at her. Skinned her. No big deal, except now the iron's busted."

"No big deal my ass," said Ruth.

She meant the iron.

Meanwhile Woofer slid the knife back down to Meg's belly. This time he nicked her just at the bottom of the ribcage.

"Whoops," he said.

He turned to look at Ruth. Ruth stood up.

She took a drag on the cigarette and flicked off the ash.

Then she walked over.

Woofer backed away.

"Dammit, Ralphie," she said.

"I'm sorry," he said. He let go of the knife. It clattered to the floor.

You could see he was scared. But her tone was as blank as her face.

"Shit," she said. "Now we got to cauterize." She lifted the cigarette.

I looked away.

I heard Meg scream behind the gag, a shrill thin muffled shriek that turned abruptly into a wail.

"Shut up," said Ruth. "Shut up or I'll do it again."

Meg couldn't stop.

I felt myself trembling. I stared at the bare concrete wall.

Hold on, I thought, I heard the hiss. I heard her scream.

I could smell the burning.

I looked and saw Ruth with the cigarette in one hand while the other cupped her breast through the gray cotton dress. The hand was kneading. I saw the burn marks close together under Meg's ribs, her body bathed in sudden sweat. I saw Ruth's hand move roughly over her wrinkled dress to press between her legs as she grunted and swayed and the cigarette drifted forward once again.

I was going to blow it. I knew it. I could feel it building. I was going to have to do something, say something. Anything to stop the burning. I closed my eyes and still I saw Ruth's hand clutch at the place between her legs. The scent of burning flesh was all around me. My stomach lurched. I turned and heard Meg scream and scream again and then suddenly Donny was saying *Mom! Mom! Mom!* in a voice that was hushed and suddenly filled with fear.

I couldn't understand.

And then I heard it. The knocking.

There was someone at the door.

The front door.

I looked at Ruth.

She was staring at Meg and her face was peaceful and relaxed, unconcerned and distant. Slowly she raised the cigarette to her lips and took a long deep drag. *Tasting her.*

I felt my stomach lurch again.

I heard the knocking.

"Get it," she said. "Go slow. Go *easy*."

She stood quietly while Willie and Donny glanced at one another and then went upstairs.

Woofer looked at Ruth and then at Meg. He seemed confused, suddenly just a little boy again who wanted to be told what to do. Should I go or should I stay? But there wasn't any help for him, not with Ruth that way. So finally he made up his own mind. He followed his brothers.

I waited until he was gone.

"Ruth?" I said.

She didn't seem to hear me.

"Ruth?"

She just kept staring.

"Don't you think . . . ? I mean, if it's somebody . . . Should you be leaving it to them? To Willie and Donny?"

"Hmmm?"

She looked at me but I'm not sure she saw me. I've never seen anyone *feel* so empty.

But this was my chance. Maybe my only chance. I knew I had to push her.

"Don't you think you ought to handle it, Ruth? Suppose it's Mr. Jennings again?"

"Who?"

"Mr. Jennings. *Officer* Jennings. The *cops*, Ruth."

"Oh."

"I can . . . watch her for you."

"Watch her?"

"To make sure she doesn't . . ."

"Yes. Good. Watch her. Good idea. Thank you, Davy." She started toward the doorway, her movements slow and dreamlike. Then she turned. And now her voice was tight sharp, her back straight. Her eyes seemed shattered with reflected light.

"You'd better not fuck up," she said.

"What?"

She pressed her finger to her lips and smiled.

"One sound down here and I promise I'll kill the both you. Not punish you. *Kill* you. Dead. You got that, Davy? Are we straight about that?"

"Yes."

"You sure?"

"Yes ma'am."

"Good. Very good."

She turned and then I heard her slippers shuffling up the stairs. I heard voices from above but couldn't make them out.

I turned to Meg.

I saw where she'd burned her the third time. Her right breast.

"Oh Jesus, Meg," I said. I went to her. "It's David. I slipped off the blindfold so she could see me. Her eyes were wild.

"Meg," I said. "Meg, listen. Listen *please*. Please don't make any noise. You heard what she said? She'll do it, Meg. Please don't scream or anything, okay? I want to help you. There's not much time. Listen to me. I'll take off the gag, all right? You won't scream? It won't help. It could be anybody up there. The Avon lady. Ruth can talk her way out of it. She can talk her way out of anything. But I'm going to get you out of here, you understand me? I'm going to get you out!"

I was talking a mile a minute but I couldn't stop. I slipped off the gag so she could answer.

She licked her lips.

"How?" she said. Her voice a tiny painful rasp of sound.

"Tonight. Late. When they're asleep. It's got to look like you did it on your own. By yourself. Okay?"

She nodded.

"I've got some money," I said. "You'll be okay. And I can hang around here and make sure nothing happens to Susan. Then maybe we can figure out some way to get her away too. Go back to the cops, maybe. Show them . . . this. "All right?"

"All right."

"All right. Tonight. I promise."

I heard the screened front door slam shut and footsteps cross the living room, heard them coming down the stairs. I gagged her again. I slipped on the blindfold.

It was Donny and Willie.

They glared at me.

"How'd you know?" asked Donny.

"Know what?"

"Did you tell him?"

"Tell who? Tell him what? What are you talking about?"

"Don't hack around with me, David. Ruth said you told her it might be Jennings at the door."

"So who the hell do you *think* it was, assface?"

Oh Jesus, I thought. Oh shit. And I'd begged her not to scream.

We could have stopped it then and there.

I had to play it through for them though.

"You're kidding," I said.

"I'm not kidding."

"Mr. Jennings? My God, it was just a *guess*."

"Pretty good guess," said Willie.

"It was just a thing to say to get her . . ."

"Get her what?"

Up there I thought.

"To get her *moving* again. Christ, you saw her. She was like a fucking zombie down here!"

They looked at each other.

"She did get pretty weird," said Donny.

Willie shrugged. "Yeah. I guess so."

I wanted to keep them going. So they wouldn't think about my being here alone with her.

"What'd you say?" I asked. "Was he after Meg?"

"Sort of," said Donny. "Said he just dropped by to see how the nice young girls were doing. So we showed him Susan in her room. Said Meg was out shopping. Susan didn't say a word of course—didn't dare to. So I guess he bought it. Seemed kinda uncomfortable. Kinda shy for a cop."

"Where's your mom?"

"She said she wanted to lie down awhile."

"What'll you do for dinner?"

It was an inane thing to say but the first thing I thought of.

"I dunno. Cook some dogs out on the grill I guess. Why? Want to come over?"

"I'll ask my mother," I said. I looked at Meg. "What about her?" I asked him.

"What about her?"

"You gonna just leave her there or what? You ought to put something on those burns at least. They'll get infected."

"Fuck her," said Willie. "I ain't sure I'm done with her yet."

He bent over and picked up Woofer's knife.

He tossed it in his hand, blade to handle, and slouched and grinned and looked at her.

"Then again maybe I am," he said. "I dunno. I dunno." He walked toward her. And then so that she could hear him very clearly and distinctly he said, "I *just don't know*." Taunting her.

I decided to ignore him.

"I'll go and ask my mother," I told Donny.

I didn't want to stay to see what his choice would be. There was nothing I could do anyway one way or another. Some things you had to let go of. You had to keep your mind on what you *could* do. I turned and climbed the stairs.

At the top I took a moment to check the door.

I was counting on their laziness, their lack of organization.

I checked the lock.

And yes, it was still broken.

Chapter Thirty-Eight

It was a time when even the guilty displayed a rare innocence.

In our town burglary was unheard of. Burglaries happened in cities but not out here—that was one of the reasons our parents had left the cities in the first place.

Doors were closed against the cold and wind and rain, but not against people. So that when the lock on a door or window snapped or rusted through over years of bad weather more often than not it got left that way. Nobody needed a lock to keep out the snow.

The Chandlers' house was no exception.

There was a screen door in back with a lock that I don't think had ever worked—not in living memory. Then a wooden door that had warped slightly and in such a way that the tongue of the lock didn't match with the lip on the doorjamb anymore.

Even with Meg held prisoner there they'd never bothered to repair it.

That left the metal icehouse door to the shelter itself, which bolted. It was a clumsy, noisy affair but all you had to do was throw the bolt.

I thought it could be done.

At three twenty-five in the morning I set out to see.

I had a penlight flashlight, a pocketknife and thirty-seven dollars in snow-shoveling money in my pocket. I wore sneakers and jeans and the T-shirt my mother'd dyed black for me after Elvis wore one in *Loving You*. By the time I crossed the driveway to their yard the T-shirt was plastered to my back like a second skin.

The house was dark.

I stepped up onto the porch and waited, listening. The night was still and clear beneath a three-quarter moon.

The Chandler house seemed to breathe at me, creaking like the bones of a sleeping old woman.

It was scary.

For a moment I wanted to forget about this, go home and get into bed and pull up the covers. I wanted to be in another town entirely. All that evening I'd fantasized my mother or my father saying, well David, I don't know how to break this to you but we're moving.

No such luck.

I kept seeing myself getting caught on the stairs. Suddenly the light would go on and there would be

Ruth above me pointing a shotgun. I doubt they even owned a gun. But I saw it anyway. Over and over like a record stuck in the final groove.

You're nuts, I kept thinking.

But I'd promised.

And as frightening as this was, today had scared me more. Looking at Ruth I'd finally seen all the way through to the end of it. Clearly and unmistakably I'd finally seen Meg dying.

I don't know how long I stood there waiting on the porch.

Long enough to hear the tall Rose of Sharon scrape the house in a gentle breeze, to become aware of the frogs croaking from the brook and the crickets in the woods. Long enough for my eyes to adjust to the darkness and for the normalcy of frogs and crickets speaking to each other in the night to calm me. So that after a while what I finally felt was not so much the sheer terror I'd started with as excitement—excitement at finally doing something, something for Meg and for myself, and something no one I knew had *ever* done. It helped me to think about that. About the moment-by-moment present tense reality of what I was doing. If I did that I could make it into a sort of game. I was breaking into a house at night and people were sleeping. That was all. Not dangerous people. Not Ruth. Not the Chandlers. Just people. I was a cat burglar. Cool and careful and stealthy. No one was going to catch me. Not tonight and not ever.

I opened the outer screen door.

It made barely a whimper.

The inner door was trickier. Its wood had expanded with humidity. I turned the handle and pressed my fingers against the doorjamb, my thumb against the door. I pushed slowly, gently.

It groaned.

I pushed harder and more steadily. I held tight to the handle, keeping a slight backward pressure so that when it did open it wouldn't pop and shudder.

It groaned some more.

I was sure the entire house was hearing this. Everybody.

I still could run if I had to. It was good to know.

Then all of a sudden it opened. With even less noise than the screen had made.

I listened.

I stepped inside onto the landing.

I turned on the penlight. The stairs were cluttered with rags, mops, brushes, pails—stuff Ruth used for cleaning, along with jars of nails and paint cans and thinner. Luckily most of it lined just the one side, the side opposite the wall. I knew the stairs were going to be firmest and least creaky right next to the wall, where they'd have support. If I was going to get caught this was the likeliest place, the place there'd be the most noise. I stepped down carefully.

At each stair I'd stop and listen. I'd vary the time between steps so there'd be no rhythm to it.

But each stair had its say.

It took forever.

Then finally I was at the bottom. By then my

heart felt ready to burst. I couldn't believe they hadn't heard me.

I crossed to the shelter door.

The basement smelled of damp and mildew and laundry—and something like spilt sour milk.

I threw the bolt as quietly and evenly as possible. Metal squealed against metal all the same.

I opened the door and stepped inside.

It was only then, I think, that I remembered what I was doing here in the first place.

Meg sat in the corner on her air mattress, her back against the wall, waiting. In the thin beam of light I could see how frightened she was. And how badly the day had gone for her.

They'd given her a thin rumpled shirt to put on and that was all. Her legs were bare.

Willie had been at them with the knife.

There were lines and scratches crisscrossed across her thighs and down her calves almost to her ankles.

There was blood on the shirt as well. Dried blood mostly—but not all. Some of it seeping through.

She stood up.

She walked toward me and I could see a fresh bruise on her temple.

For all of that she still looked firm and ready.

She started to say something but I put my finger to my lips, hushing her.

"I'll leave the bolt and the back door open," I whispered.

"They'll think they just forgot. Give me maybe a half an hour. Stay to the wall side on the stairs and try not to run. Donny's fast. He'd catch you. Here."

I dug into my pocket and handed her the money. She looked at it. Then she shook her head.

"Better not," she whispered. "If something goes wrong and they find it on me they'll know somebody's been here. We'd never get another chance. Leave it for me . . ." She thought for a moment. "Leave it at the Big Rock. Put a stone on top of it or something. I'll find it, don't worry."

"Where will you go?" I said.

"I don't know. Not yet. Back to Mr. Jennings maybe. Not too far. I want to stay close to Susan. I'll find a way to let you know as soon as I can."

"You want the flashlight?"

She shook her head again. "I know the stairs. You keep it. Go ahead. Go. Get out of here."

I turned to leave.

"David?"

I turned again and she was suddenly next to me, reaching up. I saw the tears gleam bright in her eyes just as she closed them and kissed me.

Her lips were battered, broken, chapped and torn.

They were the softest, most beautiful things that had ever touched me, that I had ever touched.

I felt my own tears come all in a rush.

"God! I'm sorry, Meg. I'm *sorry*."

I could barely get it out. All I could do was stand there and shake my head and ask her to forgive me.

"David," she said. "David. *Thank you*. What you do last—that's what counts."

I looked at her. It was as though I were drinking her in, as though I were somehow *becoming* her.

I wiped my eyes, my face.

I nodded and turned to go.

Then I had a thought. "Wait," I said.

I stepped outside the shelter and ran the flashlight beam across the walls. I found what I was looking for. I took the tire iron off the nails and walked back and handed it to her.

"If you need to," I said.

She nodded.

"Good luck, Meg," I said and quietly closed the door.

And then I was in the midst of it again, in the close jarring silence of the sleeping house, moving slowly upward to the doorway, weighing each step against the creaking of beds and the whispers of the branches of trees.

And then I was out the door.

I ran across the yard to the driveway, cut through to the back of my house and into the woods. The moon was bright but I knew the path without the moon. I heard the water rushing full by the brook.

At the Rock I stooped to pick up some stones and lowered myself carefully down over the embankment. The surface of the water gleamed in the moonlight, shattered over the rocks. I stepped onto the Rock and dug into my pocket, put the money in a pile and weighed it down with a small neat pyramid of stones.

On the embankment I looked back.

The money and the stones looked pagan to me, like an offering.

Through the rich green scent of leaves I ran home.

Chapter Thirty-Nine

And then I sat in bed and listened to my own house sleeping. I thought it would be impossible to sleep but I hadn't counted on strain and exhaustion. I dropped off just after dawn, my pillow damp with sweat.

I slept badly—and late.

I looked at the clock and it was almost noon. I got into my clothes and ran downstairs, gulped down the requisite bowl of cereal because my mother was standing there complaining about people who slept all day and where it got them as adults—mostly jail and unemployment—and bolted out the door smack into the sticky August sunlight.

There was no way I dared going straight to the Chandlers'. What if they'd figured it was me?

I ran through the woods to the Rock.

The little pyramid I'd made of stones and dollars was still there.

In the light of day it no longer looked like an offering. It looked like a pile of dogshit sitting on a pile of leaves. It sat there mocking me.

I knew what it meant. She hadn't got out.

They'd caught her.

She was still inside.

I felt this terrible sick feeling in my gut and the cereal nearly slid up again. I was angry and then I was scared and then I was plain confused. Suppose they *had* decided it was me who threw the bolt? Or suppose they'd done something to make Meg tell them?

What was I supposed to do now?

Get out of town?

You could go to the cops, I thought. You could go see Mr. Jennings.

And then I thought, great, and tell him what? That Ruth's been torturing Meg for months and I know she has for a fact because I've sort of been helping?

I'd seen enough cop shows to know what an accomplice was.

And I knew a kid—a friend of my cousin's from West Orange—who'd done almost a year in Juvenile for getting drunk on beer and stealing his neighbor's car. According to him they could beat you, they could drug you, they could stick you in a straightjacket if they wanted to. And they let you out when they were damn good and ready.

There's got to be some other way, I thought.

Like Meg said about keeping the money—we could try again. Think it through better this time.

If they didn't know about me already.

There was only one way to find that out.

I climbed over to the Rock and gathered up the fives and singles and put them in my pocket.

Then I took a real deep breath.

And then I went over.

Chapter Forty

Willie met me at the door and it was clear that even if they knew or suspected, Willie had other more urgent things on his mind.

"Come on," he said.

He looked drawn and tired, excited though, the two combining to make him uglier than ever. You knew he hadn't washed and his breath was foul even for him.

"Close the door behind you."

I did.

We went downstairs.

And Ruth was there, sitting in her folding chair. And Woofer. Eddie and Denise perched on the worktable. And Susan sat bloodlessly silent crying next to Ruth.

Every one of them sitting quiet while on the cold damp concrete floor Donny lay grunting on top of Meg with his pants down around his ankles, raping her, her naked body tied hands and feet between the four-by-four support beams.

And I guessed Ruth had finally changed her mind once and for all about touching.

I felt sick.

I turned to get out of there.

"Unh-unh," said Willie. "You stay."

And the carving knife in his hand and the look in his eyes said he was right. I stayed.

They were all so quiet in there you could hear the two flies buzzing.

It seemed like a bad sick dream. So I did what you do in a dream. Passively I watched it unfold.

Donny covered most of her. I could see only her lower body—her legs and thighs. Either they were very much bruised since yesterday or had gotten very dirty. The soles of her feet were black.

I could almost feel his weight on top of her, pressing down, pounding her to the rough hard floor. She was gagged but not blindfolded. Behind the gag I could hear her pain and the helpless outrage.

He groaned and arched suddenly and clutched her burned breast and then rolled slowly off her.

Beside me Willie breathed relief.

"There now," said Ruth, nodding. "That's what you're good for."

Denise and Woofer giggled.

Donny pulled up his pants. He zipped them. He glanced at me but wouldn't meet my eyes. I couldn't blame him. I wouldn't have met his either.

"You probably got the clap now," Ruth said. "But never mind. They've got cures these days."

Susan suddenly started sobbing.

"Mommeee!"

She kept rocking back and forth in her chair.

"I want my *mommeeee!*"

"Oh, shut up why doncha?" said Woofer.

"Yeah," said Eddie.

"Shut the fuck up," said Ruth. "Shut up!"

She kicked her chair. She backed up and kicked it again and Susan tumbled off it. She lay there screaming, scraping the floor with her braces.

"*Stay* there!" said Ruth. "You just stay there! Stay where you are." Then she looked around at the rest of us. "Who else wants a turn?" she said. "Davy? Eddie?"

"*Me*," said Willie.

Ruth looked at him.

"I don't know about that," she said. "Your brother's just had her. Seems sorta like incest to me. I dunno."

"Aw hell, Mom!" said Willie.

"Well, it *does*. Not that the little whore would give a damn. But I'd feel a whole lot better if it was Eddie or Davy."

"Davy don't *want* her for chrissake!"

"Sure he does."

"No, he don't!"

She looked at me. I looked away.

She shrugged. "Maybe not. Boy's sensible. I know I wouldn't touch her. But then I'm not a man am I. Eddie?"

"I want to cut her," said Eddie.

"Yeah. Me too!" said Woofer.

"Cut her?" Ruth looked puzzled.

"You said that we could cut her, Mrs. Chandler," said Denise.

"I did?"

"Sure you did," said Woofer.

"I did? When? Cut her how?"

"Hey. Come on, I want to fuck her," said Willie.

"Shut up," said Ruth. "I'm talking to Ralphie. Cut her how?"

"*Put* something on her," said Ralphie. "So people'd know. So people'd know she was a whore."

"That's right. Like a scarlet letter or something," said Denise. "Like in the Classic Comic."

"Oh, you mean like brand her," said Ruth. "You mean brand her, not cut her."

"You *said* cut her," said Woofer.

"Don't tell me what I said. Don't you tell your mother."

"You did, Mrs. Chandler," said Eddie. "Honest. You said cut her."

"I did?"

"I heard you. We all did."

Ruth nodded. She thought about it. Then she sighed.

"Okay. We'll want a needle. Ralphie, go up and get my sewing kit out of the . . . I think it's in the hall closet."

"Okay."

He ran by me.

I couldn't believe this was happening.

"Ruth," I said. "Ruth?"

She looked at me. Her eyes seemed to quiver, to shudder in their sockets.

"What."

"You're not really *doing* this, are you?"

"I said we could. So I guess we will."

She leaned close to me. I could smell the cigarette smoke leaking from every pore.

"You know what the bitch tried to do last night?" she said. "She tried to get out of here. Somebody left the door unlocked. We figure it was Donny because he was the last one in yesterday and besides, Donny's sweet on her. Always has been. So I finally let him have her. You have a woman, you don't much want her anymore. I figure Donny's cured now.

"But it's good to let people see and know what she is. Don't you think?"

"*Mom*," said Willie. He was whining now.

"What."

"Why can't I?"

"Can't what?"

"*Fuck* her!"

"Because I *said* so, goddammit! It's incest! Now you leave me the hell alone about it. You want to go skinnydipping into your own brother's scum? That what you want? Don't talk to me. You're disgusting! Just like your goddamn father."

"Ruth," I said. "You . . . you can't do this."

"Can't?"

"No."

"No? Why not?"

"It's not . . . it's not right."

She got up. She walked over to me and I had to look at her. I had to look straight in her eye.

"Please don't tell me what's right, boy," she said.

Her voice was a low trembling growl. I was aware of her shaking with a fury that was only barely under control. The eyes flickered like guttering candles. I stepped backward. I thought, my God, this was a woman I'd liked once. A woman I'd thought funny, sometimes even pretty. One of the guys.

This woman scared the hell out of me.

She'll kill you, I thought. She'll kill us all including her own kids and not even care or think about it till later.

If she feels like it.

"Don't you tell me," she said.

And I think she knew what was in my mind then. I think she read me completely.

It didn't concern her. She turned to Willie.

"This boy tries to leave," she said. "Cut his balls off and hand 'em over here to me. You got that?"

Willie returned her smile. "Sure, Mom," he said.

Woofer came running into the room holding a battered cardboard shoebox. He handed it to Ruth.

"It wasn't there," he said.

"Huh?"

"It wasn't in the closet. It was in the bedroom on the dresser."

"Oh."

She opened it. I caught a glimpse of jumbled

twine and balls of thread, pincushions, buttons, needles. She put it down on the worktable and rummaged through it.

Eddie moved off the table to give her room and peered down over her shoulder.

"Here we go," she said. She turned to Woofer, "we have to heat this through, though, or she'll get an infection."

She held a long thick sewing needle.

The room was suddenly crackling with tension.

I looked at the needle and then at Meg lying on the floor and she was looking at it too and so was Susan.

"Who gets to do it?" said Eddie.

"Well, I guess to be fair you can each do a letter. That okay?"

"Great. What'll we write?"

Ruth thought about it.

"Suppose we keep it simple. How 'bout we write, 'I fuck. Fuck me.' That ought to do it. That ought to tell whoever needs to know."

"Sure," said Denise. "That'll be great." To me at that moment she looked just like Ruth. The same twitchy light in her eyes, the same tense expectancy.

"Wow," said Woofer. "That's a lot of letters. Almost two each."

Ruth counted, nodded.

"Actually," she said, "if David doesn't want in on this, and I suspect he doesn't, you could make it two each and I'll just take the one over. David?"

I shook my head.

"I figured," said Ruth. But she didn't seem angry or mocking about it.

"Okay," said Ruth. "I'll take the *I*. Let's do it."

"Ruth?" I said. "*Ruth?*"

Willie moved closer to me, moving the carving knife in slow lazy circles right beneath my chin. He made me very nervous because you couldn't tell with Willie. I looked at Eddie and watched him fiddle with the blade of his own Swiss Army knife, eyes cold and dead as I knew they'd be even before I looked. Then at Donny. It was a new Donny. There was no help from him either.

But Ruth just turned to me, still not angry, sounding calm and sort of weary. Almost like she were trying to tell me something I should have known all along, strictly for my own benefit. As though she were doing something really nice for me. As though of all the people here in this room, I was her favorite.

"David," she said, "I'm telling you. Just leave this be."

"I want to go, then," I said. "I want to get out of here."

"No."

"I don't want to see this."

"Then don't look."

They were going to do it to her. Woofer had matches.

He was heating the needle.

I was trying not to cry.

"I don't want to hear it either."

"Too bad," she said. "Unless you got wax in your ears you'll hear it plenty."

And I did.

Chapter Forty-One

When it was over and they'd finished swabbing her with the rubbing alcohol I walked over to see what they'd done. Not just this but last night and this morning too.

It was the first I'd been near her all day.

They'd removed the gag once they'd finished, knowing she was too weak now to say much anyhow. Her lips were puffy and swollen. One of her eyes was closing, turning red and purple. I saw three or four new cigarette burns on her chest and collarbone and one on her inner thigh. The triangular burn from Ruth's iron was an open blister now. There were bruises on her ribs and arms and over her calves and thighs where Willie'd cut her the day before.

And there were the words.

I FUCK FUCK ME

Two-inch letters. All in capitals. Half-burned and half-cut deep into the flesh across her stomach.

Written in what looked like the shaky hesitant hand of a six-year-old schoolboy.

"Now you can't get married," said Ruth. She was sitting in her chair again, smoking, hugging her knees and rocking back and forth. Willie and Eddie had gone upstairs for Cokes. The room stank of smoke and sweat and alcohol. "See, it's there *forever*, Meggy," she said. "You can't undress. Not for anybody, ever. Because he'll see those words there."

I looked and realized it was true.

Ruth had changed her.

Changed her for life.

The burns and bruises would fade but this would stay—legible, however faintly, even thirty years from now. It was something she'd have to think about and explain each and every time she stood naked in front of someone. Whenever she looked in a mirror she'd see it there and remember.

They'd passed a rule in school this year that said showers were mandatory after gym class. How could she handle that, in a roomful of teenage girls?

Ruth wasn't worried. It was like Meg was her protégé now.

"You're better off," she said. "You'll see. No man will want you. You won't have kids. It'll be a whole lot better that way. You're lucky. You thought it's good to be cute? To be sexy? Well, I'll tell you, Meggy. A woman's better off *loathsome* in this world."

Eddie and Willie came in laughing with a six-pack of Cokes and passed them around. I took one from them and held it, trying to keep the bottle steady. The faint sweet scent of caramel was sickening. One sip and I knew I'd vomit. I'd been trying not to ever since it started.

Donny didn't take one. He just stood by Meg looking down.

"You're right, Ma," he said after a while. "It makes things different. What we wrote I mean. It's weird."

He was trying to puzzle it out. Then finally he got a handle on it.

"She ain't so much anymore," he said.

He sounded a little surprised and even a little happy.

Ruth smiled. The smile was thin and shaky.

"I told you," she said. "You see?"

Eddie laughed, walked over and kicked her in the ribs. Meg barely grunted. "Nah. She ain't much," he said.

"She ain't *nothin'!*" said Denise. She swigged her Coke.

Eddie kicked her again, harder this time, in full solidarity with his sister.

Get me out of here, I thought.

Please. Let me go.

"I guess we could string her up again now," said Ruth.

"Let her stay," said Willie.

"It's cold down there. I don't want no runny noses or no sneezing. Haul her back on up and let's have a look at her."

Eddie untied her feet and Donny freed her hands from the four-by-four but kept them tied together and looped the line over one of the nails in the ceiling.

Meg looked at me. You could see how weak she was. Not even a tear. Not even the strength to cry. Just a sad defeated look that said, you see what's become of me?

Donny pulled on the line and raised her arms above her head. He tied it off at the worktable but left some slack this time. It was sloppy and unlike him—as though he didn't really care anymore. As though she wasn't worth the effort.

Something had changed all right.

It was as though in carving the letters across her they'd stripped her of all power to excite—to elicit either fear or lust or hate. What was left was so much flesh now. Weak. And somehow contemptible.

Ruth sat looking at her like a painter studying her canvas.

"There's one thing we should do," she said.

"What?" said Donny.

Ruth thought. "Well," she said, "we got her so no man's gonna want her now. Problem is, see, Meg might still want *him*." She shook her head. "Life of torment there."

"So?"

She considered. We watched her.

"Tell you what you do," she said finally. "Go upstairs to the kitchen and get some newspapers off the pile there and bring 'em down. Bunch of 'em. Put 'em in the sink in back of us here."

"Why newspapers? What are we gonna do with newspapers?"

"*Read* to her?" said Denise. They laughed.

"Just do it," she said.

He went up and got the papers and came back down. He tossed them in the sink by the washer.

Ruth stood up.

"Okay. Who's got a match? I'm out."

"I got some," said Eddie.

He handed them to her. She stooped and picked up the tire iron I'd given to Meg last night.

I wondered if she'd had any chance to use it.

"Here. Take this," she said. She handed the iron to Eddie. "Come on."

They put down the Cokes and walked past me. Everybody wanted to see what Ruth had in mind. Everybody but me and Susan. But Susan just sat on the floor where Ruth had told her to sit and I had Willie's knife about two feet from my ribcage.

So I went too.

"Roll 'em up," said Ruth. They looked at her.

"The papers," she said. "Roll 'em up good and tight. Then toss them back in the sink."

Woofer, Eddie, Denise and Donny did as she said. Ruth lit a cigarette with Eddie's matches. Willie stayed behind me.

I glanced at the staircase just a few feet away. Beckoning.

They rolled the papers.

"Pack 'em down tight," said Ruth.

They stuffed them into the sink.

"See, here's the thing," Ruth said. "A woman doesn't want a man all over her body. No. She only wants him one place in particular. Know what I mean, Denise? No? Not yet? Well you will. Woman wants a man in one particular place and that's right down here between her legs."

She pointed, then pressed her hand to her dress to show them. They stopped rolling.

"One little spot," she said. "Now. You take out that spot, and you know what happens? You take out all of her desire.

"Really. You take it out forever. It just works. They do it some places all the time, like it's just the usual thing to do, when a girl reaches a certain age I guess. Keeps her from strayin'. Places like, oh, I dunno, Africa and Arabia and New Guinea. They consider it a civilized practice down there.

"So I figure, why not here? *We'll just take out that one little spot.*

"*We'll burn her. Burn* it out. We'll use the iron.

"And then she'll be . . . perfect."

The room was hushed as they stared at her a moment, not quite believing what they were hearing.

I believed her.

And the feeling I'd been trying to understand for days now finally came together for me.

I started to tremble as though standing naked in a rude December wind. Because I could *see* it, smell it, hear her screams. I could see all the way down into Meg's future, into *my* future—the living consequences of such an act.

And I knew I was alone in that.

The others—even Ruth, for all the impulsiveness that had made her into a jailer, for all her inventiveness with pain, for all her talk of what might have been had she kept her job and not met Willie Sr. and not married and never had kids—the others had no imagination.

None. None whatever. They had no idea.

For everyone but themselves, for everything but the moment, they were blind, empty.

And I trembled, yes. With reason. With understanding.

I was captured by savages. I had lived with them. I'd been one of them.

No. Not savages. Not really.

Worse than that.

More like a pack of dogs or cats or the swarms of ferocious red ants that Woofer liked to play with.

Like some other species altogether. Some intelligence that only looked human, but had no access to human feelings.

I stood among them swamped by otherness.

By evil.

I broke for the stairs.

I heard Willie curse and felt his knife graze the back of my shirt. I grabbed the wooden banister and twisted onto the stairs.

I stumbled. Below me I saw Ruth pointing, shouting, her mouth a wide black empty gaping hole. I felt Willie's hand grasp my foot and pull. Beside me were paint cans and a bucket. I swept them down the stairs behind me and heard him curse again and Eddie too as I wrenched my foot away. I got to my feet. I crashed blindly up the stairs.

The door was open. I flung open the screen.

The summer heat washed over me in a single heavy wave. I couldn't scream. I had to gasp for air. I heard them close behind me. I leapt down the stairs.

"Move!" Donny yelled.

Then suddenly he was on top of me, the momentum of his leap from the landing knocking me down and knocking the breath out of me and rolling him away from me. I was faster than he was. I got to my feet. I saw Willie to the side of me, blocking my way to my house. I saw the knife glint in the sunlight. I didn't try.

I ran past Donny's outstretched arms across the yard heading toward the woods.

I was halfway there when Eddie hit me, threw himself hard across the back of my legs. I went down and suddenly he was all over me, punching, kicking, trying to gouge my eyes. I rolled and twisted. I had weight on him. I wrestled him over. He grabbed my shirt. I let it tear and pulled away. I stumbled back and then Donny was on me too and then Willie and it was only when I felt Willie's knife at my throat and felt it cut that I stopped struggling.

"Inside, cunt," he said. "And not a fucking word!"

They marched me back.

The sight of my own house tormented me. I kept looking at it for signs of life but there weren't any.

We went up and then down into the cool, paint-smelling dark.

I put my hand to my throat. My fingers came up wet with just a little blood.

Ruth stood there, arms folded tight across her breasts.

"Fool," she said. "Now where the hell were *you* going?"

I didn't answer.

"Well, I guess you're with her now," she said. "Don't know what the hell we're going to do with you all."

She shook her head. Then she laughed.

"Just be glad you don't have one of them *little spots* like she does. 'Course, then, you've got something else to worry about, don't you?"

Denise laughed.

"Willie, you go get some rope. I think we better tie him up, in case he feels like wandering again."

Willie went into the shelter. He came back with a short length of rope and handed Donny the knife. Donny held it while Willie tied my hands behind me.

Everybody watched and waited.

And this time Donny seemed to have no trouble at all looking me in the eye.

When they were through Ruth turned to Woofer and handed him the matches.

"Ralphie? You want the honors?"

Woofer smiled and lit a match and leaned way over the sink. He reached back and lit a corner of one of the rolled-up papers. Then he lit another corner nearer to him.

He stepped back. The paper began to burn brightly.

"You always did like a fire," said Ruth. She turned to the rest of them. She sighed.

"Who wants to do this now?" she said.

"I do," said Eddie.

She looked at him, smiling a little. It seemed to me the very same look that once, not long ago at all, had been pretty much reserved for me.

I guess I wasn't her favorite kid on the block anymore.

"Get the tire iron," she said.

And Eddie did.

They held it to the flames. It was very quiet.

When she judged it was hot enough she told him to remove it and we all went back inside.

Chapter Forty-Two

I'm not going to tell you about this.
I refuse to.

There are things you know you'll die before telling, things you know you should have died before ever having seen.
I watched and saw.

Chapter Forty-Three

We lay huddled together in the dark.

They'd removed the work light and closed the door and we were alone, Meg and Susan and I, lying on the air mattresses that Willie Sr. had provided for his family.

I could hear footsteps passing from the living room to the dining room and back again. Heavy footsteps. Donny or Willie. Then the house was silent.

Except for Meg's moaning.

She'd fainted when they touched her with the iron, gone rigid and then suddenly limp as though struck by a bolt of lightning. But now some part of her was struggling toward consciousness again. I was afraid to think what it would be like for her once she woke. I couldn't imagine the pain. Not that pain. I didn't want to.

They'd untied us. At least our hands were free.

I could tend to her somehow.

I wondered what they were doing up there now. What they were thinking. I could picture them. Eddie and Denise would have gone home for dinner. Ruth would be lying in the chair with her feet up on the hassock, a cigarette burning in the ashtray beside her, staring at the blank screen of the television. Willie sprawled across the couch, eating. Woofer on his belly on the floor. And Donny sitting upright on one of the straight-back kitchen chairs, having an apple maybe.

There would be frozen TV dinners in the oven.

I was hungry. I'd had nothing since breakfast now.

Dinner. I thought about that.

When I failed to come home to eat my parents would be angry. Then they'd start to worry.

My parents would worry.

I doubt that it had ever occurred to me before exactly what that meant.

And for a moment I loved them so much I almost cried.

Then Meg moaned again and I could feel her tremble beside me.

I thought of Ruth and the others sitting in the silence upstairs. Wondering what to do with us.

Because my being here changed everything.

After today they couldn't trust me. And unlike Meg and Susan, I'd be missed.

Would my parents come looking for me? Sure, of course they would. But *when?* Would they look for me here? I hadn't told them where the hell I'd be.

Dumb, David.

Another mistake. You knew you might be in trouble here.

I felt the darkness press tight around me, making me smaller somehow, crimping my space and limiting my options, my potential. And I had some small sense of what it must have felt like for Meg all these weeks, all alone down here.

You could almost wish for them to come back again just to relieve the tension of waiting, the sense of isolation.

In the darkness, I realized, you tend to disappear.

"David?"

It was Susan and she startled me. I think it was the only time I'd ever heard her speak to me—or to anybody for that matter—without being spoken to first.

Her voice was a scared trembly whisper. As though Ruth were still at the door listening.

"David?"

"Yeah? You okay, Susan?"

"I'm okay. David? Do you hate me?"

"Hate you? No, 'course not. Why should I . . . ?"

"You should. Meg should. Because it's my fault."

"It's not your fault, Susan."

"Yes it is. It's all my fault. Without me Meg could have gone and not come back."

"She *tried* to, Susan. They caught her."

"You don't *understand*."

Even without seeing her you could tell how hard she was trying not to cry.

"They caught her in the *hall*, David."

"Huh?"

"She came to get me. She got out, somehow."

"I *let* her out. I left the door open."

"And she came up the stairs and into my room and put her hand here, over my mouth so I'd be quiet and she lifted me up off the bed. And she was carrying me down the hall when Ruth, when Ruth . . ."

She couldn't hold back anymore. She cried. I reached out and touched her shoulder.

"Hey, it's okay. It's all right."

". . . when Ruth came out of the boys' room—I guess she heard us, you know—and she grabbed Meg by the hair and threw her down and I fell right on top of her so she couldn't move at first and then Willie came out and Donny and Woofer and they started beating her and hitting her and kicking her. And then Willie went into the kitchen and got a knife and put it right here to her throat and said that if she moved he'd cut off her head. He'd cut her head off's what he said.

"Then they took us downstairs. Later they threw my braces down. This one's busted."

I heard it rattle.

"And then they hit her some more and Ruth used her cigarette on her . . . on her . . ."

She slid over and I put my arm around her while she cried into my shoulder.

"I don't get it," I said. "She was going to come back for you. We were going to figure something out. Why now? Why'd she try to take you? Why'd she try to take you with her?"

She wiped her eyes. I heard her sniffle.

"I think because . . . Ruth," she said. "Ruth . . . touches me. Down . . . you know . . . down there. And once she . . . she made me bleed. And Meg . . . I told Meg . . . and she got mad about it . . . real mad and she told Ruth she knew and Ruth beat her again, beat her bad with a shovel from the fireplace and . . ."

Her voice broke.

"I'm sorry! I didn't mean it. She should have gone! She *should* have! I didn't mean for her to get hurt. I couldn't help it! I hate it when she touches me! I *hate* Ruth! I *hate* her. And *I* told Meg . . . I told her what she did and that's why they got her. *That's* why she came for me. Because of me, David. Because of *me!*"

I held her and it was like rocking a baby she felt so frail.

"Shhh. Easy. It'll be . . . okay."

I thought of Ruth touching her. I could picture it. The broken, helpless little girl, unable to fight, the woman with the empty glittering eyes like the surface of a fast-running stream. Then I blocked it from my mind.

After a long while she subsided.

"I have something," she said, sniffing. "I gave it to Meg. Reach over behind the far leg of the work-table. Past where Meg is. Feel around."

I did. I came up with a pack of matches and the two-inch stub of a candle.

"Where'd you . . . ?"

"I rooked it off of Ruth."

I lit the candle. Its honey glow filled the shelter. It made me feel better.

Until I saw Meg.

Until we both did.

She lay on her back, covered to the waist with an old thin dirty sheet they'd thrown over her. Her breasts and shoulders were bare. She had bruises everywhere. Her burns were open, liquid oozing.

Even in her sleep the muscles of her face pulled her skin tight with pain. Her body trembled.

The writing glistened.

I FUCK FUCK ME

I looked at Susan and could see she was going to cry again.

"Turn away," I said.

Because it was bad. All of it was bad.

But worst of all was not what they'd done to her, but what she was doing to herself.

Her arms were outside the sheet. She slept.

And the dirty jagged fingernails of her hand worked constantly and deep against her left elbow all the way down to her wrist.

She was tearing at the scar.

Tearing it open.

The body, abused and beaten, was turning finally against itself.

"Don't look," I said. I took off my shirt and managed to bite and rip my way through the seam. I tore two strips off the bottom. I moved Meg's fingers away. I wrapped the shirt tightly twice around her arm. Then I tied it off top and bottom. She couldn't do much damage now.

"Okay," I said.

Susan was crying. She'd seen it. Enough to know.

"*Why?*" she said. "Why would she *do* that?"

"I don't know."

But I did, in a way. I could almost feel Meg's anger at herself. For failing. For failing to get free, for failing herself and her sister. Maybe even for being the sort of person this could happen to in the first place. For allowing it to happen and thinking she'd get through it somehow.

It was unfair and wrong of her to feel that way but I thought I understood.

She'd been tricked—and now that good clear mind was angry with itself. *How could I have been so stupid?* Almost as if she deserved her punishment now. She'd been tricked into thinking Ruth and the others were human in the same way she was human and that consequently it could only go so far. Only so far. And it wasn't true. They weren't the same at all. She'd realized that. Too late.

I watched the fingers probe the scar.

There was blood seeping through the shirt. Not too much yet. But I felt the strange sad irony of knowing I might have to use the shirt to tie her up again eventually in order to restrain her.

Upstairs, the phone rang.

"Get it," I heard Ruth say. Footsteps crossed the room. I heard Willie's voice and then a pause and then Ruth's voice, speaking into the phone.

I wondered what time it was. I looked at the tiny candle and wondered how long it would last.

Meg's hand fell away from the scar.

She gasped and groaned. Her eyelids fluttered.

"Meg?"

She opened her eyes. They were glazed with pain.

Her fingers went back to the scar again.

"Don't," I said. "Don't do that."

She looked at me, not comprehending at first. Then she took her hand away.

"David?"

"Yes. It's me. And Susan's here."

Susan leaned forward so she could see her and the corners of Meg's mouth turned upward in the palest ghost of a smile. Then even that seemed to pain her.

She groaned. "Oh God," she said. "It hurts."

"Don't move," I said. "I know it does."

I drew the sheet up to her chin.

"Is there anything . . . anything you want me to . . . ?"

"No" she said. "Just let me . . . Oh God."

"Meg?" said Susan. She was trembling. She reached across me but couldn't quite reach her. "I'm sorry, Meg. I'm sorry. I'm sorry."

"It's okay, Suz. We tried. It's okay. It's . . ."

You could almost feel the electric pain run through her.

I couldn't think what to do. I kept looking at the candle as though the light would tell me something but it didn't. Nothing.

"Where . . . where are they?" she said.

"Upstairs."

"Will they stay? Is it . . . night?"

"Almost. Around dinnertime. I don't know. I don't know if they'll stay."

"I can't . . . David? I can't take any more. You know?"

"I know."

"I can't."

"Rest. Just rest." I shook my head.

"What?" she said.

"I keep wishing there were something . . ."

"What?"

". . . to *hurt* them with. To get us out of here."

"There's nothing. Nothing. You don't know how many nights I . . ."

"There's this," said Susan.

She held up the arm brace.

I looked at it. She was right. It was lightweight aluminum but if you took the pole end and swung the jointed brace you could do some damage.

Not enough, though. Not against Willie and Donny both. And Ruth. You couldn't underestimate her. Maybe if they were nice enough to come in one at a time with a couple minutes' breather space in between I might have had a shot but that was damn unlikely. I was never much of a fighter anyway.

All you had to do was ask Eddie.

We'd need something else.

I looked around. They'd removed mostly everything. The fire extinguisher, radio, the food cartons, even the alarm clock and air pump for the mattresses were gone. They'd even taken the lengths of clothesline they tied us with. All we had was the worktable—almost too heavy to move alone much less throw—the mattresses, Meg's sheet, her plastic drinking cup and the clothes on our backs. And the matches and candle.

And then I saw a use for the matches and candle.

At least we could get them down here when *we*

wanted them and not whenever they felt like it. We could confuse and surprise them. That was something. Something.

I took a deep breath. An idea was forming.

"Okay," I said. "You want to try a couple things?"

Susan nodded. Weakly, so did Meg.

"It may not work. But it's possible."

"Go," Meg said. "Do it." She moaned.

"Don't move," I said. "I don't need you."

"Okay. Just do it," she said. "Get them."

I took off my Keds high-tops and pulled out the shoelaces and tied them together. Then I took off Susan's shoes and tied their laces to my own so that I had about twelve feet of line to work with. I slipped one end around the lower hinge of the door and tied it off tight and ran the line over to the first of the four-by-four support beams, and tied it off there about three inches from the floor. It gave me a tripwire running at a slight angle from door to beam, cutting off about a third of the left-hand side of the room as you entered.

"Listen," I said. "This is gonna be hard. And dangerous. I mean it's not just gonna be them. I want to build a fire here. Right over there in front of the table just short of midway through the room. They'll smell the smoke and come down. And hopefully somebody will hit that line there. Meantime I can stand on the other side over by the door with one of Susan's braces.

"But there'll be lots of smoke and there's not much air. They better come fast or we're in trouble. See what I mean?"

"We'll yell," said Susan.

"Yeah. I hope that'll do it. But we've got to wait a little while so they smell the smoke. People get panicky around fire and it'll help. What do you think?"

"What can *I* do?" said Susan.

I had to smile. "Not too much, Suz."

She thought about it, the delicate little-girl features very grave.

"*I* know what I can do. I could stand over here by the mattresses and if anybody tries to come by I can trip 'em!"

"Okay but watch yourself. No more broken bones. And make sure you give me plenty of room to swing that thing."

"I will."

"Meg? Is this okay with you?"

She looked pale and weak. But she nodded.

"Anything," she said.

I pulled off my T-shirt.

"I'll . . . I'll need the sheet," I said.

"Take it."

I drew it carefully off her.

She moved her hands to cover where they'd burned her. But not before I saw the black-red glistening wound. I winced and Meg saw me and turned her face away. Through the shirt she started working on the scar again. I didn't have the heart to stop her—to call attention to what she was doing.

And suddenly I couldn't wait to use that brace on someone. I bundled up the sheet and placed it where I wanted it in front of the table. I placed my T-shirt and socks on top.

"Mine too," said Susan.

They wouldn't make much difference but she needed to help so I took them off her and threw them on too.

"You want the shirt?" said Meg.

"No. You keep that."

"All right," she said. The fingernails kept digging.

Her body looked old, the muscles thin and slack.

I took the brace from Susan and stood it against the wall by the door. Then I picked up the stub of candle and walked over to the pile.

My stomach knotted with fear.

"Let's go," I said and brought the candle down.

Chapter Forty-Four

The fire burned low but there was smoke all right. It plumed to the ceiling and billowed outward. Our own mushroom cloud, inside the shelter.

In seconds it filled the room. I could hardly see across to Meg lying on the floor. Our coughing was for real.

As the smoke got thicker so did our shouting.

You could hear the voices up there. Confusion. Fear. Then the tumble of footsteps down the stairs. They were running. They were worried. That was good. I held tight to the brace and waited just beside the door.

Someone fumbled at the bolt. Then the door flew open and Willie stood in the light from the cellar swearing while the smoke washed over him like a sudden fog. He lurched inside. He hit the line of shoelaces and stumbled, fell and skidded across the floor into the pile headfirst, screaming, flailing at the rag burning on his cheek and the sizzling greasy flattop that was melting down his forehead.

Ruth and Donny pushed in shoulder to shoulder, Donny closest to me, trying to make out what was happening through the smoke. I swung the brace. I saw blood fly off Donny's head flecking Ruth and the doorway as he fell, grabbing for me. I brought the brace down like an ax but he pulled away. The brace crashed to the floor. Then suddenly Ruth was darting past me heading for Susan.

Susan. Her pawn. Her shield.

I whirled and swung the brace and caught her across the ribs and back but it wasn't enough to stop her.

She was fast. I was after her, swinging the brace up from the floor like a backhand shot at tennis, but she reached for Susan's scrawny chest and pushed her against the wall, then reached into her hair and jerked it back. I heard a thump like a dropped pumpkin and Susan slid down the wall. I whipped the brace across Ruth's lower back with everything I had. She howled and fell to her knees.

I saw a movement out of the corner of my eye. I turned.

Donny was up, coming at me through the thinning smoke. Then Willie.

I whipped the brace back and forth in front of me. They moved slowly at first, carefully. They were close enough so I could see how Willie's face was burned, one eye closed and streaming tears. There was blood on Donny's shirt.

Then Willie came in low, rushing me. I swung the brace and it slammed across his shoulder, ran up and clattered to a jarring stop against his neck. He screeched and fell.

I saw Donny lurch forward and pulled the brace around, I heard a scrabbling sound behind me.

Ruth hurled herself at my back, clawing at me, hissing like a cat. I stumbled under the twisting weight. My knees buckled. I fell. Donny moved forward and I felt a sudden searing pain across my cheek and my neck snapped back. I suddenly smelled of leather. Shoe leather. He'd kicked me like you kick a football. I saw a blinding light. My fingers tried to tighten against the brace but it wasn't there anymore. It was gone. The bright light faded fast to black. I scrambled to my knees. He kicked me in the stomach. I went down, gasping for air. I tried to get up again but my balance was wrong. I felt a wave of sickness and confusion. Then someone else was kicking me too, my ribs, my chest. I pulled myself into a ball, drew my muscles tight and waited for the dark to clear. And still they were kicking me and swearing. But it was beginning to work, I was beginning to see, finally enough so that I knew where the table was so I rolled to it, rolled beneath it, looking out and up at Ruth's legs and Donny's in front of me—and then I was confused again because there were another pair of legs standing where Meg should be, right where Meg should be lying on the mat.

Naked legs. Burned and scarred.

Meg's.

"No!" I yelled.

I moved out from under. Ruth and Donny turned, moved toward her.

"You!" Ruth screamed. "You! You! *You!*"

And I still don't know what Meg thought she was doing, if she actually thought she could help—maybe she was just sick of this, sick of Ruth and sick to death of the pain, sick of everything—but she should have known where all Ruth's fury would go, not toward me or toward Susan but straight to her like some evil perfect poison arrow.

But there wasn't any fear in her. Her eyes were hard and clear. And weak as she was she managed one step forward.

Ruth rushed against her like a madwoman. Grabbed her head between both hands like an evangelist, healing.

And then smashed it against the wall.

Meg's body began to tremble.

She looked at Ruth, straight into her eyes, and for a moment her eyes held a puzzled expression, as though even now she was asking Ruth *why. Why.*

Then she fell. Straight to the air mattress like a boneless sack.

She trembled a little longer and then stopped.

I reached for the table for support.

Ruth just stood staring at the wall. Like she didn't believe Meg wasn't still standing there. Her face an ashy white.

Donny and Willie were standing too.

The silence in the room was sudden and immense.

Donny bent down. He put his hand to her lips, then onto her chest.

"Is she . . . breathing?"

I'd never heard Ruth so small.

"Yeah. A little."

Ruth nodded. "Cover her up," she said. "Cover her. Get her covered."

She nodded again to no one in particular and then turned and walked across the room as carefully and slowly as though walking through broken glass. At the doorway she stopped to steady herself. Then she walked away.

And then it was just us kids.

Willie was the first to move. "I'll get some blankets," he said.

He had his hand to his face covering his eye. Half his hair was burned away.

But nobody seemed angry anymore.

In front of the table the fire still smoldered, sending up wisps of smoke.

"Your mother called," Donny muttered.

He was staring down at Meg.

"Huh?"

"Your mother," he said. "She called. Wanted to know where you were. I answered the phone. Ruth talked to her."

I didn't have to ask what she'd told her. They hadn't seen me.

"Where's Woofer?"

"He ate at Eddie's."

I picked up the arm brace and brought it over to Susan. I don't think she knew or cared. She was looking at Meg,

Willie came back with the blankets. He looked at each of us a moment and dumped the blankets on the floor and then turned and went out again.

We heard him trudging up the stairs.

"What are you gonna do, Donny?" I asked him.

"I dunno," he said.

His voice seemed flat and unfocused, stunned—as if he'd been the one kicked in the head instead of me.

"She could die," I said. "She *will* die. Unless you do something. Nobody else will. You know that. Ruth won't. Willie won't."

"I know."

"So do something."

"What?"

"Something. Tell somebody. The cops."

"I dunno," he said.

He took one of the blankets off the floor and covered her as Ruth had told him to. He covered her very gently.

"I dunno," he said. He shook his head.

Then he turned. "I gotta go."

"Leave us the work light, huh? At least do that? So we can take care of her?"

He seemed to think a moment.

"Yeah. Sure," he said.

"And some water? A rag and some water?"

"Okay."

He went out into the cellar and I heard the water

running. He came back with a bucket and some dust rags and put them on the floor. Then he hung the work light from the hook in the ceiling. He didn't look at us. Not once.

He reached for the door.

"I'll see you," he said.

"Yeah," I said. "See you."

And then he closed the door.

Chapter Forty-Five

The long chilly night drew on.

We received no more visits from above.

The house was quiet. We could dimly hear the radio going in the boys' room, the Everly's singing "All I Have To Do Is Dream," Elvis's "Hard Headed Woman." Every song mocked us.

By now my mother would be frantic. I could imagine her calling every single house on the block to see if I was there, camping out or just staying overnight somewhere without telling her. Then my father would call the police. I kept expecting that official-sounding knock at the door. I couldn't imagine why they hadn't come.

Hope turned to frustration, frustration to anger, anger to a dull resignation. Then the cycle began again. There was nothing to do but wait and bathe Meg's face and forehead.

She was feverish. The back of her head was sticky with crusting blood.

We drifted in and out of sleep.

My mind kept latching on to singsongs, jingles. *Use Ajax! The foaming cleanser-da-da-da-da-da-dum-dum. Wash the dirt right down the drain-da-da-da-da-da-dum. Over the river and though the woods . . . the river and through the woods . . . the river and through the* . . . I couldn't hold on to anything. I couldn't let go of anything, either.

Sometimes Susan would start to cry.

Sometimes Meg would shuffle and moan.

I was happy when she'd moan. It meant she was alive.

She woke twice.

The first time she woke I was running the cloth over her face and was just about to quit for a while when she opened her eyes. I almost dropped it I was so surprised. Then I hid it behind me because it was pink with blood and I didn't want her to see. Somehow the idea really bothered me.

"David?"

"Yeah."

She seemed to listen. I looked down into her eyes and saw that one of her pupils was half again as large as the other—and I wondered what she was seeing.

"Do you hear her?" she said. "Is she . . . there?"

"I only hear the radio. She's there, though."

"The radio. Yes." She nodded slowly.

"Sometimes I hear her," she said. "All day long.

Willie and Woofer too . . . and Donny. I used to think I could listen . . . and hear and learn something, figure out why she was doing this to me . . . by listening to her walk across a room, or sit in a chair. I . . . never did."

"Meg? Listen. I don't think you ought to be talking, you know? You're hurt pretty bad."

It was a strain, you could see that. There was a slurring to her words, as though her tongue had suddenly become the wrong size for her.

"Unh-unh," she said. "No. I want to talk. I never talk. I never have anybody to talk to. But . . . ?"

She looked at me strangely. "How come *you're* here?"

"We're both here. Me and Susan both. They locked us in. Remember?"

She tried to smile.

"I thought maybe you were a fantasy. I think you've been that before for me sometimes. I have a lot . . . a lot of fantasies. I have them and then they . . . go away. And then sometimes you try to have one, you want one, and you can't. You can't think of anything. And then later . . . you do.

"I used to beg her, you know? To stop. Just to let me go. I thought, she's got to, she'll do it a while and then she'll let me go, she'll see she should like me, and then I thought no she won't stop, I've got to get out but I can't, I don't understand her, how could she let him *burn me?*"

"Please, Meg . . ."

She licked her lips. She smiled.

"You're taking care of me though, aren't you."

"Yes."

"And Susan too."

"Yes."

"Where is she?"

"She's sleeping."

"It's hard for her too," she said.

"I know. I know it is."

I was worried. Her voice was getting weaker. I had to bend very close now in order to hear her.

"Do me a favor?" she said.

"Sure."

She gripped my hand. Her grip was not strong.

"Get my mother's ring back? You know my mother's ring? She won't listen to me. She doesn't care. But maybe . . . Could you ask her? Could you get me back my ring?"

"I'll get it."

"You promise?"

"Yes."

She let go.

"Thanks," she said.

Then a moment later she said, "You know? I never really loved my mother enough. Isn't that strange? Did you?"

"No. I guess not."

She closed her eyes.

"I think I'd like to sleep now."

"Sure," I said. "You rest."

"It's a funny thing," she said. "There's no pain. You'd think there would be. They burned me and burned me but there's no pain."

"Rest," I said.

She nodded. And then she did. And I sat listening for Officer Jennings's knock, the lyrics to "Green Door" riding absurdly through my head like a garish painted carousel, round and round: . . . *midnight, one more night without sleepin'/watchin', 'til the morning comes creepin'/green door, what's that secret you're keepin'?/green door?/*

Until I slept too.

When I woke it was probably dawn.

Susan was shaking me.

"Stop her!" she said, her voice a frightened whisper. "Stop her! Please! Don't let her *do* that!"

For a moment I thought I was home in my bed.

I looked around. I remembered.

And Meg wasn't there beside me anymore.

My heart began to pound, my throat tightened.

Then I saw her.

She'd thrown off the blanket so she was naked, hunched over in the corner by the worktable. Her long matted hair hung down across her shoulders. Her back was streaked with dull brown stains, crisscross channels of drying blood. The back of her head gleamed wetly under the work light.

I could see the muscles pull along her shoulders and outward from the elegant line of vertebrae as she worked. I heard the scrabble of fingernails.

I got up and went to her.

She was digging.

Digging with her fingers at the concrete floor where it met the cinderblock wall. Tunneling out. Tiny sounds of exertion escaping her. Her fingernails broken back and bleeding, one gone already, the tips of her fingers bloody too, her blood mixing with the grit she dug from the flaking concrete in an uneven yielding of the substances of each. Her final refusal to submit. Her final act of defiance. The will rising up over a defeated body, to force itself on solid stone.

The stone was Ruth. Impenetrable—yielding just grit and fragments.

Ruth was the stone.

"Meg. Come on. Please." I said.

I put my hands under her arms and lifted her up. She came away as easily as an infant child.

Her body felt warm and full of life.

I laid her back on the mattress again and covered her with the blanket. Susan handed me the bucket and I bathed her fingertips. The water turned redder.

I began to cry.

I didn't want to cry because Susan was there but it wasn't anything I could help or hinder. It just came, flowed, like Meg's blood across the cinderblock.

Her heat was fever. Her heat had been a lie.

I could almost smell the death on her.

I had seen it in the expanded pupil of her eye, a widening hole into which a mind could disappear.

I bathed her fingers.

When I was finished I shifted Susan over so she could lie between us and we lay together quietly watching her shallow breathing, each breath of air flowing through her lungs another moment binding the moments together, another few seconds' grace, the flickering of her half-open eyelids speaking of the life that roiled gently beneath the wounded surface—and when she opened her eyes again we weren't startled. We were happy to see Meg there looking out at us, the old Meg, the one who lived before this in the very same time as we did and not in this fevered dream-space.

She moved her lips. Then smiled.

"I think I'm going to make it," she said, and reached for Susan's hand. "I think I'll be fine."

In the artificial glare of the work light, in the dawn that for us was not a dawn, she died.

Chapter Forty-Six

The knock at the door could not have come more than an hour and a half later.

I heard them rising from their beds. I heard masculine voices and heavy unfamiliar footsteps crossing the living room to the dining room and coming down the stairs.

They threw the bolt and opened the door and Jennings was there, along with my father and another cop named Thompson who we knew from the VFW. Donny, Willie, Woofer and Ruth stood behind them, making no attempt to escape or even to explain, just watching while Jennings went to Meg and raised her eyelid and felt for the pulse that wasn't there.

My father came over and put his arm around me. *Jesus Christ* he said, shaking his head. *Thank God we found you. Thank God we found you.* I think it was the first time I'd ever heard him use the words but I also think he meant it.

Jennings pulled the blanket up over Meg's head and Officer Thompson went to comfort Susan, who couldn't stop crying. She'd been quiet ever since Meg died and now the relief and sadness were pouring out of her.

Ruth and the others watched impassively.

Jennings, who Meg had warned about Ruth on the Fourth of July, looked ready to kill.

Red-faced, barely controlling his voice, he kept shooting questions at her—and you could see it wasn't so much questions he wanted to shoot as the pistol he kept stroking on his hip. *How'd this happen? how'd that happen? how long has she been down here? who put that writing there?*

For a while Ruth wouldn't answer. All she'd do was stand there scratching at the open sores on her face. Then she said, "I want a lawyer."

Jennings acted like he didn't hear her. He kept on with the questions but all she'd say was, "I want to call a lawyer," like she was preparing to take the Fifth and that was that.

Jennings got madder and madder. But that didn't help. I could have told him that.

Ruth was the rock.

And following her example so were her kids.

I wasn't. I took a deep breath and tried not to think about my father standing beside me.

"I'll tell you everything you want to know," I said. "Me and Susan will."

"You saw all this?"

"Most," I said.

"Some of these wounds occurred weeks ago. You see any of that?"

"Some of it. Enough."

"You saw it?"

"Yes."

His eyes narrowed. "Are you kept or keeper here, kid?" he said.

I turned to my father. "I never hurt her, Dad. I never did. Honest."

"You never helped her, either," said Jennings.

It was only what I'd been telling myself all night long.

Except that Jennings's voice clenched at the words like a fist and hurled them at me. For a moment they took my breath away.

There's correct and then there's right, I thought.

"No," I said. "No, I never did."

"You tried," said Susan, crying.

"Did he?" said Thompson.

Susan nodded.

Jennings looked at me another long moment and then he nodded too.

"Okay," he said. "We'll talk it over later. We better call in, Phil. Everybody upstairs."

Ruth murmured something.

"What?" asked Jennings.

She was talking into her chest, mumbling.

"I can't hear you, lady."

Ruth's head shot up, eyes glaring.

"I said she was a *slut*," said Ruth. "*She* wrote those words! *She* did! 'I FUCK. FUCK ME.' You think I wrote 'em? She wrote 'em herself, *on* herself, because she was *proud* of it!

"I was tryin' to teach her, to discipline her, to show her some decency. She wrote it just to spite me, 'I FUCK. FUCK ME.' And she did, she fucked *everybody*. She fucked him, that's for sure."

She pointed at me. Then at Willie and Donny.

"And him and him too. She fucked 'em all! She'd have fucked little Ralphie if I hadn't stopped her, hadn't tied her up down here where nobody had to see her legs and her ass and her cunt, her *cunt*—because, mister, that's all she was was a cunt, woman who don't know any better than to give in to a man any time he asks her for a piece of pussy. And I did her a goddamn *favor*. So fuck you and what you think. Goddamn meat in a uniform. Big soldier. Big shit. Fuck you! I did her a goddamn favor . . ."

"Lady," said Jennings. "I think you should shut up now."

He leaned in close and it was like he was looking at something he'd stepped in on the sidewalk.

"You understand my meaning, lady? Mrs. Chandler? Please, I really hope you do. That piss trap you call a mouth—you keep it *shut*."

He turned to Susan. "Can you walk, honey?"

She sniffed. "If somebody helps me up the stairs."

"Just as soon carry her," said Thompson. "She won't weigh much."

"Okay. You first, then."

Thompson picked her up and headed out through the door and up the stairs. Willie and Donny followed him, staring down at their feet as though unsure of the way. My dad went up behind them, like he was part of the police now, watching them, and I followed him. Ruth came up right behind me, hard on my heels as if in a hurry to get this over with now all of a sudden. I glanced over my shoulder and saw Woofer coming up practically at her side, and Officer Jennings behind him.

Then I saw the ring.

It sparkled in the sunlight pouring in through the backdoor window.

I kept on going up the stairs but for a moment I was barely aware of where I was. I felt heat rushing through my body. I kept seeing Meg and hearing her voice making me promise to get her mother's ring back for her, to *ask* Ruth for it as though it didn't belong to Meg in the first place but was only on loan to her, as though Ruth had any right to it, as though she wasn't just a fucking thief, and I thought of all Meg must have been through even before we met her, losing the people she loved, with only Susan left—and then to get this substitute. This parody of a mother. This evil joke of a mother who had stolen not just the ring from her but everything, her life, her future, her body—and all in the name of raising her, while what she was doing was not raising but pushing down, pushing her further and further and loving it, exulting in it, *coming* for God's sake—down finally into the very earth itself which was where she'd lie now, *un*-raised, erased, vanished.

But the ring remained. And in my sudden fury I realized I could push too.

I stopped and turned and raised my hand to Ruth's face, fingers spread wide, and watched the dark eyes look at me amazed for a moment and afraid before they disappeared beneath my hand.

I saw her *know*.

And want to live.

I saw her grope for the banister.

I felt her mouth fall open.

For a moment I felt the loose cold flesh of her cheeks beneath my fingers.

I was aware of my father continuing up the stairs ahead of me. He was almost to the top now.

I pushed.

I have never felt so good or so strong, then or since.

Ruth screamed and Woofer reached for her and so did Officer Jennings but the first step she hit was Jennings's and she twisted as she hit and he barely touched her. Paint cans tumbled to the concrete below. So did Ruth, a little more slowly.

Her mouth cracked open against the stairs. The momentum flung her up and around like an acrobat so that when she hit bottom she hit face-first again, mouth, nose and cheek bursting under the full weight of her body tumbling down after her like a sack of stones.

I could hear her neck snap.

And then she lay there.

A sudden stink filled the room. I almost smiled. She'd shit herself like a baby and I thought that was most appropriate, that was fine.

Then everybody was downstairs instantly, Donny and Willie, my dad and Officer Thompson minus the burden of Susan pushing past me, and everybody yelling and surrounding Ruth like she was some sort of find in an archaeological dig. *What happened? What happened to my mother!* Willie was screaming and Woofer was crying, Willie really losing it, crouched over her, hands clutching her breasts and belly, trying to massage her back to life. *What the fuck happened!* yelled Donny. All of them looking up the stairs at me like they wanted to tear me limb from limb, my father at the base of the stairs just in case they tried to.

"So what *did* happen?" asked Officer Thompson.

Jennings just looked at me. He knew. He knew damn well what happened.

But I didn't care just then. I felt like I'd swatted a wasp. One that had stung me. Nothing more and nothing worse than that.

I walked down the stairs and faced him.

He looked at me some more. Then he shrugged.

"The boy stumbled," he said. "No food, lack of sleep, his friend dying. An accident. It's a damn shame. It happens sometimes."

Woofer and Willie and Donny weren't buying that but nobody seemed to care about them much today and what they were buying and what they weren't.

The smell of Ruth's shit was terrible.

"I'll get us a blanket," said Thompson. He moved past me.

"That ring," I said. I pointed. "The ring on her finger was Meg's. It belonged to Meg's mother. It should go to Susan now. Can I give it to her?"

Jennings gave me a pained look that said enough was enough and not to push it.

But I didn't worry about that either.

"The ring belongs to Susan," I said.

Jennings sighed. "Is that true, boys?" he asked. "Things'll go better from here on in if you don't lie."

"I guess," said Donny.

Willie looked at his brother. "You fuck," he muttered.

Jennings lifted Ruth's hand and looked at the ring.

"Okay," he said and then all at once his voice was gentle. "You go give it to her." He worked it off her finger.

"Tell her not to lose it," he said.

"I will."

I went upstairs.

All at once I felt very tired.

Susan lay on the couch.

I walked over to her and before she could ask what was going on I held it up for her. I saw her look at the ring and see what it was and then suddenly the look in her eyes brought me down to my knees beside her and she reached for me with her thin pale arms and I hugged her and we cried and cried.

Epilogue

Chapter Forty-Seven

We were juveniles—not criminals but delinquents.

So that under the law we were innocent by *definition*, not to be held accountable for our acts exactly, as though everybody under eighteen were legally insane and unable to tell right from wrong. Our names were never released to the press. We had no criminal record and no publicity.

It struck me as pretty strange but then as we were excluded from the rights of adults I suppose it was the natural thing to exclude us from the responsibilities of adults as well.

Natural unless you were Meg or Susan.

Donny, Willie, Woofer, Eddie, Denise and I went to juvenile court and Susan and I testified. There was no prosecutor and no defense attorney, just the Honorable Judge Andrew Silver and a handful of psychologists and social workers earnestly discussing what to do with everybody. Even from the beginning what to do was obvious. Donny, Willie, Woofer, Eddie and Denise were placed in juvenile detention centers—reform school to us. Eddie and Denise for just two years since they hadn't any hand in the actual killing. Donny, Willie and Woofer until they turned eighteen, the stiffest sentence you could get in those days. At eighteen they were to be released and their records destroyed.

The child's acts could not be held against the man.

They found a foster home for Susan in another town, up in the lakes district, far away.

Because of what she'd said about me at the hearing and the fact that under juvenile law there was, strictly speaking, no such thing as an accomplice, I was remanded to the custody of my parents and assigned a psychiatric social worker, a bland school-teacherly woman named Sally Beth Cantor who saw me once a week and then once a month for exactly a year and who always seemed concerned with my "progress" in "dealing with" what I'd seen and done—and not done—yet always seemed half asleep as well, as though she'd been through this a billion times before and wished against all reason and evidence that my parents would be far more unforgiving with me or that I'd go at them with an ax or something, just to give her some issue or occurrence to sink her teeth into. Then the year was up and she just stopped coming. It was a full three months before I missed her.

* * *

I never saw any of them again. At least not in person.

I corresponded with Susan for a while. Her bones healed. She liked her foster parents. She had managed to make a few friends. Then she stopped writing. I didn't ask why. I didn't blame her.

My parents divorced. My father moved out of town. I saw him infrequently. I think he was embarrassed by me in the end. I didn't blame him, either.

I graduated school in the low middle third of my class, which was no surprise to anybody.

I went to college for six years, interrupted by two years in Canada to avoid the draft, and came out with a masters in business. This time I graduated third in my class. Which was a big surprise to everybody.

I got a job on Wall Street, married a woman I'd met in Victoria, divorced, married again, and divorced again a year later.

My father died of cancer in 1982. My mother had a heart attack in '85 and died on the kitchen floor by her sink, clutching at a head of broccoli. Even at the end, alone and with no one to cook for, she'd kept the habit of eating well. You never knew when the Depression would be back again.

I came home with Elizabeth, my fiancée, to sell my mother's house and settle her estate and together we poured through the cluttered relics of her forty years of living there. I found uncashed checks in an Agatha Christie novel. I found letters I'd written from college and crayon drawings I'd made in the first grade. I found newspaper items brown with age about my father opening the Eagle's Nest and getting this or that award from the Kiwanis or the VFW or the Rotary.

And I found clippings on the deaths of Megan Loughlin and Ruth Chandler.

Obituaries from the local paper.

Meg's was short, almost painfully short, as though the life she'd lived hardly qualified as a life at all.

LOUGHLIN—Megan, 14, Daughter of the late Daniel Loughlin and the late Joanne Haley Loughlin. Sister of Susan Loughlin. Services will be held at Fisher Funeral Home, 110 Oakdale Avenue, Farmdale, NJ, Saturday, 1:30 p.m.

Ruth's was longer:

CHANDLER—Ruth, 37, Wife of William James Chandler, Daughter of the late Andrew Perkins and the late Barbara Bryan Perkins. She is survived by her husband and her sons William Jr., Donald, and Ralph. Services will be held at Hopkins Funeral Home, 15 Valley Road, Farmdale, NJ, Saturday 2:00 p.m.

It was longer but just as empty.

I looked at the clippings and realized that their services had been just half an hour apart that day, held in funeral homes about six or seven blocks from each other. I had gone to neither. I couldn't imagine who had.

I stared out the living room window at the house across the driveway. My mother had said a young couple lived there now. Nice people, she said. Childless but hoping. They were putting in a patio as soon as they had the money.

The next clipping down was a photo. A picture of a young, good-looking man with short brown hair and wide-eyed goofy smile.

It looked familiar.

I unfolded it.

It was an item from the Newark *Star-Ledger*, dated January 5, 1978. The headline read "Manasquan Man Indicted for Murder" and the story told how the man in the picture had been arrested December 25th along with an unidentified juvenile in connection with the stabbing and burning deaths of two teenage girls, Patricia Highsmith, 17, of Manasquan, and Debra Cohen, also 17, of Asbury Park.

Both victims exhibited signs of sexual assault and though both had been stabbed repeatedly, the cause of death was burning. They'd been doused with gas and torched in an abandoned field.

The man in the photo was Woofer.

My mother had never told me. I looked at the photo and thought I could see at least one good reason why—I might have looked in the paper and seen the picture.

In his twenties Woofer had come to look so much like Ruth it was frightening.

Like all the other clippings this one had been stuffed in a shirt box and put on the attic stairs and the edges were dry and brown and crumbling. But I noticed something along the margin. I turned it and recognized my mother's writing. She'd written in pencil, which had faded, but it was readable.

Just beside the headline and rising up along the

side of the picture she'd written with fine irony *I wonder how Donny and Willie are doing?*

And now, on the uncertain, unsettled eve of my third marriage, to a woman who would have been exactly Meg's age had she lived, plagued with nightmares all of which seem to concern failing again, failing *somebody*, carelessly leaving them to the rough mercies of the world—and adding to those names she'd scrawled along the side of the clipping the names of Denise and Eddie Crocker, and my own name—I wonder too.

Author's Note: On Writing the Girl Next Door

"*Who loves ya, baby?*" says Kojak.

Well, with the world's most trusted Greek selling Atlantic City gambling, who knows? But I do know who and what *scares* me.

The *what*, broadly speaking, is the unpredictable. Not that some chance encounter with a redhead has me racing back to my apartment for a crucifix and garlic. More along the lines of Alzheimer's, AIDS, or geese in the jet props. I was walking down Broadway one day when an entire oak dresser came plummeting to the sidewalk two steps ahead of me. *That* scared me. Scared me and made me mad.

And I feel the same way about the people who frighten me. They piss me off. I resent sharing my planet with creeps like Bundy who look like me and talk like me and who are very charming except that they have this one funny thing about them, gee, they like to bite the nipples off people.

This is not just empathy with the victim. I mean, I have nipples too.

Sociopaths scare me and make me mad. Not just the big-league sociopaths—the Mansons and Gary Tisons—but also the guys who rip off old ladies with land scams in Florida. All these types without a conscience. I know a woman whose husband got thrown off his seat at the Stock Exchange and to cover his debts forged her name to loans totalling over a quarter million dollars, not to mention IRS forms, and now all hell is breaking loose with liens against the house and back taxes and she—with a kid to support who, tragically, still loves the guy the way an eight-year-old almost *has* to love his father—hasn't seen or heard from him since March of 1989. Neither has anybody else. He skipped. Nobody can touch him. While the world descends on wife and son like swarms of flies.

I'd wanted to write about one of these bastards for a long time. Their otherness. And what happens to us real people when we believe them to be human.

I found one in Jay Robert Nash's *Bloodletters and Badmen*.

Her crime was unusual and wholly repellent.

Over the course of months and with the help of her teenage son and daughters—and eventually, the neighborhood kids as well—she had tortured a sixteen-year-old girl to death, a boarder, in view of her little sister, ostensibly to "teach her a lesson" about what it was like to be a woman in the world.

Her kids reminded me of something out of *Lord of the Flies*. But forget the kids—because here's this *woman*, this adult, giving them permission, orchestrating things and leading them every step of the way in some sick game of *instruction* that had something to do with a fundamental loathing of her sex and inability to see any suffering but her own. Then transmitting that to a bunch of teenagers. The girl's *friends*.

There was a picture of her in the book. Her crime took place in 1965, when she was thirty-six years old. But the face in the book was sixty. Sagging blotchy skin—deeply lined—thin bitter mouth, a receding hairline and dingy hair worn in the style of a full decade earlier.

Deep-set big dark eyes that managed to look both haunted and empty at once. Scary. Right away I was mad at her.

She stayed with me.

Then some years later my mother died, well-loved, in the same New Jersey home I'd grown up in and had known since infancy. In almost every way that counted it was still home base for me. I dealt with both losses gradually, leaving my apartment at intervals and spending a lot of time out there going through her effects, getting to know the neighbors again, remembering.

At the time I was reworking *She Wakes*, my only supernatural novel to date. I'd shelved it for a while. And it was good to go back to it then because I was in no condition to start something new—or something real—for the moment. A reincarnated goddess on a sunny Greek isle felt just about right to me.

But gradually that woman started to insinuate again.

Maybe it was the 1950s hairdo. I dunno.

But when I was growing up, my street was a dead-end street and every house was filled with war-babies. I could imagine her *doing* it there. And then, if you lived through the 1950s you know its dark side. All those nice soft comfy little buboes of secrecy and repression black and ripe and ready to burst. There was the perfect kind of isolation and built-in cast of characters I could shapeshift after the real ones.

So I thought, kick it back to 1958, when you were twelve. Instead of the midwest, where it really happened, use New Jersey.

And being there, especially through the summer, things kept coming back to me. The smell of the woods, the bleeding damp walls of the basement. Things I'd been too busy to remember for years were keeping me awake nights now. There was too much detail surfacing to resist and I didn't try. I could even give a nod now and then to what I liked about the time. We had brooks and orchards and unlocked doors. We had Elvis.

But I wasn't doing *Happy Days* either. Not since *Off Season*, my first book, had I worked on a subject this grim. And *Off Season* was about cannibals on the coast of Maine for godsakes. Nobody was going to take it too seriously no matter now gut-churning I made the thing. Whereas this was about child abuse. Abuse so extreme that writing it

I eventually made the decision to soften some of what happened and leave some out altogether.

It's still pretty extreme.

There wasn't any getting around that, not that I could see. The problem in fact was to *keep it* extreme without ripping off all those real live kids who are abused every day in the process.

Posing technical problems helped. I used a first-person voice for one thing, with the boy next door as narrator. He's a troubled but not insensitive kid who vacillates between his fascination at the very *license* involved and what his empathy's telling him. He sees plenty. But not everything. Which allowed me to sketch a few things rather than go at them close-up and full-throttle.

He's also speaking some thirty years later. He's an adult now so he can edit. So at one point when the going gets roughest I have him say, *Sorry, I'm just not going to show you this. Imagine it for yourself if you care and dare to. Me, I'm not helping.*

The first-person voice in a suspense book can automatically shift the reader's sympathy directly to the object of violence. I'd used it in *Hide and Seek* to that effect. You know whoever's talking to you is going to survive so you don't tend to worry much about his physical safety. (Though you can worry about his moral safety and hopefully that's what happens here.) But if it's done right, you'll worry about the safety of the people he *cares* about. In this case, *The Girl Next Door* and her sister.

It's tricky. Because if the people he cares about are insufficiently drawn or sympathetic or you as a reader just don't like lawyers or dogs the way he does, you'll wind up just watching the bad guys, the violence, or both. Or closing the book forever.

But I'm not too worried about that (he says, quaffing deep his cup of hubris.) If the book has a moral ambiguity to it, a moral tension, it's supposed to. That's the problem this kid has to solve throughout, a problem with his view of things. And I'm not too worried because I like these girls and I think that's clear. They're not just victims. In some ways—especially as they relate to each other—I think they're pretty heroic.

And because, by contrast, these other types scare me.

Scare me and yes, for being in my face every time I open a paper or turn on the evening news or talk to some woman whose drunken husband's slugged her again, royally piss me off.

Do You Love Your Wife?

"Sometimes I feel like you're . . . I don't know, not really *there* anymore," she said. "Like no matter what I do, it wouldn't make any difference, would it. Know what I mean?"

They were lying in bed. He was tired and a little buzzed from the scotches after work. Greene's *The Power and the Glory* lay open on her lap. He was halfway through Stone's *Bay of Souls*.

She was right. Stone could obviously rouse himself. He could not.

She was heading to California in a few days, leaving behind the chill of New York and his own chill for a week or so. Her ex-lover beckoned. Perhaps he'd become her lover all over again. Bass hadn't asked.

"I'm not complaining," she said. "I'm not criticizing. You know that."

"I know."

"And it's not just you and me. Seems like it's everything. You used to write. Hell, you used to paint. It's not like you."

"It's like *part* of me obviously."

"Not the best part."

"Well. Maybe not."

She didn't say the rest of it. *Even after three whole years it's still her isn't it.* She hadn't the slightest urge to hurt him with it. She was simply observing and leaving him an opening should he wish to talk. He didn't. It wasn't precisely the loss of Annabel that was bothering him these days anyhow. It was what was left of him in her absence. Which seemed to amount to less and less—a subtle yet distinct difference. He continued to feel himself rolling far beneath the whitewater wake of their parting. Way down where the water was still and deep and very thin.

"Confront her," Gary said.

"Annabel?"

"Yes, Annabel. Who else?"

"After all this time?"

"My point exactly. You're not getting any younger."

"It's easier said than done. She's married now, remember?"

"So are you and Laura. In your very odd way."

He was referring to Laura seeing her old lover again. Gary didn't approve and didn't mind saying so. It was four in the morning. They were closing *The Gates of Hell*. It was a hot summer night and the thirtysomething crew had come at them fast and furious despite the nine-dollar well-drinks.

"Confront both of them then, what the hell."

"I don't even know him. We met once when she was bartending for all of about five minutes. I'm not sure I'd recognize him if he were sitting right in front of me."

"So maybe that's part of the problem. You don't know the guy. So you don't know what he offers her. You don't know *why him*. I mean, sometimes you meet the other guy and he's not all that much, you know? Brings *her* down a notch. Sometimes that's just what you need.

"You miss her and you think you're missing this . . . enormous personality. But you're only seeing her in the context of the two of you. You've got no perspective. You're in there yourself, churning things up. Messing with the perspective. You think you know somebody but you don't—not until you either live with them or see them in some whole new situation, like with somebody else. That's my take on it, anyway. And I still think you're fucking crazy letting Laura fly away to some clown in California."

He ignored the last bit. He couldn't tell Laura what to do and wouldn't want to anyway. He had to figure that she knew what she was doing.

But he thought it possible that Gary might be on to something regarding Annabel. When she left she'd insisted on cutting him off completely. No phone calls, no e-mails, no letters. A clean break she called it. He remembered wincing at the raw cliche.

At first he didn't believe she was capable of such draconian thinking—not when it came to them—so he tried anyway. But it became apparent that no confrontation, no follow-up of any sort short of appearing at her apartment was about to happen.

He knew where *that* little visit would lead. Access to her home was by invitation only. It would only earn him the humiliation of having a door once wide open to him slammed shut in his face.

The very last e-mail she'd sent him was calm and deliberate—informing him that she'd thrown out all her photos of them and suggesting he do the same. That it would speed up the healing process. Yet another cliche but he let it pass. Three months later she'd married a guy she'd known and dated off and on for a long time before they met and that was the last he'd heard of her.

He'd been angry, hurt and surprised over both developments. First the cutoff and then the marriage. But there was to be no court of appeals nor any use howling in the wind. It had seemed intolerable to simply stop, to surrender all communication. For a while Bass damn near hated her.

Yet three years later he felt no anger anymore. He could only wonder where it had gone. Because back then *you'll get over it in time* along with *making a clean break of it* and *speeding up the healing process* had seemed the Father, Son, and Holy Ghost of useless psychobabble. They disgusted and infuriated him.

But maybe in the long run they'd obtained after all. *Victory through inanity.*

Because here he was.

Curious in a passive sort of way about what if anything could possibly wake his dead ass up again, ressurect his sense of engagement in Life After Annabel. But the operative word was still *passive.* Confrontation? Three years ago, in a minute. But now he wasn't even sure he had the energy anymore. It was possible that the time for explanation and understanding and that most odious of all suspender-and-bowtied words *closure* had simply come and gone.

He'd never thrown out his own photos.

So he went through them for the first time in a long time over a corned beef on rye for lunch the following day. He felt a brief twinge looking at them. The pinch of a muscle you could stretch a moment later and be rid of.

Still it was something.

He decided to search her out on the Internet. He'd thought of doing that before but resisted it, wary of any further humiliation.

He punched in her maiden name and got nothing. Then tried her married name. What came back was a single photo. A wedding picture two and a half years old—Annabel and her husband, Gerard, standing smiling beneath a canopy of healthy green palm fronds in front of some old New Orleans hotel. Annabel looking lovely in a pale green shoulderless gown, her husband slightly shorter than she and balding, wearing a white silk short-sleeved shirt, lopsided grin and a crisp new panama hat. She gazed not at the camera but into the sky. And that was exactly like her. Annabel was a painter and the sky was her true north, her canvas.

It was the only thing familiar.

The caption read INTRODUCING MR. AND MRS. GERARD POPE AT MARDI GRAS. LOOK WHAT WE WENT AND DID!

The photo was off her husband's Web site. Bass had no reason to think he even had one. No idea that what he did for a living was write detective novels—fairly successful ones from the look of it. He roamed the site. Book covers and reviews and a bibliography and message board and quotes from *Publishers Weekly* and Lawrence Block. Not too shabby at all. He had a series character who'd appeared first in six paperback originals and then more recently in two hardcovers, presumably with paperbacks forthcoming.

There was that twinge again.

Possibly the twinge was jealousy. Bass had seriously hoped to write one day himself—the bartending was supposed to have been temporary.

Or perhaps it was the fact that she and Bass had talked about New Orleans together too, while the farthest south they'd ever gotten was Cape May in the spring their very first year.

But more likely he was beginning to experience what Gary had talked about.

Context.

Here she was, Annabel embraced within the photo. Another, different Annabel. Far beyond the scope or influence of that entity which had once been Annabel and Bass together. With a man he barely recognized, to all purposes a total stranger. And in this man's presence—on that day at least—she was happy.

So it seemed that she could be perfectly happy without him.

He'd known that of course. Any cerebrum worth its salt could fire up that conclusion. But he thought the twinge came not from there but from some less apollonian area of the brain. The part men shared with snakes and birds and dinosaurs. That part which holds a single thing above all self-evident—*eat or be eaten*. Take or be taken.

Just a twinge.

But enough so that when a few days later Laura smiled and kissed him good-bye at the door to their apartment and lugged her bags downstairs to the taxi headed for LaGuardia, it began—unexpectedly—to move from twinge to throb. To leak through into this brand-new *second* void in his life created by her absence like a beaver dam broken slowly apart by a heavy upstream rain.

Its immediate focus was Gerard, not Annabel. Which seemed strange to him because, Web site aside, he had no idea who Gerard even was. Bass bought one of his paperbacks but he hated thrillers so beyond reading the first few pages to ascertain that the man was capable of handling line and paragraph with more than meager skill he delved no further. So how could he feel such a growing *animus*—because that's what it was—toward somebody he'd never shaken hands with? Whose habits, tastes, voice, wit *or lack of wit* he knew nothing of?

How could you begin to dislike what amounted to a human abstraction?

Good question, he thought.

But his dream life wasn't asking.

And Gerard was beginning to show up there on a pretty regular basis.

In one dream he and Gerard were trying to decipher blurred-out cooking directions printed on a bag of frozen food—some kind of stuffed Italian bread. They needed to know the oven time and couldn't read the damn thing. It was very frustrating.

In another they were playing chess. Pieces kept disappearing. A pawn here, a bishop there. Bass suspected himself of cheating.

In yet another they were seated beneath a shade tree in Central Park watching a little girl play on the monkey bars and the little girl was Annabel. This did not seem strange to either of them. Bass lit a Winston and inhaled and Gerard leaned over smiling and plucked it from his lips and tossed it. Annabel laughed and jumped off the monkey bars and crushed it underfoot. Bass was furious with both of them.

Then there was the really bad one.

There's Gerard, seated in front of an old bare country-style oak table, massive, and he's tied to a heavy wooden armchair. His legs are tied to the chair legs and his arms are tied to the chair arms. Annabel is nowhere to be seen. Gerard stares at Bass, his brow furrowed with anxiety. Bass asks him, do you love your wife? He nods in the affirmative.

Then suddenly there's Annabel, similarly tied to a similar chair at the other end of the table. Behind her is a screen door open to the starry night. Moths drift through the doorway, attracted by the light. A luna moth, the color of her wedding dress, settles on the knuckles of her right hand where it grips the chair. Bass brushes it away and his carving knife immediately replaces it, big and sharp and elegant in its way and poised to sever all four fingers and maybe the thumb too for good measure.

He asks Gerard again, Do you love your wife? *and presses the knife gently to her flesh.*

He nods yes and Bass sees that he is gagged now, as is she.

Bass lifts the knife off her fingers and transfers it to Gerard's right hand and asks him a third time, Do you love your wife? *and he nods again slowly, sadly it seems, almost a polite bow to him and full of understanding. He reaches over to place his free hand on top of the knife and push suddenly down and the screams behind the gag and the sound and feel of knife breaking through bone are what wake him.*

He replayed the dream off and on all night long at the *Gates of Hell*. He didn't court it. It just wouldn't go away. Should Gary have asked him even so much as a how's it going? he'd have told him about the dream in an instant in as much detail as he could muster but he didn't ask and Bass couldn't very well blurt it out between banana daiquiris and bijou cocktails.

It was the dream though and dwelling on the dream that goaded him into action the next day.

The Official Gerard Pope Web Site carried no e-mail address but it did have a message board where readers could discuss his work, swap observations and opinions and Bass noted at first visit that Gerard tended to log on once a week over the weekend and answer whatever questions had been put to him. He was regular about it.

His style in these messages was encouragingly open and unaffected. He was even funny. Approachable. Bass reflected that though Annabel had forbidden him any contact with her she'd said nothing about Gerard.

Bass sat down, lit a cigarette, took a deep drag and dropped him a line Thursday night after work.

Good photo. She looks great in green. I like the far-away sky-look, of course. Know it well. Care to catch up on old times we never had? If you're curious, e-mail's above. Bass

By Sunday he had a reply.

She'd probably kill me for doing this but yeah, I guess I am curious. You still on the West Side? If so, how about 1:00 Tuesday, lunch at the Aegean? Best, Pope

So he used his last name too. Interesting.

He e-mailed back saying Tuesday was fine.

Monday night he dreamed about something else entirely. At least he thought it was about something else entirely. It was a bright beautiful day and he was driving along a highway when another car pulled up alongside him and Bass and the driver glanced at one another. The driver was a woman, a blonde, slightly overweight he thought, but she gave him a gap-tooth smile that simply beckoned.

The next thing he knew he was in her car, in the passenger seat, and the next thing after *that* they were parked along the roadside and the car had become a trailer and they were naked on her bed making love and even though her body had a fleshy quality it was pretty good, really—not bad at all. It got even better when she morphed into a slim beautiful brunette, the model Paulina Porizkova, who Bass had wanted since he first laid eyes on her. And she kept doing that—morphing from Paulina to the blonde with the gap in her teeth and back again.

"I think maybe you should stay the night," she said as the blonde.

He said, "I thought you'd never ask."

He woke with barely enough time to shower and shave and grab a cup of coffee along the way.

The Aegean was doing a moderate lunch business and there were plenty of open tables but Pope was at the bar at the corner facing the door. He immediately smiled and offered his hand. "Gerard Pope," he said.

"John Bass. How'd you know it was me?"

"What? Oh, the photos."

"Photos?"

"Yeah."

"She kept the photos?"

"Some, I guess. I don't know how many. I just know you from the ones she showed me. Cape May, mostly. You know how it is with the ladies—the ones *she* looked really good in."

He smiled and shook his head. "Damn."

"What'll you have?" said the bartender. Pope was drinking an O'Doul's non-alcoholic.

"Amstel Lite."

"Coming right up."

"I thought she destroyed them all."

"Annabel? Annabel can't throw away a burned-out light bulb."

His beer arrived complete with frosted mug and they asked for menus and talked trivia, about his Web site for the most part, which Bass said he admired and which was handled for him by a fan in Colorado in exchange for collectables, first editions and such and they ordered and then gradually the conversation began to get more personal and Bass learned that they had moved twice in three years into larger better apartments from Hell's Kitchen to the West Side and finally to Soho. He learned two of Pope's books had movie options but that Pope wasn't necessarily counting on anything to come of them. He learned that Annabel was working in mixed-media now, seascapes like stylized beachcombings and that they were selling fairly well out of their Soho loft. They were currently working on a Web site to promote her stuff too.

By the time he'd finished his broiled squid and calamari salad and Pope his chicken *lemoni* Bass realized something that didn't make him happy at all. He kind of liked the guy. What a pain in the ass. And he guessed that Pope could see it on his face because he laughed.

"Disappointed? That I'm not some prick you could just keep on hating?"

"I never. . . ."

"Come on. If you didn't hate me you were sure working on it. Look, I'm a writer. I'm good at body language. There was a definite poker up your ass when you walked in. You only just relieved yourself of it a while ago."

He thought of the dream, Gerard's sad nod to him that was almost a bow. He was pretty good at body language himself. But he only now realized what the nod was telling him. Not resignation to the knife, which was what he'd thought it to be the following morning. *Recognition*. Recognition of the Other.

In his mind he spoke the dream words *do you love your wife?* but what came out of him was "You love her, don't you."

"Of course I do. She's pretty damn easy to love. Which you of all people ought to know. She was trying to do you a favor, Bass."

"Oh yeah? How so?" He hoped it didn't come out as bitter as it sounded.

"Telling you she'd thrown out the photos, for one thing. Telling you to do the same. But cutting you off. That was the main thing."

Cutting you off. He thought of his dream and suddenly it clarified and almost startled him. He realized that in the subtle inversions dreams will make it hadn't been Gerard sitting tied to the chair at all. *It was Bass.* Unable to move or defend himself, unable to speak or argue his position. Waiting, nodding sadly in recognition *of Gerard.* And finally cut off at the very moment of awakening.

"She knew it wouldn't work. She was trying to do you a kindness by not letting it go any further. And herself a kindness too. Me, too, of course."

Bass thought about it. Finally he nodded.

"I had a dream about you," he said. "I lit a cigarette. You took it from me and threw it away."

"Pushy little bastard, huh?"

"No. It was for my own damn good."

They split the bill.

"You asked me if I loved my wife," Gerard said—*though he hadn't, exactly.* "If *you* love her you'll do the same as she tried to do for you. Metaphorically at least, throw those damn pictures away. Tear them into little pieces. Maybe someday when we're old and grey, you can take a new one."

"Or maybe not."

"Or maybe not. Nice meeting you, Bass. This never happened but I'm sort of glad it did, if you know what I mean."

Bass ordered another beer and sipped it slowly, thinking things through.

A little while later he switched to scotch.

Midway through the second one he stepped outside for a smoke and watched the street life. Nannies and brisk young mothers with double-wide strollers. Truckers delivering paper goods and dairy. A woman across the street jogging in place at a stoplight and shouting furiously into a cellphone. A guy in a mohawk, moccasins and fur earmuffs, stripped to the waist, all buff and tanned. *What's with that?* he wondered. *Tonto Nuevo?* Earmuffs in August? It seemed there were people out here way more strange and obsessive than he was.

He went back inside and finished his scotch and had another. He sipped this one for a long time. The bartender made no effort to engage him in conversation. Sometimes they just knew.

He paid for the beer and scotches and headed home

Home was as he knew it would be. Empty. Empty of Laura, mostly.

He poured himself a final scotch he certainly didn't need and sat back heavily on the couch and sipped it and he supposed he must have dozed for a little while because the next thing he knew his face was wet with tears, *he was crying in his sleep now for chrissake, that was different* and he thought of the dream and what the dream maybe wanted him to do so he went to the kitchen and opened the drawer and took out the knife.

He looked at the long heavy blade. It needed honing but he guessed it would do the trick. He looked at his fingers spread out on the counter. A symbol, he thought. That was what dreams were all about, weren't they? Symbols for what still needing doing in your life? He lit a cigarette and thought about it some more. *Nah*, he thought. That's more loco than the earmuffs. Not even the tip of a pinkie. You didn't want to take this dream terminology too damn literally.

Besides, something else had occurred to him. In his dream, the end of his affair with Annabel was loss, pure and simple. Symbolized by a few missing fingers. He thought it was more complex than that.

You lost something, sure. But when you did you added something too.

Scar tissue.

He could live with that.

He put down the knife and stripped off his shirt, pulled deeply on his cigarette and then pressed it slowly to the flesh directly over where he imagined his heart to be. He wanted the burn to last. Here's to you, Annabel, he thought. He smelled his chest hair burning and another sweeter smell beneath it and felt something like a hornet's sting, sharp and abrupt and then fading to a bright throb as the ember gutted out.

He tossed the butt into the ashtray and headed for the bacitracin.

Roughly seven years later preparatory to Annabel and Gerard's tenth anniversary party he stepped out of a steaming shower and admired the pale white circle that stood out plainly against his glowing flesh.

Laura was already waiting, dressed and ready to go.

She always was a bit ahead of him.

Returns

"I'm here."

"You're what?"

"I said I'm here."

"Aw, don't start with me. Don't get started."

Jill's lying on the stained expensive sofa with the TV on in front of her tuned to some game show, a bottle of Jim Beam on the floor and a glass in her hand. She doesn't see me but Zoey does. Zoey's curled up on the opposite side of the couch waiting for her morning feeding and the sun's been up four hours now, it's ten o'clock and she's used to her Friskies at eight.

I always had a feeling cats saw things that people didn't. Now I know.

She's looking at me with a kind of imploring interest. Eyes wide, black nose twitching. I know she expects something of me. I'm trying to give it to her.

"You're supposed to feed her for godsakes. The litter box needs changing."

"What? Who?"

"The cat. Zoey. Food. Water. The litter box. Remember?"

She fills the glass again. Jill's been doing this all night and all morning, with occasional short naps. It was bad while I was alive but since the cab cut me down four days ago on 72nd and Broadway it's gotten immeasurably worse. Maybe in her way she misses me. I only just returned last night from God-knows-where knowing there was something I had to do or try to do and maybe this is it. Snap her out of it.

"Jesus! Lemme the hell *alone*. You're in my goddamn head. *Get outa my goddamn head!*"

She shouts this loud enough for the neighbors to hear. The neighbors are at work. She isn't. So nobody pounds the walls. Zoey just looks at her, then back at me. I'm standing at the entrance to the kitchen. I know that's where I am but I can't see myself at all. I gesture with my hands but no hands appear in front of me. I look in the hall mirror and there's nobody there. It seems that only my seven-year-old cat can see me.

When I arrived she was in the bedroom asleep on the bed. She jumped off and trotted over with her black-and-white tail raised, the white tip curled at the end. You can always tell a cat's happy by the tail language. She was purring. She tried to nuzzle me with the side of her jaw where the scent-glands are, trying to mark me as her own, to confirm me in the way cats do, the way she's done thousands of times before but something wasn't right. She looked up at me puzzled. I leaned down to scratch her ears but of course I couldn't and that seemed to puzzle her more. She tried marking me with her haunches. No go.

"I'm sorry," I said. And I was. My chest felt full of lead.

"Come on, Jill. Get up! You need to feed her. Shower. Make a pot of coffee. Whatever it takes."

"This is fuckin' crazy," she says.

She gets up though. Looks at the clock on the mantle. Stalks off on wobbly legs toward the bathroom. And then I can hear the water running for the shower. I don't want to go in there. I don't want to watch her. I don't want to see her naked anymore and haven't for a long while. She was an actress once. Summer stock and the occasional commercial. Nothing major. But god, she was beautiful. Then we married and soon social drinking turned to solo drinking and then drinking all day long and her body slid fast into too much weight here, too little there. Pockets of self-abuse. I don't know why I stayed. I'd lost my first wife to cancer. Maybe I just couldn't bear to lose another.

Maybe I'm just loyal.

I don't know.

I hear the water turn off and a while later she walks back into the living room in her white terry robe, her hair wrapped in a pink towel. She glances at the clock. Reaches down to the table for a cigarette. Lights it and pulls on it furiously. She's still wobbly but less so. She's scowling. Zoey's watching her carefully. When she gets like this, half-drunk and half-straight, she's dangerous. I know.

"You still here?

"Yes."

She laughs. It's not a nice laugh.

"Sure you are."

"I am."

"Bullshit. You fuckin' drove me crazy while you were alive. Fuckin' driving me crazy now you're dead."

"I'm here to help you, Jill. You and Zoey."

She looks around the room like finally she believes that maybe, maybe I really *am* here and not some voice in her head. Like she's trying to locate me, pin down the source of me. All she has to do, really, is to look at Zoey, who's staring straight at me.

But she's squinting in a way I've seen before. A way I don't like.

"Well, you don't have to worry about Zoey," she says.

I'm about to ask her what she means by that when the doorbell rings. She stubs out the cigarette, walks over to the door and opens it. There's a man in the hall I've never seen before. A small man, shy and sensitive looking, mid-thirties and balding, in a dark blue windbreaker. His posture says he's uncomfortable.

"Mrs. Hunt?"

"Uh-huh. Come on in," she says. "She's right over there."

The man stoops and picks up something off the floor and I see what it is.

A cat-carrier. Plastic with a grated metal front. Just like ours. The man steps inside.

"Jill, *what are you doing?* What the hell are you *doing*, Jill?"

Her hands flutter to her ears as though she's trying to bat away a fly or a mosquito and she blinks rapidly but the man doesn't see that at all. The man is focused on my cat who *remains focused on me*, when she should be watching the man, *when she should be seeing the cat carrier, she knows damn well what they mean for godsakes, she's going somewhere, somewhere she won't like.*

"Zoey! Go! Get out of here! *Run!*"

I clap my hands. They make no sound. But she hears the alarm in my voice and sees the expression I must be wearing and at the last instant turns toward the man just as he reaches for her, reaches down to the couch and snatches her up and shoves her head-first inside the carrier. Closes it. Engages the double latches.

He's fast. He's efficient.

My cat is trapped inside.

The man smiles. He doesn't quite pull it off.

"That wasn't too bad," he says.

"No. You're lucky. She bites. She'll put up a hell of a fight sometimes."

"*You lying bitch,*" I tell her.

I've moved up directly behind her by now. I'm saying this into her ear. I can *feel* her heart pumping with adrenalin and I don't know if it's me who's scaring her or what she's just done or allowed to happen that's scaring her but she's all actress now, she won't acknowledge me at all. I've never felt so angry or useless in my life.

"You sure you want to do this, ma'am?" he says. "We could put her up for adoption for a while. We don't *have* to euthenize her. 'Course, she's not a kitten anymore. But you never know. Some family . . ."

"I *told* you," my wife of six years says. "*She bites.*"

And now she's calm and cold as ice.

Zoey has begun meowing. My heart's begun to break. Dying was easy compared to this.

Our eyes meet. There's a saying that the soul of a cat is seen through its eyes and I believe it. I reach inside the carrier. My hand passes *through* the carrier. I can't see my hand but she can. She moves her head up to nuzzle it. And the puzzled expression isn't there anymore. It's as though this time she can actually *feel* me, feel my hand and my touch. I wish I could feel her too. I petted her just this way when she was only a kitten, a street waif, scared of every horn and siren. And I was all alone. She begins to purr. I find something out. Ghosts can cry.

The man leaves with my cat and I'm here with my wife.

I can't follow. Somehow I know that.

You can't begin to understand how that makes me feel. I'd give anything in the world to follow.

My wife continues to drink and for the next three hours or so I do nothing but scream at her, tear at her. Oh, she can hear me, all right. I'm putting her through every torment as I can muster, reminding her of every evil she's ever done to me or anybody, reminding her over and over of what she's done *today* and I think, so this is my purpose, this is why I'm back, the reason I'm here is to get this bitch to end herself, end her miserable fucking life and I think of my cat and how Jill never really cared for her, cared for her wine-stained furniture more than my cat and I urge her toward the scissors, I urge her toward the window and the seven-story drop, toward the knives in the kitchen and she's crying, she's screaming, too bad the neighbors are all at work, they'd at least have her arrested. And she's hardly able to walk or even stand and I think, *heart attack maybe, maybe stroke* and I stalk my wife and urge her to die, *die* until it's almost one o'clock and something begins to happen.

She's calmer.

Like she's not hearing me as clearly.

I'm losing something.

Some power drifting slowly away like a battery running down.

I begin to panic. I don't understand. *I'm not done yet.*

Then I feel it. I feel it reach out to me from blocks and blocks away far across the city. I feel the breathing slow. I feel the heart stopping. I feel the quiet end of her. I feel it more clearly than I felt my own end.

I feel it grab my own heart and *squeeze*.

I look at my wife, pacing, drinking. And I realize

something. And suddenly it's not so bad anymore. It still hurts, but in a different way.

I haven't come back to torment Jill. Not to tear her apart or to shame her for what she's done. She's tearing herself apart. She doesn't need me for that. She'd have done this terrible thing anyway, with or without my being here. She'd planned it. It was in motion. My being here didn't stop her. My being here afterward didn't change things. Zoey was mine. And given who and what Jill was what she'd done was inevitable.

And I think, *to hell with Jill. Jill doesn't matter a bit. Not one bit. Jill is zero.*

It was Zoey I was here for. Zoey all along. That awful moment.

I was here for my cat.

That last touch of comfort inside the cage. The nuzzle and purr. Reminding us both of all those nights she'd comforted me and I her. The fragile brush of souls.

That was what it was about.

That was what we needed.

The last and the best of me's gone now.

And I begin to fade.

•